MU

ta es

Root

MURDER
takes
Root

ROSIE SANDLER

embla
books

First published in Great Britain in 2024 by

Bonnier Books UK Limited
4th Floor, Victoria House, Bloomsbury Square, London, WC1B 4DA
Owned by Bonnier Books
Sveavägen 56, Stockholm, Sweden

A CIP catalogue record for this book is available from the British Library.

ISBN: 9781471416200

This book is typeset using Atomik ePublisher.

Embla Books is an imprint of Bonnier Books UK.
www.bonnierbooks.co.uk

For Andrew: with love always

Prologue

The specimen has taken days to track down, but he has it in his sights at last, gleaming jewel bright against the lush vegetation. Gabriel inserts his trowel carefully into the rich soil. It's early enough that there's still dew on the ground, a mist in the air. A scorpion has not yet gone to bed for the day; it scuttles past, and Gabriel watches it for a moment, noting that it's the type with venom that can kill a man. The beast safely past, Gabriel turns back to his delicate task.

As he plunges his trowel into the ground a second time, he freezes at the sound of a twig snapping behind him. His heart thumping hard, he draws his knife and whirls around.

But the new arrival is ready for him. The man slits Gabriel's throat in one neat movement and sets his body carefully to one side, before stepping in to claim the prize.

1

'You'll be telling me next you're out of flour.' Lady Clara Fanshawe is frowning at her cook: a short, stout woman called Vicky, of indeterminate age, with skin the sallow shade of frozen milk.

'No, ma'am, just the truffles. Beanie in the village is laid up with the shingles at the moment, and he's our only source. He won't tell anyone where he finds them.'

Her ladyship sighs, as if this is a crisis of giant proportions. 'I had so hoped to serve truffles to Sally and Herbert, when they come on Tuesday. Their own cook is so unimaginative. What do we have instead?' she asks, in the resigned voice of one who is accustomed to crushing disappointment.

It's the second Sunday in November, and we are in the front study at Ashford Manor in Derbyshire, where Lady Clara presides behind a large walnut desk. This highly polished item is a thing of beauty in a room filled with similar treasures and – if it weren't for my poor dog awaiting release from the van after our four-hour journey, and the fiercely blazing fire in the hearth – I would be enjoying my surroundings. I've been waiting at least twenty minutes in this suffocating space for her ladyship's full attention, but there has been one interruption after another.

'I need to—' I try, but Lady Clara holds up a hand.

'I am so sorry to keep you waiting, Ms Williams,' she says. And she sounds genuinely contrite – even offering me a sweet smile.

At that moment, there's a knock on the door, and a tall, white man in his thirties steps inside. He has strawberry-blond hair and striking green eyes. Wearing an open-collar shirt beneath an expensive-looking suit, he gives off the air of being completely

2

at ease in his body. From the breadth of his shoulders, I suspect he was – perhaps still is – a rugby player. He bears more than a passing resemblance to Lady Clara, so I'm guessing he's her brother.

'Oh, Dickie,' she says, 'I've been held up but I shouldn't be much longer. Are you OK to wait for me in the great parlour? Rupert's around somewhere . . .' She looks at Vicky, 'Are we still on schedule for family dinner at seven?'

Vicky nods, 'All prepared, ma'am.'

Dickie nods, 'No probs.' He smiles at me, and nods to Vicky, before exiting.

Lady Clara turns back to Vicky, 'Well, see what you can do. If we really can't get the truffles – and surely *someone* locally must know where to find them, even if this "Beanie" won't reveal his source – then please try to come up with something suitably enticing in their place.'

Vicky nods. 'Yes, ma'am.'

'That will be all.' As Vicky leaves, Lady Clara turns back to me and flashes me another gracious smile. She has deep-blue eyes, blonde hair in a chignon and a svelte figure that's emphasised by the form-fitting cut of her navy skirt suit, and I would estimate she's in her mid-forties. She is chic, in an old-money, old-world way. 'Now, Ms Williams,' she says, 'we are so grateful to have you here. We are in great need of your horticultural expertise. I will have Saliha show you to your rooms.'

'I mentioned that I have a dog?'

She smiles. 'Oh, yes. I'm sure he won't be a problem. He had a curious name. What was it again?'

'Mouse.'

She laughs. 'That's right! Is he tiny?'

I shake my head. 'No, that's kind of the point – he's big and black, and as un-mouse-like as they come.'

'I see . . .' She regards me for a moment, as if I, myself, am a curious breed. At last, she says, 'Right, well, come by in the morning, after breakfast, and we'll talk game plans.' She nods to show our meeting's over, and I take my leave.

I'm not sure where I'm supposed to go but, as I turn, I see a slight figure, waiting just inside the door.

'Saliha?' I ask, as I reach her. I would guess she's eighteen or nineteen and of South Asian heritage, with large eyes, framed by a neat, dark bob. She has a nose stud: a pretty, turquoise gemstone.

She nods and smiles shyly. 'Yeah. I've been asked to show you the way to your rooms.' Her accent is solid Mancunian.

'Thanks. I'll just fetch my dog from my van.'

Saliha walks over to the garages with me. She watches as I let Mouse out. He's overjoyed to be freed from the confines of the vehicle, and runs in large circles for a moment, before racing towards Saliha, who takes a step back in alarm.

'Mouse! Here!' I call. He stops and looks at me. I can see he's weighing up the rewards of obedience to me, versus the pleasure of making a new friend.

'Does he bite?' asks Saliha.

I shake my head. 'Oh, no.' This is only a small lie: he won't bite Saliha. He might, however, bite anyone he believes to be a threat to me. She bends forward and holds out a hand, and Mouse trots over, drops his beloved rabbit toy at her feet and licks her hand.

'Aw! He's lovely!' she says, with a smile.

I open the back of the van and grab the bag that contains my immediate necessities. I sling it over my shoulder before drawing out Mouse's bed and blanket.

'Here,' says Saliha, 'I can carry those.' She takes the dog's bed and bedding and leads us from the garages along the front of the house.

Mouse and I examine our new environment as we follow her. According to the local history website I found, Ashford Manor is a 'small' manor house, built in the late-seventeenth century from local limestone, to which it owes its yellow hue. It boasts twelve bedrooms, and was once honoured by a visit from King George II. The manor's extensive grounds take in the small village of Larkham. Luckily for me, I have been hired to oversee only the formal gardens, which make up the portion of land closest to the house.

Mouse trots ahead of me, following Saliha, and I have to keep watch to avoid tripping over him each time he stops to examine a dead leaf or sniff a new smell. We round the corner of the building, and Saliha stops at the foot of what can only be described as a tower.

She glances at me, 'What d'you reckon?'

I start to grin. 'Are you serious? When Lady Clara said she was putting me up in the "Round Wing", I didn't realise she meant a literal tower.'

She beams back. 'I know, right?'

I take a step back and look up at the impressive cylinder of limestone, which runs up all three storeys of the great house. 'Wow.'

'We're all dead jealous. I mean, we have to sleep in the "servants' quarters" at the top of the house.' She makes air quotes around the words 'servants' quarters'.

I'm not sure how to respond, so I just say,

'Is it not nice?'

'It's freezing up there right now, and it was boiling all summer.'

I gesture to the tower. 'What makes you think this won't be the same?'

'Well, I mean, your windows all open, for starters. Most of ours have been painted shut.'

'And now?' There's a distinct chill in the November air.

'You've got central heating. They didn't bother fitting it in the staff bedrooms, which have all these draughts down the chimneys and round the windows. Oh, and the fireplaces in the tower actually work.'

'Yours don't?'

She shakes her head. 'I mean, I tried to light a fire back in May, and the whole room filled up with smoke.' She unlocks the heavy oak door and pushes it open, then looks at me. 'I hope you like climbing.'

Mouse has already pushed past her, and is bounding up the stairs, taking several at a time. I glance around and see that there are no rooms on the ground floor. Saliha and I start to climb slowly; the stairs are steep and made of stone – not to be rushed by us mere bipeds, especially with full arms.

Part way up, the staircase takes a ninety-degree turn to the left, where there's a door to the first floor, before the stairs continue up. Mouse is sitting at this first door, awaiting ingress. Saliha lets him through and he races into the room, his claws click-clacking on the wooden floor and his long legs struggling to maintain coordination on the smooth, polished surface. He's like a cartoon of a dog on an ice rink. She laughs at the sight.

She gestures for me to go ahead of her. As I walk into the living room, I'm struck by how light it is. There's a cushioned window seat built into the wide, curved window at the front, to make the most of the views. A large, woven rug, in rich shades of red and green, lies in the centre of the oak floor. A big, teal sofa and two matching armchairs with brightly coloured cushions look cosy and inviting. There are framed landscapes on the walls, depicting hills and woodland; I suspect these are local scenes.

She opens a door off the living room. 'Your kitchen's in here.'

I poke my head inside the room. The kitchen is also well served by windows. Despite its awkward shape, it has fitted units, set around an oven, plus a microwave, a little table and two chairs. Someone has set out a painted floral jug, containing a pretty posy of seasonal flowers, presumably from the garden. There are stems of pink viburnum, plus yellow jasmine and a few purple Michaelmas daisies, all backed by fern leaves.

'That's lovely,' I say, pointing to the flowers.

Saliha nods. 'Jamie's great at that stuff.'

'Jamie is . . .?

She puts her head on one side while she considers this. 'I'm not sure . . . I mean, he does, like, everything that isn't somebody else's job.'

'I see. Are there a lot of staff?' I have learnt not to use the word 'servant' to refer to those in the employ of big houses.

She counts on her fingers. 'I make it nine all together.'

I raise my eyebrows. 'That seems quite a few.'

'There is, like, loads to be done.' She looks earnest. 'When we arrived back in February, at the same time as Lady and Mr Fanshawe, the furniture was all in storage, and poor Sir Angus was living in just a couple of rooms.'

'Who's Sir Angus?'

'Oh! He's the . . . great-uncle,' she considers this, 'or maybe just uncle, of Lady Clara. He spends most of his time in the Scottish Room, even though he's always complaining the tartans aren't real – you know, like, they're not based on any actual Scottish wotsits.'

'Clans?' I suggest.

'Yeah. He says it's all "utter poppycock".' She pauses, thinking for a moment. 'But he says that about a lot of things.'

I'm not following much. The long journey has taken its toll, and I realise I'm smiling in a fixed, dim-witted fashion.

She notes my lack of engagement. 'Sorry!' she says. 'You must be knackered. Do you need help getting the rest of your stuff in?'

I shake my head, gesturing to my bag. 'I've got everything for now, thanks. And you've brought in the dog bed.' I glance around for Mouse, and see he's sitting upright on the window seat, staring out.

'Where are the bedroom and bathroom?' I ask her. She points to the ceiling.

'One level up, at the top. You've got this shower room with a toilet off the bedroom.' I nod and she says, 'Oh! Dinner's at six thirty, so Vicky can feed the family at eight. Which is brilliant for me, cos I'm always starving by then.'

'I think I'll skip it this evening, if Vicky won't mind. I'm shattered, and I need to take Mouse out for some exercise, as he's been cooped up all day. I've still got some sandwiches left over from lunch.'

She nods. 'OK. I'll let her know.'

'I'll come to breakfast, though. Remind me what time?'

'Seven thirty. Waaaay too early,' she says.

I don't tell her that, by seven thirty, I'll already have been for a run with Mouse.

At nine that night, my phone starts ringing with a WhatsApp video call. I'm slumped wearily on the sofa, where I've been trying to decide whether to read a book or go to bed early. I click the green button, and my brother Danny's face comes up on my screen.

'Hiya,' he says. 'How was the journey?'

I pull a face. 'We got stuck in roadworks around Nottingham, so it took four hours.'

'Shit! Can't believe it took you that long to get to the Midlands from just the other side of London! You must be knackered.'

'Pretty shattered.'

'Daddy you're blocking the way!' comes a child's voice from the screen.

'Is that Alice still up?' I ask.

My niece's face pops up in place of her father's. 'Yes! Daddy said I could stay up to say hello.'

'I see. Well, it's very nice to see you.'

'Frankie wanted to stay up, too. But he fell asleep on the sofa, so Daddy carried him up to bed.'

'Give him a hug from me in the morning. And Luke and the baby, too. Has the baby got a name yet?'

'He's just called Baby still,' says my niece, frowning. 'Frankie calls him "Screamer".' Alice, who recently turned eight, now has three younger brothers. Frankie is six. There's also Luke, who's three.

'Weren't you going to name him?' I ask her.

She looks indignant. 'Mummy wouldn't let me call him "Storm" or "Diamond".'

'They'd be good names for a horse,' I say, and she brightens.

'When Mummy and Daddy get me a horse, that's what I'll call him: "Storm Diamond".'

'Perfect,' says Danny. 'I'd better start saving. With any luck, I'll have enough for a horse by the time you're eighty.'

'Eighty! Daddy! That's . . .' she pauses, counting on her fingers, '. . . seventy-two years away.'

'Anyway, time for bed, young lady,' says Danny.

Alice shakes her head, uttering a long-suffering sigh, before wishing me goodnight.

'Night, love,' I say.

Danny comes back into view and asks, 'What's the accommodation like? Are you missing Gardener's Cottage?'

The pretty stone cottage was my accommodation at my last placement, and it was a wrench to leave it. But I can't get over the novelty of my new premises. 'I'm living in a tower,' I tell him. 'And I have it all to myself – with Mouse, of course.' He lets out a low whistle. 'I'll send you pics tomorrow, in daylight. The kids would love it.'

'Sounds great! Right, I'd better let you get some rest after that journey,' he continues. 'I hope everyone's friendly when you meet them tomorrow.'

'Thanks. I'll be fine,' I say, to reassure him. I know he's probably worrying about me, after my run-in with the residents' committee at my last place.

As we finish the call, I look around at my tower accommodation, at the curved window seat where Mouse is dozing, and the huge windows. It really is an amazing space for our fresh start.

I had expected to be aware of nothing but the occasional owl, fox or badger in my private quarters in this rural spot. But, at around half-ten, as I'm lying in bed, I hear a raised voice. Mouse hears it, too, and comes running up the stone stairs. He appears in my room and trots over to the wall at the head end of the bed. We are next to the attic, I realise – where Saliha said the staff are housed.

'It sounds like an argument,' I say.

There's a loud thump, like a piece of furniture being thrown or overturned, and then everything goes quiet. Mouse continues to sit beside the wall. He's making a soft, guttural sound, his head on one side. 'Can you still hear something?' I ask. He glances at me, then returns his gaze to the wall. I don't know what he can hear but, from where I'm lying, it sounds like the worst of the row is over, and I'm exhausted.

'Too late to do anything now,' I tell him, though I feel guilty. 'We'll look into it tomorrow,' I add, as much for myself as for him.

The whole bed rocks as Mouse lands beside me and makes a nest for himself. He's not often allowed on my bed. For tonight, though, it's nice to have the company. Tomorrow, we can re-establish separate sleeping arrangements.

Mouse is asleep before me, but he whimpers occasionally, as if the dregs of the argument remain in the air, permeating his dream world. I lie awake for a while, worrying that I really should go to investigate. But it's all quiet now – and I'm so tired. Eventually I, too, am dragged down into sleep.

2

I wake the next morning even earlier than my usual six o'clock. The thick damask curtains reveal nothing, but it's early November and will be dark out in any case. I'm still determined to get in a run before breakfast. Mouse is asleep on his side on top of my duvet, his feet kicking as he runs through dream fields. All is quiet from next door.

I say softly, 'Hey, boy. Ready for our run?'

Mouse lifts his head and yawns extravagantly, then gets to his feet and trots down to the living room to fetch his lead, which I've not yet unpacked. I follow him down and rummage in the large holdall that's still on the living-room floor, fishing out his blue lead. It's not his favourite, but I finally had to consign that one to the dustbin after it frayed to bits. We had a little ceremony for it, Mouse and I standing beside the bin, while he whined and I said a few words: 'Dear lead, you have served us faithfully. Go well into the afterlife of dogs and their loyal accessories.' Mouse took it remarkably well. He's still not keen on the blue one though, and I suspect we'll have to shop for a new one before too long, so that he can make his own choice.

I put on my head torch and we start downstairs to our front door – Mouse trotting ahead on nimble feet – and I clip on the objectionable lead as we leave the tower. He shoots me a reproving look, but there is too much to explore for him to sulk for long.

It's dark and chilly out, with a faint smell of bonfires, mingling with damp earth and rotting leaves. We pass out of the grounds through a gate in a hedge, to a footpath that leads across fields. I'm pleased to see that there are no sheep for him to chase, so I let him off. He bounds away through stubble, running back every few minutes and trotting around me in a circle, as if to say, 'Well, come on, then – keep up!'

I do a few calf and shoulder stretches, then begin to jog. Mouse returns to me, and yaps in excitement at seeing I've picked up my pace. We run together, through the stubble field, to one full of cabbages, then another, of broccoli. We cross a river via an old limestone bridge, and continue on, towards the foothills. In the distance, the first pink-and-gold fingers of the sun are climbing up the far side of the mountains. When I check my watch, I see it's getting on for seven.

'We'd better get back for breakfast,' I tell my running buddy. He barks at the mention of food, and heads back willingly with me towards the manor.

After a quick shower, I pull on gardening trousers, layer a sweatshirt over a T-shirt, and tie back my dark, wiry curls. Then I put out food for Mouse, before donning a warm gardening jacket and boots, and walking around to the front of the house, where I find the door unlocked. There's no one in the entrance hall to ask for directions, so I have to hunt for my breakfast. I walk along a corridor to the right of the grand staircase. This passage leads towards the back of the house. I open doors as I go, glimpsing first a strangely tartan-filled room, which must be the 'Scottish Room', inhabited by Sir Angus. This is followed by a second study, a parlour, a large dining room (with all the furniture covered in white dust cloths, and a magnificent chandelier suspended above the long table) and another parlour. The house grows emptier and quieter as I pass through it, until I finally accept that I must be in the wrong section.

Retracing my steps to the hall, I select the corridor to the left of the stairs, and soon begin to smell food cooking, plus the delectable scent of freshly brewed coffee. This time, I pass through a swing door, and the corridor narrows. The decor also changes, from the richly ornate to something closer to the puritan, the floors turning from decorative tiles to dingy linoleum. I arrive at an open door to my left. Inside this room, I can see men and women, seated around a long, wooden table.

'You're meant to come in at the back door,' mutters a man seated near the centre of the table, in front of a plate of sausages, bacon, eggs and all the trimmings. He's sporting a long, grey beard and a scowl. His voice is so quiet, it takes me a moment to realise he's addressing me.

'Oh – sorry,' I say.

He shrugs, 'No skin off my nose,' he mumbles, returning his focus to his laden plate.

'That wasn't very welcoming,' says the woman beside him, shooting me an apologetic smile. She's white, and dressed in a charcoal skirt suit and emerald-green silk blouse, her light-auburn hair drawn into a sleek bun. I would guess she's close to me in age – early thirties – and, from her dress, that she works on the administrative side.

'You can sit here, if you want.' It's Saliha, offering me her shy smile and pulling out the chair beside her.

My stomach is rumbling at the scent and sight of food and coffee. 'Thanks,' I say, smiling back, as I walk around the table to join her.

As soon as I've taken my seat, a young white man comes in, and sets down a plate in front of Saliha, saying, 'Here you go, Sali.' She has eggs and what look like vegetarian sausages, with hash browns, tomatoes and mushrooms. He turns to me. 'You must be the new gir . . . woman,' he says, blushing as he corrects himself.

'That's me: the new girwoman. Or you can call me Steph.' I smile at him.

He laughs. 'Soz! I'm Jamie.' His accent is pure Liverpudlian. 'What can I get you? Michael's in bed with a bug, so I've stepped in as your waiter for the day.' He gives a mock bow. He's quite tall, with carefully coiffed blond hair and deep-blue eyes.

'What's on offer?' I ask him.

'Full English with toast?'

'Sounds great. And is there coffee?'

He points to a pot further down the table. 'I've just refilled that one.' He turns and leaves to take my order back to the kitchen.

Someone passes me the pot, and I fill my cup with the rich, dark brew, breathing in the scent. It's not quite as refined as some of the coffee I had at my previous workplace, but it still smells like a decent blend. I sip it and sigh with pleasure.

'Have you just got up?' Saliha asks me.

I shake my head. 'No – Mouse and I have been out for our morning run.'

She draws a pyjama collar out from beneath the neck of her sweatshirt. 'Still in my pjs. It's one of the bonuses of living where you work. I can get washed after.'

'What time do you start?'

She tips her head to one side. 'I think it's supposed to be eight thirty, but no one fusses. Lady C hasn't got round to hiring a . . .' she squints, looking for the word.

'. . . house manager?' I suggest.

She smiles. 'Yeah!' She leans towards me, lowering her voice, 'I mean, I'm new to all this and I'm still not used to it. Like how we're meant to only use the back door. They call us "the staff" but really we're servants – like in *Downton Abbey* or something. It's a bit weird.'

I whisper back, 'It's very weird.' We laugh.

'Where did you work before?' she asks.

'A gated community of five grand houses. Not as grand as this place, obviously.'

She rolls her eyes. 'Obviously.'

'What about you?'

'I just finished my foundation course last July, and, like I said, I've been here since Feb. It's good to be earning some dosh, till I work out what I want to do.'

'What did you study?'

'Art.' She pulls a face. 'It doesn't qualify you for much.'

'No, but it's a lovely skill to have.'

'Do you draw up your garden plans?'

'I tend to use modelling software, to be honest. But this job's going to involve referring back to old garden plans on paper, and working out how to realistically reimpose them on the current garden.'

Someone down the table calls to Saliha, and she turns her attention to them. I take the opportunity to study my new colleagues. Who did Mouse and I hear shouting last night? It's not obvious. There's Mr Beardy Scowler, who told me off for coming in via the front door. I have a worrying suspicion that he might be the head gardener. He's clearly the oldest member of staff present.

But he doesn't seem like the type to be getting into a screaming match. There's another young, white man, around the same age as Saliha, who looks, from his slumped posture and dishevelled hair, as if he could do with an injection of caffeine. A shy-looking black girl in an apron and hair net comes in, carrying her own breakfast plate, and sits down at the far end, beside Sleepy Boy. I'd say she's about sixteen.

So, that's three teenagers, plus Jamie, who took my order, and who I'd guess to be about twenty. As I glance around the table, the woman in the charcoal suit catches my eye and nods a greeting. I notice that she has startling amber eyes. I nod back, and we smile briefly. There's a sense of camaraderie, and I wonder if she's pleased to finally have a more mature – but not too mature – colleague.

My food arrives, and I tuck straight in. It's well cooked, with mushrooms that are tender rather than soggy, and tomatoes that are fresh, sweet and deliciously charred rather than out-of-a-tin and bitter. Vicky the cook clearly knows what she's doing, and I find myself already looking forward to dinner.

I'm buttering my toast when chairs start scraping back.

'I've got to get dressed,' says Saliha, standing up. 'See you later.'

I lower my voice. 'Before you go – I heard quite a lot of noise last night—'

She bends down and whispers close to my ear, 'That'll be Simon. He cries a lot.'

'Which one's Simon?'

She nods towards Sleepy Boy.

'Why does he cry?' I ask quietly.

She shrugs. 'I think he's homesick. He's from . . .' she wrinkles her face in thought, and I wait for her to name some distant land. Instead, she says, 'Croydon?'

'I guess that's quite far away. But this wasn't crying. It was shouting, and maybe throwing things?'

Her big brown eyes widen. 'Really? Shit.'

'Any ideas?'

She shakes her head, then says, 'I mean, unless it's maybe Jamie, on Skype with his dad? They have this dead explosive relationship, cos his dad wants him to go to uni and be a lawyer, but Jamie wants to do stage school.'

I think back to earlier this year, when my mum refused to speak to me for months, because I wanted to trace my birth parents. While I'd understood that she felt hurt and threatened, those were some of the toughest months of my life. 'Poor Jamie,' I say.

'Yeah,' she says, with a sigh. 'Anyway, I've got to get on. See you later.'

I watch her and the two other young people leave the room. Saliha and the kitchen girl chat animatedly, joined by the elegant woman in the grey suit. Sleepy Boy – *Simon*, I correct myself – trails sluggishly behind them.

Mr Scowler is the last to leave, muttering to himself.

Jamie comes in a moment later, with his own plate of food. Seeing me, he says, 'Oh, hiya! Did they all run off and leave you on your ownsies?'

'They did, I'm afraid. I am officially friendless.'

'Awww. And I've got to get this down me and get straight out of here. I'm running late, like.'

'What work do you do?'

'Er . . . what *don't* I do?' He grins. 'I'm your dogsbody-cum-waiter-cum-skivvy-cum-chauffeur. Or I will be, like, when I pass me driving test.'

I watch, as he tucks happily into his plate of food. He doesn't look like someone who's just had a major falling out with his dad, or anyone else.

'I heard someone shouting last night,' I say tentatively.

'Did you?' I nod. 'Who was it?'

'I don't know. Did you hear them?'

He shakes his head. 'I didn't hear anything,' he says, through a mouthful of food. 'But I can ask around, if you want?'

'No, don't worry. It was probably a one-off. Everyone looked all right this morning. Unless Michael, who you said wasn't well . . .?'

He shakes his head again. 'Michael's all right.' He lowers his voice. 'He just had too many bevvies last night, so he's married to the toilet this morning, like. He doesn't learn,' he says, in the tone of someone far older and wiser than his years.

'Are you and Michael good friends?'

'Yeah. Me and him have worked together for the last few years. Part time during A levels, then full time at another big house, where the pay was crap. That's where we met Vicky, though, so it wasn't all bad.'

'Vicky the cook?'

'Yeah, she's me surrogate mum.' He grins.

I finish my toast and gulp down the last of my coffee, pushing back my chair and standing up. 'Well, I'd better get to work myself. Nice to meet you, Jamie. Thanks for the breakfast.'

'Ta'ra,' he says, through another mouthful of food. He raises a hand in farewell.

I need to check in with Lady Clara, so I head through the house to her study, where she welcomed me the previous day. Approaching from the staff dining room, it's the room to the right of the front door. The dark-oak study door is surrounded by a beautiful frame, carved with acorns and oak leaves. I knock and wait, but there's no sound from inside. On the other side of the hall, the door to the Scottish Room is ajar, so I walk over and peer inside again. It appears empty, and I decide to explore.

Despite Saliha's description – and my brief glimpse through the door before breakfast – I'm not prepared for quite how much tartan can be squeezed into one room. It's everywhere: checks of blues, greens and reds in a multitude of shades, intersected with thin stripes in contrasting colours. There are tartan rugs on the parquet floor, all of them different, and there's even tartan on the walls, in the form of flock wallpaper. Every piece of upholstered furniture in the room – from the many upright sofas to the various wing-back armchairs – has its own version of tartan, complete with contrasting (*clashing* might be more accurate) cushions. There are glassy-eyed stag heads on the walls, and glass cabinets displaying sets of bagpipes alongside empty bottles of Scotch malt whisky. It's as if someone who'd never visited Scotland had searched, 'Scottish memorabilia' on eBay, and bought it all.

A loud snore informs me I'm not alone in the dimly lit room. Glancing around, I spot a tiny man, seated in one of the armchairs.

He's wearing a green kilt, a sporran, knee-high forest-green socks with a red garter flash, and even a tam-o'-shanter perched on his head.

Not wanting to disturb the sleeping figure – Sir Angus, I presume – I turn to tiptoe out. But a floorboard creaks loudly beneath my feet and he sputters to life like a clockwork doll.

'You, there!' he says, pointing a bony figure in my direction. 'What're you doing, tiptoeing around like a petty thief?' I'm pretty sure his accent is the only authentically Scottish thing in the room.

'Sorry. I'm the new gardening consultant, Steph Williams.'

'Yer a long way from the garden,' he says, in his reedy voice. I'd hazard a guess that his accent hails from Edinburgh. 'Unless you thought I was a weed as needed removing?' he suggests. He makes a strangled sound, and I start towards him in concern, before realising he's laughing at his own joke.

'I suppose you might be a Scotch thistle,' I say. 'As for the rest of the room . . .' I gesture to the surplus of 'Scottish' furnishings.

''Tis like a tourist shop that's spewed out all its contents,' he says in disgust. 'None of this is real. It's all poppycock!' He lowers his voice. 'It's just for the Americans.' I'm not sure which Americans he means: to the best of my knowledge, Ashford Manor doesn't receive tourists.

'What clan are you?' I ask.

'Fraser,' he says, drawing himself up and puffing out his chest in a way that suggests I should be impressed, so I nod reverently.

'I don't suppose you've seen Lady Clara?' I ask him.

He snorts. 'She'll be around. She always is. Like a wee speck of dirt you cannae wash out.'

'Right . . . Well, nice to meet you.' I turn to leave.

'Dinnae be a stranger now,' he calls after me.

As I head back towards the hall, I hear him making his strange choking laugh and murmuring, 'A weed as needs removing!'

I knock on Lady Clara's study door again, but there's still no response, so I decide to get on with my day. In any case, I'll need to survey the gardens fully before any restoration work can begin.

I start by making two trips to the garages, to fetch the rest of my belongings from the van. I collect all my books and clothes, but leave my crockery and pans behind, as I've noticed these are supplied in my new kitchen. Once my possessions are installed in my new residence, I take a few snaps of the tower from inside and out, and message them over to Danny. He responds almost instantly with: I'd better not show this to the kids when they get home, or they'll be on the next train.

I grin and type back: I'll roll out their sleeping bags.

I dig out my preliminary notes on the gardens, before waking Mouse. He's been snoozing on the living-room floor, a slant of rare November sunshine creating a warm patch on the rug. He shakes off his drowsiness and trots happily downstairs, his soft toy, Mr Rabbit, swinging from his mouth. As soon as we're outside, though, he deposits Mr Rabbit at my feet and bounds away, vanishing among the trees.

I tuck the toy into my jacket pocket and seal the Velcro flap, before beginning my own explorations. There's a chill wind and I pull out my lime-green woolly hat and draw it down over my ears. I have two of these hats; the other is citrus orange. I like brightening up my surroundings on dull, wintry days with this small splash of colour.

I know from the plans that there's a formal parterre close to the house: small, intricately shaped flowerbeds, surrounded by – in this case – box hedging. I was a little surprised by the discovery of the box hedging when Lady Clara first sent over copies of the original plans by the celebrated landscaper, George London. By the time these beds were created, in the late-seventeenth century, most parterres were being built using boundaries constructed from non-plant materials, such as sand, wood or gravel. Perhaps the box hedge was a preference specified by the incumbents of the manor house at the time.

I walk over to this area, where I find the interior of the parterre beds so overgrown they've lost their precise geometry. Where the plants should be spaced out, with bare soil between them, there is just an expanse of plants – much of which is still visible even now, so late in the year.

What's more, a lot of the box hedging is dead. My heart sinks as I crouch to examine a nearby specimen, and see the telltale webbing that indicates an infestation of box tree caterpillar. I had trouble with this towards the end of my time down south at my last place, when box tree caterpillars infested the plants of a beautiful topiary garden. Luckily, I caught it in time to intervene, and break the moths' cycle.

Here, though, the infestation has progressed too far for moth traps and fertiliser. It's going to have to be a complete replacement job – both costly and time-consuming. The Japanese holly, *Ilex crenata*, would make a decent, pest-resistant substitute, although it favours acid soil, and Ashford is on limestone, so the soil is alkaline. I'll have to talk to a specialist at one of the nurseries. Whatever replacement we opt for, I'm not happy at being forced to deviate so soon from London's original plans.

I make a note and walk on, through a yew arch. This is healthy, thank goodness, with only a few areas of brown foliage – no doubt caused by the harsh Derbyshire frosts. I'm pretty sure this is the original yew hedge, planted more than three hundred years ago. As yew can live for thousands of years, this is not as remarkable as it might sound.

I hear a regular thudding that suggests someone is chopping wood, and I follow the sound through a door in a wall to a small, cobbled courtyard. There, I see Mr Scowler, raising an axe above his head and bringing it down to split a log. He has a neat pile of split logs on one side, with others awaiting the chop stacked close to his feet.

I move away, but he catches sight of me and stills the axe, dropping his arm to his side.

'You're the new gardening consultant,' he says. His speech surprises me, by being intelligible. From his appearance and demeanour – and mutterings – at breakfast, I'd had some expectation of his speaking in some ancient dialect that I'd strain to understand. Instead, his Derbyshire-accented speech is pleasant and clear.

'That's right,' I say. 'Steph Williams.' I step towards him, offering a hand.

At that moment, Mouse comes running through the open door. The man catches sight of him and sets down the axe, crouching to Mouse's level. The dog runs straight over to greet him.

'Hey, boy,' the man says softly, his scowl vanishing as he makes a fuss of Mouse, rubbing his fur and ears and talking to him in a voice too low for me to make out.

'You're a dog whisperer,' I say, after a few minutes of watching the pair of them bond. Mouse is naturally friendly, but this is a whole other level of trust.

Mr Scowler looks up, as if only just remembering my presence. 'He's a beautiful dog,' he says. 'I lost my poor boy last year.'

'Oh, I'm so sorry to hear that. How sad.'

He nods, still petting Mouse. 'He was thirteen, so it was the kindest thing to let him go.'

'Still hard, though.'

'My wife died the year before.'

I feel shame for having judged this man on his grumpy appearance.

'Should I leave Mouse here with you for a bit?' I suggest.

His face brightens. 'We'll have a grand old time, won't we, boy?' Mouse, who's now lying on his back in a blissed-out state from having his tummy rubbed, makes the rumble in his throat that is his form of assent.

As I step back through the door in the wall, I realise I still haven't discovered the man's name, or his role here. Oh, well: there will be plenty of time for that. I return to my explorations. There are some beautiful trees, and I note them as I walk, checking each one for signs of disease or dead branches for removal. Whereas George London was known for his formal avenues of largely native trees, these specimens have been introduced since his time, and planted in a more natural-looking arrangement, forming a fine arboretum, rather like a wood.

I round a large border, filled with evergreen shrubs, and arrive at a lake. Although I knew from the plans that it was here, it's still a surprise to be greeted with such a large expanse of water. There's a little jetty, with a rowing boat tied to it, and even a small, wooded island at the lake's centre. I walk to the edge. The water is so clear, I can see minnow flitting through the fronds of oxygenating pond weed.

'Lovely, isn't it?'

I jump at a deep, male voice close by. Turning, I see a young white man I don't recognise. He's around my height – five ten – with a tanned face, dark, curly hair and brown eyes. He smiles.

'Sorry. I didn't mean to startle you.' He holds out a hand. 'Miles Spencer, Julian's cousin.'

'Julian?'

'The wayward son,' he says, with a smile.

'I didn't know there was one,' I say.

'Oh, there's always a wayward son.'

'I'm Steph Williams,' I say, accepting the proffered hand. 'I've been brought in to consult on the garden designs.'

He's in his early twenties, and dressed simply in black jeans and a hoodie, but it all looks expensive. There's a brand name I don't recognise on the hoodie, and on his feet are trainers that I suspect cost several hundred pounds.

'You're here for the garden?' he asks. 'William won't like that.'

'Who's William?'

'You really don't know anyone, do you?'

'I arrived yesterday. So far, I've met Lady Clara, seen Vicky the cook, and encountered a couple of other staff members.'

'Ah. Well, William is the head gardener.'

'Is he the older guy with the beard?'

'That's Samuel Finch. He's the maintenance chap. William is late-thirties-ish and very territorial. He won't appreciate anyone invading his space.'

'Great.' I sigh.

'Hey, maybe he'll go easy on you,' he says, with a grin. A shout comes from the direction of the house and he calls back, 'Coming!' then looks at me. 'Just stroke William's ego. We men are simple souls.' Then he lopes off down the path, leaving me more concerned than ever about the elusive head gardener.

Despite my big, cooked breakfast, I'm hungry by twelve thirty, so I head over to the house, where I obediently make my way in through the staff entrance at the back. This turns out to lead directly to the kitchen and staff dining room. The latter has been laid out with several large platters of fresh sandwiches, plus bowls of fruit, and pots of various delicious-looking chutneys. There are homemade raisin flapjacks for dessert. There's no one else around, so I make myself up a plate of food, which I take up to the tower, before heading over to the courtyard to retrieve Mouse.

There's no sign of either Samuel Finch – as I now know he's called – or Mouse, when I reach the cobblestone area. I walk around the courtyard, glancing inside a large barn, which is full of rusting farm machinery, including an old John Deere 4020 six-cylinder tractor, which I'll have to check out at some stage: I love a good piece of kit, and this one is a collectable piece of farming history.

The loud revving of engines causes me to turn quickly. I have to leap out of the way of two motorbikes, each with two helmeted riders, all in leathers. I'm pretty sure the driver of the first bike is Miles; he raises a hand in greeting, before they speed off down a track and out of sight. I whistle as they pass, taking in the gleaming Harley-Davidsons.

I'm just wondering where else I can look for Mouse and his new friend, when the besuited woman from breakfast comes into the courtyard, bearing a plate of food.

She smiles. 'Hi! You must be Steph. I'm Olivia, the estates administrator.'

'Yep, I'm Steph. But right now, I seem to have lost my dog.'

She grins. 'So high?' She places her hand rather high on her torso for even my tall dog – but, as I hesitate, she adds, 'Black, wiry coat, surprisingly long legs, and very inquisitive?'

'That's the one!'

'Samuel has him in the quad.'

'The quad?'

'It's a grassy seating area. Head that way, and you'll find the pair of them.' She points past the courtyard, and around to the right.

'Got it! Thanks.'

I follow her directions, walking down a passage between the far end of the barn and a brick outbuilding, and arriving at an area of raggedy grass filled with moss.

Mouse comes running over, greeting me as if I've been gone for months.

'Hi, boy.' I bend to stroke him.

'He's a sweetheart, that one,' comes Samuel Finch's voice. He's sitting on a bench beneath the wide spread of an ornamental cherry tree, which must be glorious in spring, and even now is flouting some spectacular autumnal foliage in shades of orange and copper.

'It looks like you and he have been getting on well.'

'We have at that. Haven't we, boy?'

Mouse barks again, running back to Samuel and then over to me, before racing around in large loops.

'I'd have thought he'd be worn out by now,' says Samuel. 'He's been with me all the morning and I've had jobs to do all over the place.'

'I heard you're the maintenance person?'

He draws himself up and I realise I've offended him. 'I'm the estates manager.'

'Oh, sorry!'

He shakes his head. 'No matter. I'm Samuel Finch, by the way.'

'Good to meet you,' I say. 'Is it OK if I take Mouse back? He's due a rest.'

'Of course. Thanks again for letting me keep him for the morning. He's a grand fellow.'

'You did me a favour; it meant I could take a proper look at the gardens, without worrying what Mouse was up to.'

'Oh, you'll have no worries about him here: Ashford is as dog friendly as they come. But I'll be more than happy to dog-sit whenever you need it.'

We smile at each other, then Mouse and I head back to the tower.

I spend the afternoon in the living room, bent over the original garden plans at a little desk that's set beneath the window in the side wall. From time to time, I get up to take a look through the window above the built-in seat, comparing the current garden layout with the original. This spot, where Mouse has settled for his afternoon snooze, offers a good view over a section of the neglected parterre, and takes in some of the extensive gardens beyond.

From my online research, together with the notes I've received from Lady Clara, I know that the gardens were designed by George London, who was appointed royal gardener by William and Mary.

From 1670 until his death in 1714, he worked at a number of parks and gardens, creating intricate parterre plantings, inspired by the embroidery on contemporary clothing. Also influenced by the beautiful gardens of France, including Versailles, he often included a labyrinth in his designs, and I'm eager to check out the yew maze that features on his plans for Ashford.

Sadly, London's original avenues of lime and oak trees – which radiated out from the house like the rays of the sun – were torn out at some point in the intervening centuries. I am not planning on reinstating these, as the scale of the project would be phenomenal, and it would be many years before the trees matured.

On one of my trips to the front window, my attention is caught by two figures, a male and a female, who seem to be deep in conversation. She's leaning towards him, her hand on his chest, and I see him lift a strand of hair off her face, and tuck it behind her ear. The gesture is so intimate that I feel like an interloper. I move to step away from the window, but it's too late – she looks up and catches my eye. And then, she tugs at his sleeve and draws him out of sight, behind a tree. I feel myself blush at the impression I've given, of being a curtain-twitcher. But I can't deny that I'm curious. Despite the late-afternoon dusk, I caught a glimpse of russet hair, and I'm sure the woman was Olivia. I was unable to identify her companion, but the encounter was clearly a tryst.

It occurs to me that I still haven't met William Blythe, the head gardener. This strikes me as a little odd, as we'll need to work closely together: I would have hoped he'd seek me out. I make a mental note to redress that situation tomorrow, if he doesn't show up at dinner tonight.

Later, as I'm finishing up my notes for the day, my mobile rings. My heartbeat increases and I answer quickly when I see it's Caroline, the girlfriend of my ex-husband, Ben.

'Is there some news?' I ask her. Ben has been missing for months now – ever since he paid me a visit, asking for money, and I turned him down.

'There's been a sighting in Salford.'

I'm not sure what to say to this. There have been many 'sightings' since his disappearance went out on Facebook and missing persons' noticeboards. All of them have, so far, proved false.

'Well?' she demands in her high, nasal tones.

'Are they sure it's him?' I ask quietly.

'Actually, this time there's a photo,' she says. 'And it's definitely him, living it up in some bar. So it looks like the bastard has just buggered off and left me.' Her voice breaks and she sobs loudly, still talking. I can't make out what she's saying through the crying, so I don't even attempt a response. At last, she blows her nose loudly and says, 'Good riddance.'

'Absolutely,' I say. 'Listen, Caroline, would you mind forwarding that photo? I'd like to see it.'

'All right.'

There's a long silence. I want to feel relieved but, until I see the picture for myself, I'm still uneasy.

'I'll send it later,' she says. 'I'm busy cutting up his clothes.'

'Have fun,' I say.

We end the call and I check my watch. It's six twenty-five: time to head over for dinner.

In the dining room, I find myself seated between Simon and Jamie. The latter regales me with stories of other places he's worked, providing all of the characters' voices, while the others look on in amusement and call out requests for various tales from his repertoire.

'Jamie, do the head cook at Chatsworth!'

'Jamie, do that one-eyed cat that stole the chicken at that chateau in France!'

'Do the house manager that smoked in the guest bathroom and set off the sprinklers!'

Jamie is clearly in the wrong job – he should be on stage. I hope he manages to sort things out with his father so that he can pursue his theatrical dreams.

The food is delicious, in an unpretentious way: a hearty meal of shepherd's pie, followed by jam roly-poly and custard. It's like a finessed version of a school dinner. The table is decorated with many small jam jars, each filled with Michaelmas daisies amid the fluffy white seed heads of *Clematis vitalba* (old man's beard) and the orange seed pods of *Physalis franchetii* (Chinese lanterns), some of which have become finely skeletal with age, forming a delicate cage around their central fruit. Jamie is clearly a young man of many talents.

At bedtime, I settle Mouse in his own bed with Mr Rabbit, before mounting the stairs to mine. There's no argument through the walls tonight, but my dreams are unsettled. In one of them, Miles Spencer is insisting, 'We need a wayward gardener.'

'Well, that's not me,' I protest.

'If it's not you, it will just have to be your dog.'

'But Mouse doesn't know how to garden!'

'Then he'll just have to learn. It's either that or the doghouse for both of you.'

When I wake in the night, it's with the conviction that Mouse and I have been locked in the doghouse: a small, dark shed, with no way out.

3

I check my phone when I wake at six the next morning. Caroline has sent over the photograph, as promised. The image is quite grainy. I zoom in, but really it just looks like a generic shot of a man with red hair – I'm not at all sure it's Ben. I send her a message to that effect, and start to dress for my jog.

At that moment, my mobile rings. Expecting it to be Caroline, I grab it from my bedside table. It's my father.

'Hi, Dad. Everything OK?'

'We need to talk about sprouts,' he says.

I'm getting used to these impromptu calls. For most of his life, Dad had expressed no interest whatsoever in horticulture – so it came as a surprise when a mild heart attack led to this sudden urge to retire and take up vegetable gardening.

'How do I know when they're ready to pick?' he asks.

I perch on the edge of the bed. 'Did you stagger the sowing and planting out, like I suggested, so you get a continuous crop, rather than having them all ripen at once?'

'That sounded tedious, so I just sowed them all together.' I sigh inwardly. 'So, how do I know?' he persists.

'If they look the right size to eat, then they're the right size to pick. They should feel quite firm to the touch. But I hope you like sprouts – you're about to have a glut.'

'Right. Your mother can't stand them, as you know. But I've been looking up recipes and I'm hoping to win her round. Now, I was looking into greenhouses . . .'

'Dad, can this wait? I've just got time to fit in a run before breakfast.'

'Oh. OK. But call me back, won't you?'

'Will do.'

I was adopted as a baby, so Dad and Mum are my adoptive parents. And I've recently received notification through the National Adoption Register that my biological mother would like to make contact with me. But, given the amount of attention Dad requires for his allotment lessons, I keep wondering whether I'd have time for another parent in my life.

I'd been so keen to discover my 'origin story', as they say in comic books, but now that that possibility is close, I'm also getting nervous. What if my birth mother just didn't like the look of me when I was born? What if her reason for giving me up was that she couldn't love me? I'm not sure I'm ready for that kind of rejection. Mum and Dad did a pretty decent job of raising me, and maybe that's enough?

Deep down, I know it isn't. I have a file from Mum which breaks down my heritage: Eastern European Jewish on one side and Scottish Presbyterian on the other, with an African great-grandmother. But that's not the same as really knowing who I am and where I come from.

I call to Mouse, and we head downstairs and out, to the arable fields, where he races off in the darkness, after rabbits and imaginary beasts.

Jamie sits next to me at breakfast. In a low voice, I ask him, 'Who's William Blythe?' I glance around the table, but I know the identity of everyone present; none of them can be William.

'Oh, Mr Blythe doesn't eat with the likes of *us*.' He puts a dramatic hand to his chest.

'Really?'

Simon is seated opposite me, slumped in his chair. He chimes in, 'I have to work for him sometimes. He's dead jumped-up. I'm not even allowed to call him by his first name.'

'No one's allowed to call him by his first name,' says Jamie.

Oh, the joy. 'So, where can I find him?'

'I'll take you,' says Olivia, unexpectedly. She's sitting on the far side of Simon, and I hadn't realised she was listening. 'He has a desk in the office where I'm based, and he always starts the day there.'

'Oh, right. That would be great, thanks.'

Olivia waits for me to finish my toast and coffee before escorting me out of the dining hall. As we walk down the corridor towards the main part of the house, I wonder whether to bring up the previous afternoon – to tell her I didn't mean to spy on her from my window. But, as I pretty much was spying on her, albeit by chance rather than intent, I can't think how to phrase it.

We pass through a door to our left, that leads to another corridor. Again, the contrast between this and the staff corridor is stark. This passageway is broad, and boasts plush burgundy carpeting and old paintings in ornate wooden frames, set against gilded wallpaper.

We walk on, passing unmarked doors, until we reach the end of the passage, where a carved plaque on the wall announces that we have arrived at the office.

'Here we go.' She turns the doorknob and holds the door open for me to enter first.

I barely notice the room itself, because my eye is immediately caught – and held – by a man of around my age, seated behind a desk. He's white, with thick, glossy black hair, green eyes, a clean-shaven face and a sage tweed waistcoat. What arrests me is not his appearance, however, but his expression, which can only be described as hostile.

I consider putting on a sinister voice and saying, 'Ah, William. We meet at last,' but decide against it. Instead, I say, 'Hi. I'm Steph Williams.'

'I know perfectly well who you are.' He looks down at some paperwork on his desk, to make it clear how unimportant I am. His speech has the formal structure and careful enunciation of someone who has worked hard to lose their regional accent.

I step closer, until he can't ignore me. 'And I'm guessing you're William Blythe, the head gardener?'

He looks up and meets my eye. 'I am *Mr* Blythe, yes.'

I sigh. 'Well, Mr Blythe, I think we need to have a chat, don't you?'

He humphs, but I draw up a chair, and set it in front of his desk. I glance towards Olivia, who has taken her seat behind her own desk, to my right. She is watching our encounter with fascination, like a wildlife documentary, in which two would-be alpha-beasts fight for dominance.

Thinking of beasts, I decide to confront the elephant in the room. 'Do you have a problem with my being here?' I ask Blythe.

He sits back in his curved wooden desk chair and folds his arms. 'I just don't see why we need you. I've been gardening at Ashford for nearly twenty years, and the late Lady Irene never saw the need to bring in someone from outside.'

'Twenty years?' I question. He looks too young for that to be possible, but he nods and says,

'That's right. I started my training here at sixteen, and I'm now thirty-five.'

'You do know I'm not here to take over your job?'

He leans forward, clasping his hands on the leather-inlaid desktop. 'Then why are you here, exactly?'

'Because Lady Clara has hired me to reinstate the gardens, according to George London's original plans.'

He humphs again. 'Exactly: a task I could have carried out perfectly well, without any outside intervention.' He puts emphasis on the word 'intervention', lest I fail to grasp that I am the one intervening.

I feel anger rising like bile in my throat, and I struggle to keep it down. Pushing back my chair, I stand up and say, 'I'll make a survey of the gardens and put my proposals into new plans, and oversee the renovation project. After that, I will be out of your hair and you can go back to reigning unchallenged over your tiny kingdom.'

Do I imagine it, or does Olivia let out a snigger, as I stride towards the door?

I've just exploded out of the house and am taking deep breaths of ice-cold air in a bid to calm myself down, when I feel a hand on my shoulder. Assuming it's Blythe, I whirl to confront him. I pull up short when I see it's Lady Clara.

She takes a step back and puts up her hands. 'My goodness!' She laughs. 'You certainly don't take prisoners!'

'Sorry! I was expecting someone else.'

She's not wearing a coat, and she crosses her arms over her thin blouse and shivers, saying, 'It's freezing out here. Let's go inside, and you can tell me what on earth's going on. I saw you through the window, storming out of the house.'

I follow her back indoors, where she leads me straight into her study and gestures for me to take one of the two seats in front of her desk. She walks around to her own chair and sits down. Once again, there's a fire crackling in the grate behind her, and the room is stifling. I wish I hadn't agreed to come indoors.

'I'm parched,' she says. 'Will you join me for a cup of tea?'

I'd prefer coffee, but I politely say, 'That sounds good.' She nods and strides over to a long rope, which she pulls before returning to her seat behind the desk.

Jamie appears within what feels like seconds – although that might just be because I'm distracted by my rage, replaying the exchange with Blythe in my head.

'Two teas, please, Jamie,' says Lady Clara.

'Yes, ma'am.' He nods to her, then winks at me as he turns to leave.

She clasps her hands on her desk and smiles brightly. 'Now that the really important topic of tea has been taken care of, would you care to enlighten me? Who has you so riled up?'

I hesitate. I have no idea of her relationship with Blythe. If she thinks him wonderful, I could be starting off on the wrong foot if I bad-mouth him.

'I'll tell you what,' she continues, 'shall I guess, and you can tell me if I'm close?'

This elicits an involuntary smile from me. 'You can try.'

'I suspect that you've had your first encounter with our personable head gardener. Am I right?'

I stare at her. 'How did you know?'

'Oh . . . One gets to know one's staff. William is a gifted gardener. Sadly, he's . . .' she hesitates, 'a little deficient in people skills. I should probably have warned you, but I'd naively hoped he might respect your expertise and treat you in an appropriate fashion.'

'He thinks I'm an interloper, who's after his job.'

'Oh dear. I'm so sorry. I did explain the situation to him . . .'

I shake my head. 'It's not your fault . . .' I manage to bite back, *that your head gardener's an arse.*

Jamie knocks once and enters with a round tray, set with china.

'Just place it on my desk, please, Jamie, and I'll sort it out.'

'Very well, ma'am.'

This time, as he passes me on his way out, he twists his face into a grimace of such comedic brilliance, I have trouble keeping my own face straight.

'How do you take it?' asks Lady Clara, holding up the teapot.

I refocus. 'With milk and no sugar, please.'

She pours my tea and passes it to me. I hadn't banked on it being Earl Grey; the scent hits me before I put the cup to my lips. I hate Earl Grey: it's like drinking perfume.

'So, tell me, what are your thoughts on the garden so far?' she asks, eyeing me over the rim of her own cup.

'The parterre—' I begin.

'Oh, I know!' she breaks in. 'Just awful, isn't it? All that meticulous planning and planting, simply allowed to go to rack and ruin. I'm afraid my mother – who was a wonderful woman – inherited a garden that had already strayed quite far in places from London's original vision. And sadly she didn't do any restoration work during the sixty-odd years she lived here.'

'It's not just that,' I say. 'The box hedging is infested.'

She frowns. 'Is it treatable?'

'Some of it's already dead. And the rest can't be treated without also killing off every beneficial insect in the vicinity. I'm afraid the box plants will all need digging out and replacing. I've been wondering if it might be worth referring to some of London's other gardens, and substituting the box with chippings of a local stone.'

'That's an interesting idea . . .'

'I'll find some photographs, so you can see the effect.' I hesitate, then say, 'Meanwhile, I hope you don't mind my asking, but Mr Blythe . . . Did you consider approaching him first, to see if he wanted to restore the gardens?'

She sips her tea, then sets her china cup down in its saucer. 'I did talk to him about it, when I took over from Mother, but William simply stressed how much work was needed, to keep the rest of the grounds in order, without introducing extra projects. I did give him first refusal.'

'He has a point. There is a lot to do in a garden like Ashford.'

'I meant it, when I said he's a wonderful gardener. He has the greenest fingers – everything he touches flourishes. I think he's rather better with plants than with people.' She offers me a wry smile, and I smile back, somewhat mollified. She continues, 'Sadly, he doesn't have an eye for the design side. When he plants up a new bed, there will inevitably be some ghastly colour clashes, and the plants at the front often outgrow those at the back. Poor Mother didn't have it in her to object, so he went unchecked, allowed to do as he wished.' She takes a deep breath. 'That's why it felt so important to consult a restoration expert for the parterre, where the design needs to be spot on.' She smiles again. 'I'm sorry he's so pig-headed.'

I laugh. 'At least everyone else seems friendly.'

She nods. 'We've been lucky with our team.'

'Right, well, I'd better get on.' I stand to leave, discreetly placing my full cup of Earl Grey on a side table on my way out.

4

After my talk with Lady Clara, I fetch Mouse from the tower – still not quite believing I live in an actual tower. I expect him to run off to explore but, in fact, after sniffing around near the house for a few minutes, he curls up to sleep beneath a large eucalyptus, clearly worn out from his morning run. He has good taste: this specimen has beautiful, pale, peeling bark.

I'm keen to see what state the yew maze is in, so I walk through the parterre, and then cross a formal water garden, where a bubbling fountain in white limestone is set at the centre of an octagonal pond built from the same stone. According to the original designs, there should be a partner to this fountain elsewhere in the grounds, forming a symmetry to the overall design when viewed from above. I wonder if the first-floor bedrooms – where the family sleeps – offer such a view.

After the water garden comes a walled garden, well stocked with tea roses. This late in the year, pruned back, without their blooms and losing their leaves, they make a striking spectacle: dark, jagged shapes against the warm orange of the aged brick walls.

There are tall, metal scroll gates set into the wall at either side of the rose garden. I know from the plans that the right-hand one leads out to the wildflower meadow – which I shall leave to Blythe's ministrations. I take the left-hand gate and realise I'm close to the lake. So, where is the maze?

As I look around, I see a young woman, emerging from a clutch of trees. She has long, honey-coloured hair and a short skirt that's caught up in the back. Miles Spencer appears behind her, and they laugh as he tugs her hem straight and plucks a leaf from her fringe.

He catches my eye and murmurs something to her before striding over to me.

'Ms Williams,' he says.

'Mr Spencer.'

He grins. 'Can we pretend you didn't see this?'

'Didn't see what?'

He looks confused for a moment, before understanding dawns. 'Thank you. I appreciate it.'

'But you have to help me.'

He raises an eyebrow. 'So, that's the way it is.'

'You have to direct me to the maze. I thought it would be here.'

'Ah!' He points. 'It's further along, past the croquet lawn. Now, if you'll excuse me . . .' He gestures towards the young woman.

'Of course.'

I continue on my way, passing the croquet lawn – an addition since London's original design – until I reach the maze. It's taller than I'd expected, and Blythe has maintained it well. I have a good sense of direction, so I step inside, pretty sure I will find my way out.

I don't think I've ever been in such a dense maze before. The hedging is so tall as to block any chance of seeing over the top, and no light makes its way through the rows.

I'm sure some would find it claustrophobic, but I love the sense of plunging into green darkness. The scent of the yew is strong and rich. I can hear birds rustling and singing all around me, but I feel shut off from humanity, calm and serene.

I walk fairly quickly, making three wrong turns, until I eventually reach the centre. Checking my watch, I see it's taken me ten minutes to reach this spot. There's a bench, and I sit for a few minutes. A robin flies down and comes quite close, head on one side, surprisingly tame.

'I don't have anything for you, I'm afraid,' I tell it. After a few minutes, it gives up and flies away, and I get to my feet and start back towards my work. I love a big project like the parterre, where the results will be dramatic.

After my walk through the maze, the day passes quickly. I grab my lunch from the dining hall, and make sure Mouse has a bowl of water. He drinks it quickly, before heading off to explore.

At around 3 p.m., he returns and stops in front of me with a single bark. I'm standing in a wooded area close to the lake, noting the type and condition of each tree, including its likely age. There are a number of hazel trees, which I'm sure have been 'planted' by squirrels hiding their nuts.

'What is it, boy?' I ask Mouse. 'Oh, who's this?'

Behind him, there's a wolfhound. She stands still, regarding me, and I say, 'Well, hello there.'

Mouse comes to me for a stroke and looks back at her, encouraging her to join us. She walks closer and sits politely, allowing me to read her name on the engraved disc attached to her collar. She is dark grey, and the size of a small pony. I don't know what it is about wolfhounds, but they always look scruffy to me. I have a weakness for scruffy dogs.

'Mirabelle,' I say, reading her name aloud. 'How lovely to meet you.' She lifts a paw and I am smitten. She has soft ears, coarse fur and a gentle, intelligent face.

'Belle!' comes a shout from close by. Mirabelle turns as a figure approaches through the trees. It's Lady Clara.

'I hope she's not bothering you,' she says, panting. 'She's my brother Dickie's dog. He doesn't live at Ashford, but as his place is only a few miles away, he drops her off whenever he has a long day in the office. My nephew Miles is supposed to keep an eye on her when she's here, but you know what these boys are like. He and my son are no doubt off gallivanting somewhere on their motorcycles.'

'She's not bothering me at all,' I say. 'It looks like she's been keeping Mouse company. She can hang out with us. When does your brother want her back?'

Lady Clara consults her watch, which is a delicate piece: rose gold with diamonds around the face. I can't help thinking how impractical it would be in a job like mine. 'Oh, it's only just gone three,' she says. 'Dickie won't be back until nine tonight. Are you sure you don't mind keeping her with you?'

'Not at all. She and Mouse can come inside the tower once it gets too dark to work outside.' I can't bring myself to refer to my new home as the 'Round Wing'.

Lady Clara's relief is palpable. 'Thank you,' she says. 'In that case, I think I'll treat myself to another cup of tea.'

As she walks away, Mirabelle lets out a small whine, which I at first take to be sorrow at the departure of Lady Clara, but then I realise she's just urging Mouse to get moving. He licks my hand in farewell, and the pair of them bound off into the woodland.

'Don't stay out too late,' I call, as if they're a pair of teenagers with a curfew.

And then I hear a distinct pair of splashes, and my heart sinks. They're going to be covered in stinking mud and pond weed by the time they come inside.

With a shake of my head, I refocus my attention on the tree survey. There are some beautiful imported specimens, plus a number of natives, including oaks, hornbeams and copper beeches. Most are well established and, although they weren't in the original plans, I will allow them to remain; they're such beautiful trees, and so important for wildlife. Alongside the errant hazels, there are a number of opportunistic elders and blackberries, all of which will have to come out. I'm making a note about a sickly horse chestnut, when I catch a glimpse of movement to my right. I walk towards it and see William Blythe, pushing a wheelbarrow.

It's time to swallow my pride and make nice. I walk over and call to him, 'Mr Blythe?'

He starts. I notice the barrow has a frame, supporting a tarpaulin that's concealing the contents. I don't think I've ever seen a covered wheelbarrow before. Once again, Blythe's expression is far from friendly. 'Oh, it's you.'

Determined not to let him rile me, I say, 'I just wanted to apologise. I feel like we got off on the wrong foot this morning.'

'You keep to your lane and we'll be fine,' he says.

I push a curl back from my forehead. 'The trouble is, my lane will keep crossing yours. It's inevitable.'

'I don't agree,' he says. 'You draw up your *tiny* plans and I'll sign off on them.'

I sigh. 'I'm sorry. I lost my temper and was rude. I hope you can forgive me. I'd like to start afresh.' I hold out a hand, which he regards as if it's covered in manure.

'If you'll excuse me, I need to get on,' he says, keeping his own hands firmly on the handles of the barrow.

I watch him walk away. Despite my dislike of the man, my interest is piqued by his covered barrow. It looks like he's heading for the courtyard and the outbuildings there. What might a gardener have to hide? The amateur detective in me considers following him and finding out. But I've transgressed quite enough in the eyes of Mr Blythe for the time being.

The dogs refuse to come in with me when the light's fading at four, so I leave them to roam, and call them again at five. As predicted, they arrive filthy, coated in mud like they've been dipped in foul-smelling chocolate. I take them straight up the stone staircase to my little en-suite shower room, where Mirabelle shows Mouse how an impeccably behaved dog comports herself at wash time, standing still for her entire wash. He likes to shake himself vigorously when he's covered in lather, and I often end up soapier than he is. Once I've towelled them both dry, I feed them and settle them in the living room, where they somehow manage to both squeeze on to the warm window seat above the radiator. Mouse rather sweetly shares Mr Rabbit with Belle.

Then I call Dad. Mum answers his mobile: 'Hi, Louise! How's it going?'

Mum, Dad and my brother, Danny, all refuse to call me Steph. Louise is a name I've tried to leave behind, since I changed it more than two years ago – after my ex, Ben, lost all our money in bad deals.

'OK, thanks,' I tell her. 'Pretty good, actually. My accommodation is in a tower.'

'The "Round Wing" is a tower? How wonderful, love. Oh – here's your dad now. I'll put him on.' I rarely get a proper chance to chat to Mum since Dad got his allotment.

Dad comes on the line. 'You getting to grips with your new place?' he asks. 'Anyone accuse you of blackmail yet?' Unsurprisingly, none of my family took well to this incident at my last place, although that doesn't stop dad from joking about it..

'Nope. I'm allegation free so far.'

'Oh well, plenty of time,' he says jovially.

'Thanks for that. So, what did you want help with?'

'Oh, don't worry. I thought there might be room in the garden for a greenhouse, but your mother has vetoed it.'

I can hear Mum's voice in the background, 'Yes, I bloody well have.'

'Onward and upward,' says Dad, in a jovial tone.

'OK, well I'll be off, then,' I say. 'Dinner shortly.'

We finish the call and I head over to the house.

There's no one else in the dining room when I get there, but the long table has been set, so I take a seat near the middle and wait.

A tall, middle-aged white man enters the room, stopping when he sees me.

'Oh!' he says. From his dress – an expensive, navy suit with a purple silk tie – I infer that this is Mr Fanshawe, Lady Clara's husband. 'I don't think we've met?'

I stand up. 'Steph Williams, the gardening consultant.'

'Of course, of course! Splendid!' he says, walking over and shaking my hand across the table. 'Rupert Fanshawe.'

'Good to meet you.'

'And you. Actually, I was looking for Becky. Have you seen her?'

I don't even know who Becky is. 'I'm afraid not. And I'm starting to wonder if something is happening somewhere else.'

'FOMO,' he says, nodding sagely. 'My son Julian has told me all about it.' There's a crash from the kitchen, and he whirls around. 'Good lord,' he says, as the kitchen door flies open and Vicky storms out, shouting,

'I'm not putting up with any more of this crap.' She stops in the corridor, her mouth open in horror at the sight of my companion. 'Oh, Mr Fanshawe, sir, I'm terribly sorry . . .'

Our boss puts up a hand to fend off her apologies. 'Sometimes we all need to vent, Vicky. Now, tell me, what's troubling you?'

Her face has turned bright red. 'I'm afraid I can't tell you that, sir. But heads will roll, mark my words.'

'Fighting talk indeed,' says Mr Fanshawe in a jocular tone. 'Come in here and have a seat, while I pour you a sherry.' He opens the sideboard and pours her a drink from a glittering crystal decanter, which seems too fine an item for a mere staff dining room.

'There, now.' He hands it to her and she takes it and sits down, sipping from the tiny glass.

'I just can't work in these conditions,' she says. 'I'm sorry, sir, but it's impossible.'

He unbuttons his lower jacket button, then pulls out the chair beside her and sits down. 'I'm afraid you'll have to enlighten me, Vicky.'

As I admire Mr Fanshawe's excellent people skills, it occurs to me that William Blythe could learn a lot from his boss.

Vicky draws in a breath and says, 'Michael always says he'll be here and then he never turns up, so there's just Becky, who as you know, sir, isn't trained yet. And meanwhile I've got all these mouths to feed.' At that moment, she seems to register that the mouths are largely absent from the dining table. 'Where is everyone?' she asks me.

'I was wondering the same thing. Shall I go and find out?'

Mr Fanshawe says, 'That would be very helpful. Thank you, Ms Williams.'

I get to my feet and head outside via the staff door. At first I don't see anyone, but then I hear a shout from the nearby kitchen garden. As I hurry over, I realise there are several voices, all talking and shouting at once. The door in the wall is open, and I'm treated to a preview of the scene within, before I join the throng. Miles Spencer and a young man I don't recognise – Julian, perhaps – are fighting. Both are dressed in rugby shirts. Miles's shirt is red, and Julian's dark blue, as if they're playing for opposing sides. As they grunt and continue to take swings at one another, some of the staff keep trying to separate them. Others are watching, with expressions ranging from horror to glee. Jamie is practically cheering them on.

I walk over to him. 'What's going on?'

'Only the best entertainment we've had all year,' he says. 'I'd have sold tickets if I'd known, like.'

'But, why are they fighting?'

'Dunno. Looks dead serious, though,' he says with a grin.

'Who is that with Miles? Is it Julian?'

'Yep, our young lord and master.'

'How long's this been going on?'

Jamie checks his watch. 'Getting on for an hour. Michael tried to talk them out of it but got nowhere, so he went for Mr B. He keeps getting them separated, but they just run at each other again.' He grins again. 'It's boss.'

At that moment, Julian gives his cousin a swift, sharp kick to the shins, and Miles collapses to the ground. William Blythe takes this opportunity to step between the young men and place his hands on Julian's shoulders, looking him in the face and talking quietly. But Julian is too far gone for logic and keeps trying to shove Blythe to one side, so he can get back to his attack. While this is going on, Saliha and Michael are helping Miles to his feet and supporting him in a bid for escape via the door in the wall. The three of them nearly make it, but Miles is clearly in a lot of pain from that tackle. He sinks back to the ground, clutching his injured leg and groaning. At that moment, Julian gets free of Blythe and starts charging towards his cousin with a scream of 'Arrrrggghhhh!' worthy of a berserker.

I quickly weigh up Saliha's slightness versus the force of a charging Julian, and rush over to push her safely out of the way. This leaves Michael and me on the front line. Keeping my centre of gravity low, I step forward, directly into the path of the assailant. I see the confusion on Julian's face as he gets close and realises he's about to plough into someone he doesn't even know. He tries to stop, but he's picked up too much momentum, so I reach out both arms to slow him down, and we manage to stagger to a clumsy, hugging standstill.

At that moment, a loud voice interrupts, 'What in god's name ...? Julian! What on earth do you think you're doing? I've never in my life seen such a display ...' Lady Clara is standing in the garden doorway, a look of horror on her face.

'But, Mummy—' begins Julian.

She shakes her head. 'I do not want to hear it. Brawling in front of the help . . . ! Get inside, this instant.' She turns her attention to Miles, who is still groaning on the ground. 'Are you all right, Miles?'

His eyes are shut but he says, 'Yes, Auntie,' in a weak voice.

'Very well,' she says. 'William, if you and one of the others wouldn't mind helping Miles inside?'

'Of course, ma'am.' Blythe gestures to Michael to help him, and they haul Miles back to his feet and start towards the house, one on each side of the injured man as he hobbles along.

With a guilty jolt, I remember Vicky's distress, and wave to attract the attention of Jamie, who is now in mid re-enactment of some of the fight scenes – playing both sides while others look on laughing. He stops when he sees me gesturing, and walks over. 'Everything all right?'

'Vicky's having trouble in the kitchen, trying to get everything done without Michael.'

He slaps his forehead. 'I should have thought of that. I'll go and help out.'

Now that there's no entertainment, everyone starts to notice how cold it is outside. The air has a dampness which infiltrates our clothing. I wish I hadn't left my jacket in the house. We traipse inside, to the dining room, where we sit around the table and the conversation returns inevitably to the scene we've just witnessed.

After a few minutes of laughing along with the others, I ask, 'What was the fight about?'

This is met mainly with shrugs, until Simon says, 'Maybe Master Miles broke one of his cousin's toys,' and everyone laughs.

'Is that common?' I ask. 'The two of them falling out like that?'

Olivia shakes her head. 'Normally, they're inseparable.'

'They've been thick as thieves since they were little ones,' agrees Samuel.

'How strange,' I say, and there are murmurs of agreement.

Michael and Jamie bring in our plates of food, then they and Vicky join us at the table. Vicky catches my eye as she sits down, and smiles ruefully. I smile in sympathy. She's followed a minute later by the girl I saw at breakfast on Monday. She has big eyes and a heart-shape face; her hair is worn in long twists, tucked beneath her hair net. I realise that this must be Becky. She looks as if she's on the verge of crying. She takes a seat beside Vicky, near the end of the table, and I see the head cook give the girl's hand a reassuring squeeze, which elicits a smile. Hopefully, Becky hasn't been too traumatised by Vicky's earlier meltdown.

I suddenly realise that it's Tuesday evening. I call down the table: 'Vicky, isn't it tonight Lady Clara wanted you to feed truffles to her dinner guests?'

She turns towards me and nods. 'Everything's prepped but the Abingers can never make it till late, thank god. And they're getting soufflé instead. It's one of my signature dishes, and it always gets a good reaction.'

'Sounds tasty.'

Despite the chaotic build-up, the food is delicious: a chicken breast in a creamy sauce with potato dauphinois and green beans. I try not to think about the cholesterol content – especially when dessert turns out to be apple and blackberry pie with thick custard. We eat largely in silence, savouring the meal. Occasionally, Jamie makes reference to the fight, and everyone laughs, especially when he mocks Blythe's ineffectual attempts at intervention. I can't help wishing I'd arrived sooner, and witnessed these first hand.

Later, back in the tower, the dogs snooze contentedly while I look through my notes, pondering whether new hedging plants or limestone chippings would make a better surround for the parterre.

Just after nine, Belle and Mouse start barking. Belle runs to the top of the stairs, her tail wagging frantically, so I deduce her human must have arrived.

I'm already on my way down when the knock sounds.

Opening the door, I see the broad-shouldered man from Lady Clara's study the night I arrived.

He holds out a hand. 'Hi. Dickie Spencer, Clara's brother.' His voice is deep and resonant.

I shake the proffered hand. 'Steph Williams.' Belle flies out of the door and leaps up at him. I laugh. 'I don't need to ask why you're here.'

'Steady, Belle,' he says. 'Where are your manners? What do we say to Ms Williams?'

Belle charms me anew by turning to me, sitting on her haunches, and lifting a paw. 'Aw! You're very welcome, darling, any time,' I tell her.

I hear Mouse behind me and step out of the way so that he can meet Dickie. 'And who is this fine young man?' Dickie asks.

'This is Mouse.'

Dickie bends down to make a fuss of Mouse.

'I'll let you get on,' says Dickie after a moment, standing up and pushing back his blond fringe. 'Thanks again for having Belle.'

'No worries.'

We say goodnight and I close the door. Mouse whines softly.

'I know,' I tell him. 'I miss Belle, too.'

I take him back upstairs, where he leaps on to the window seat. Although I attempt to distract him with his favourite programme – an Attenborough documentary on ocean wildlife – he refuses to budge from the window, as if hoping that Belle will reappear if he stays there long enough.

I make a big fuss of him until bedtime, giving him extra cuddles and kind words.

At around ten forty that night, when I'm trying to sleep, a voice starts shouting again on the other side of the wall. The walls are too thick for me to make out any words, but I'm not prepared to ignore the situation a second time. I get up and walk down to the first floor, where I put on my head torch and don my trainers.

Mouse wakes up as I'm grabbing my coat from the hook on the living-room door. Sleepy though he is, he stumbles to his feet and tries to accompany me, but I don't want to take him into a potentially volatile situation, in case he tries to weigh in.

'Wait here, boy.' He whines, but nonetheless sits obediently at the top of the stairs as I walk down them and out of the door.

The great house is in darkness as I make my way around to the staff entrance. I try the handle, but it's locked, so I jog to the front, where I find the door also locked. I hesitate. I don't want to wake people up by ringing the bell – which is an actual bell, like a small version of the ones they have in churches, and will, I suspect, make quite a lot of noise. So, instead, I walk around the whole mansion, trying the various doors along the way, but they are all fast.

Despite my concerns for the safety of those involved in the row, it looks like any intervention will have to wait until tomorrow.

5

When I walk into the dining room the next morning, Jamie is even livelier than usual. He's wearing a serviette as a chef's hat, and appears to be 'doing' Vicky. He has her voice down perfectly. As she's standing just inside the room, doubled up with laughter, there's obviously no malice in it.

She smiles at me. 'Morning. Full English?'

'Yes, please.'

'I've got a belly ache from laughing,' she says, nodding towards Jamie, who, with a dramatic hand to his forehead, is exclaiming, 'I simply can't cook in these conditions. Take me back to my trailer this minute!' Vicky goes to give Jamie a hug, snorting with laughter, before she turns back to the kitchen to make my breakfast.

I take a seat next to Saliha, and reach for the coffee pot. 'Jamie's on good form,' I say.

'He's off from Friday for the weekend,' she says. 'He's dead excited. Lucky sod.'

'I heard the shouting again last night. Did you not hear it?'

She shakes her head. 'But I'm at the other end of the passage.'

'Does Jamie have the end room near the tower?'

She thinks for a moment. 'Actually, that room's empty. Jamie's, like, second from the end.'

'So, I have a ghost?'

She shudders. 'Maybe. I mean, I reckon this place has a few of those.' She thinks for a moment. 'Or maybe someone's using it as an extra room or something. Our bedrooms are dead tiny.'

'I'll have to ask around. It sounded pretty serious.'

She raises her eyebrows. 'There's a heap load of drama in this place. I mean, you saw Master Julian and his cousin Miles.'

We both watch Jamie, who is now slumped in his chair, pretending to snore loudly. As we watch, he starts awake, points at Simon, and exclaims, 'You there! Fetch ma whisky this minute!' Everyone laughs.

'Is there anyone he can't impersonate?' I ask Saliha.

'I don't think so. He's amazing.' From the way she says this, I wonder if she has a crush on him.

'Where's Jamie going this weekend?' I ask.

'He's got his brother's thirtieth. There's going to be this party boat filled with booze.'

'That's a big age gap – isn't Jamie only about twenty?'

'Yeah. But he's from this massive family. I mean, he's got about fifty brothers.'

'That's a lot.' I laugh and she joins in.

'Well . . . at least four,' she says.

I look along the table. Jamie is still in performance mode, and the staff around him are loving it.

There's a sudden, loud thump, and we all look over towards the source. Simon, who was sitting opposite Jamie, has laughed so hard that he's fallen off his chair, which has come crashing down on top of him.

It's obvious he's unharmed, as he's still laughing. Samuel and Olivia rush to his aid, righting the chair and helping him to sit safely back down.

'I think that's enough now, Jamie,' says Olivia. 'We don't want any more casualties.'

There's a chorus of, 'Awww!' but Jamie grins and starts tucking into his breakfast.

I sit, drinking my coffee, until Becky brings my food. I thank her, and then turn back to Saliha. 'Have you got any tips for getting along with Mr Blythe?' I ask her quietly.

She pulls a face. 'He's well snide,' she says.

'Snide?'

'Like dead mean. He screamed at me for just going in one of his sheds my first week here. And Lady C had sent me to look for him! He said I had, "no business trespassing on his property". She deepens her voice for this last part.

'You poor thing.'

'Vicky told me to ignore him. She said he's a bully and I shouldn't let him get to me. She gave me a piece of cake.'

'She seems really nice.'

'She is. Jamie loves her – he doesn't mean anything by it when he takes the mick. His own mum died a while back, and she's like his substitute.' She glances at her watch, then stands up. 'I need to get on. See you.' I watch her join the now-familiar exodus of staff from the dining room.

Samuel is the only other person still at the table, finishing his drink. He glances over from a few seats away. 'I saw your Mouse with Lady Mirabelle yesterday,' he says.

I laugh. 'The title suits her.'

'Has she gone back now?' he asks.

'Yes – Dickie came for her last night.'

'Young Master Miles is meant to look after her when she's here, but he's too busy with his assignations,' he says, landing slowly on the final word.

'You mean his girlfriend?'

He raises an eyebrow. 'Not only *his* girlfriend, if you catch my drift?'

Understanding dawns as I remember the furtive way in which Miles emerged from the trees with a girl. 'Is that what the fight was about? Is he sleeping with Julian's girlfriend?'

'Oh, I don't know about that. He and Master Julian are like brothers. But there's a couple of young men in the village who are not best pleased at having their girlfriends lured away, I can tell you.'

'So, what was the fight about?'

'Do you know, I've been racking my brains since it went down, but I can't think of anything. They've never got into it like that before.'

I finish my coffee and stand up. 'Would you like a visit from Mouse today? He's going to be at a loose end, now his playmate's gone home.'

Something close to joy spreads across Samuel's face. 'That would be smashing.'

'Where will you be this morning?'

'I need to check the state of the tiled roofs on the old outbuildings today. I'll wait for you in the courtyard.'

I head back to the tower, where I find Mouse on the window seat, staring out. He turns at my entrance, and makes a sad little questioning sound in his throat.

I walk over and pat him. 'I know, boy. I'll have to ask if she can come again soon.' He licks my hand, as if he understands. 'Would you like to see Samuel instead?' The name is not yet familiar to him, and he tilts his head questioningly. But he accompanies me downstairs, and speeds up when he sees we're going towards the courtyard, where we met his new human friend. He stops at the door and gives an excited bark.

A voice comes from the other side, 'Is that my little friend?' And then the door opens, and Mouse hurls himself at Samuel.

I leave them to their joyful reunion and walk over to the parterre. I want to get started on my detailed survey, comparing the current planting to the original plans. This is an absorbing task. It's November, so not much is in flower but, going by the foliage, there are a number of plants that I'm sure didn't feature in the original planting.

Mouse starts barking in the distance mid-morning, while I'm kneeling to inspect an area of the parterre, where one particularly vigorous plant has taken over. As I've left him with Samuel, I figure he's in good hands, and continue my examination of the thug. It's an evergreen, *Campanula portenschlagiana*, which definitely shouldn't be here, having only been introduced to Britain in the twentieth century, long after George London laid out his plans. In general, I've decided not to be too rigid with the planting – after all, if a more recently introduced, or bred, variety of a plant has proven especially resilient to pests and diseases, or simply has a longer flowering season, it will be worth considering in place of London's original. But anything that is crowding out other plants will need to be restricted or even removed. I make a note about this campanula, and get to my feet.

Mouse is still barking, so I go to investigate.

I find him in the courtyard, where he's cornered Blythe, who is backed against the wall of one of the outbuildings, beside a standpipe. Samuel is standing beside Mouse, holding his collar and murmuring soothingly, but to no avail. I run over.

Blythe sees me and shouts, 'Can't you call off your bloody dog?'

'Sorry! Mouse! Hey, boy!' But Mouse merely glances at me, then back to Blythe, still barking.

Samuel looks at me in a panic. 'I don't know what's wrong. I've tried to calm him, but he's not listening.'

I crouch down to stroke Mouse, taking his collar from Samuel, who steps out of the way. 'Mouse won't hurt you,' I tell Blythe.

'Can you tell him that?'

It's true that Mouse has his lip drawn back in a snarl. 'It's OK, boy. It's OK.' He starts to calm down as I stroke him, his barks easing to grumbles.

I look up at Blythe. 'What did you do?'

'What do you mean, what did *I* do? Your fucking dog came straight for me.'

'It's true,' says Samuel. 'I was up on the roof and he suddenly went off.'

This is so unlike Mouse, I look around for clues. There's a bucket close by. 'What's in that?' I ask Blythe.

'None of your damn business.'

I sigh. 'Look, something must have worried Mouse for him to react like that – it's out of character. Is there something in that bucket that might have upset him?'

Although Mouse has stopped barking, his eyes are still fixed on Blythe, his body tense and alert. I keep my hand under his collar.

Blythe steps sideways, watching the dog warily, and bends down to the bucket, picking it up and tilting it, to show me the contents. Mouse starts to growl.

Kittens. Three of them, tiny and wet.

'What's happening?'

The voice comes from close by. It's Olivia, who has walked over without my noticing, a lit cigarette at her side.

'Mr Blythe is drowning kittens,' I say.

'Oh, William! Lilibeth didn't have more?'

He nods. 'Why her Ladyship won't get that Persian spayed . . .'

Olivia drops her cigarette and stubs it out neatly beneath the toe of a black court shoe. 'I'll take them.'

Blythe and Samuel stare at her. 'They're newborn,' says Blythe. 'They'll need constant care.'

'I'll take them,' she says again.

Samuel says softly, 'They'll be a lot of work, Livvy. Are you sure?'

She rolls her eyes. 'I'm not going to nurse them myself, Sam. You remember that cat in the village?'

'Oh! Grand plan!'

Blythe places the bucket on the ground and walks away, without another word. Olivia reaches in and takes out a kitten. 'Well, hello there,' she says softly, stroking its head with one finger.

I take out the other two and place them at Mouse's feet. He curls around them and licks them, nuzzling them gently.

'Will you look at that?' says Samuel in amazement.

Olivia addresses Mouse: 'What a brave dog! You saved the kittens.' She looks at me, 'I've never seen a dog defend a cat before.'

'Mouse loves cats,' I say. 'He's a rescue dog, but his first home was overrun with cats, and one of the mother cats adopted him. What are you going to do with the kittens?'

'I'll take them down to the village,' she says. 'One of the residents has a cat that's just lost her kittens. I'll see if she'll accept them.'

She goes to find a basket. While she's gone, Mouse tends to all three and, when she returns, he has to be persuaded to give them up. He whines beside Olivia as she puts them into the basket.

'I promise they'll be well looked after,' she tells him.

Samuel looks at me. 'I'm sorry I didn't manage that situation better,' he says.

'It's not your fault.' He shakes his head. 'Hey,' I say, putting a hand on his arm. 'You couldn't know why he was barking like that.'

But Samuel shakes his head and walks away, shoulders stooped, the epitome of dejection.

Mouse, meanwhile, is still marking Olivia, as she checks the kittens are comfortable in the lined basket. I lead him away, before he can try to stop her from leaving with them.

* * *

Late morning brings an ominously dark sky, which splits opens to release hailstones: fat, cold and hard. I run indoors, calling to Mouse, who is asleep beneath a nearby horse chestnut. He overtakes me on the way to the tower, where I open the door, and he races upstairs. By the time I reach the living room, he's already on the window seat. I sit beside him, where we watch and listen as the stones slap the windows and ground. Seeing the poor plants beneath us being pelted, I have to remind myself that the majority of them have been here for years, withstanding everything that Derbyshire skies can throw at them.

I take a seat at my desk. I've drawn up the outlines of the parterre beds on sheets of paper, and I'm gradually filling them in with the current planting, labelling what needs to come out or be restrained. I also have a coded map, with the position of each bed within the overall scheme.

I pencil in the results of the morning's survey, including the errant campanula. There are a lot of gaps in the beds I've inspected so far, not all of which are merely plants that are lying dormant until spring. Although parterres traditionally incorporate areas of bare soil between the plants, many of these patches are too large, marking spots where specimens have died. These areas will all need filling in with the appropriate selection. At some point, I'll be paying a visit to a local nursery, which will be benefiting from a large order from Ashford Manor.

A glow from outside has me look up from the plans in front of me. The sky is still the colour of slate, but there's a curious golden light, illuminating the tops of the trees. I get to my feet and walk over to the window seat, where Mouse has fallen asleep, Mr Rabbit beneath his head. There's a rainbow, striping the sky.

The whole scene is so beautiful and strange, that I take my mobile up to my bedroom, to get a clear shot from above the trees. And that's when I hear it: more shouting. And a thud so loud, my metal bed-frame shakes.

I run downstairs and out of the tower, then sprint around to the back of the house, to the staff entrance, where I jog down the corridor to the main staircase, and up to the first floor. I'm looking around for the stairs to the second floor, when a deep voice close by says, 'Erm . . . excuse me, but this part of the house is private. Can I help you with something?'

I turn to look at the speaker. It's Julian Fanshawe. His tone isn't unpleasant, just authoritative. This is slightly undermined by the substantial purple bruising to his cheekbone and chin, and the fact that his left eye is swollen shut. It looks like Miles got in a few more punches than I'd realised yesterday.

I stand my ground. 'I'm sorry, but I don't know my way around yet. I'm looking for the second floor.'

He frowns. 'Aren't you staying in the Round Wing? You know you can't reach that internally?'

'I do know that, but right now I'm looking for the staff rooms on the second floor. I'm in a bit of a hurry, actually – please can you point me in the right direction?'

He gestures towards a door. 'There's a corridor through there, and down the end there's a door to the second-floor staircase.'

'Thank you.'

Just as I'm turning to leave, he sticks out a hand and says, 'Julian Fanshawe. We met in a rather . . . awkward fashion yesterday. Sorry about that.'

'No worries, but can we do this later?'

'Sure, sure.' He runs a hand through his fine brown hair and moves to one side.

'Sorry!' I call as I jog away, in the direction he showed me. At the end of the corridor, I push open a plain white door and run up the wooden staircase to the top, where I jog along a white-painted corridor, as unadorned as the staff area by the kitchen. It has windows all along the left-hand side, and doors on the right. When I reach the end of the corridor, I knock on the door closest to my bedroom in the tower. There's no response, so I try the handle. It's locked. I go to the next door along – Jamie's room – and knock there.

A voice says, 'I'm busy.' Although I'm sure it is Jamie, he sounds distinctly un-Jamie in his lack of warmth.

'It's Steph,' I say.

'Who?'

'Steph. The gardening consultant.'

I hear footsteps, and Jamie opens the door. His blond hair – normally immaculately styled – is sticking up in all directions, and he has a cut on his lip, which he's dabbing with a tissue.

'What's going on?' I ask him. 'I could hear the row from my bedroom.'

He stares at me. 'From your . . .? Oh, shite!'

'Can I come in?'

'Look, it's not a good time. Sorry I bothered you, like.'

'You didn't. I mean, that's not why I'm here. I just wanted to check on you.'

He tries to smile, but winces. 'Ow, shit!'

'How did you get that cut?' I ask him.

'Shaving,' he says, not even bothering to come up with a convincing lie. He looks exhausted and . . . defeated somehow.

'Jamie, you can talk to me. Who were you arguing with?'

'I weren't rowing. I were just venting.'

'You mean . . . You were quarrelling with yourself?

'Look, I know it sounds soft, but it helps to get things straight in me head, you know?'

'So, you're telling me that every night you go into the room next door to shout at yourself and smash things?' I try not to sound passive aggressive, but it's difficult.

He meets my eye. 'Just, please don't say anything to anyone here. They'll be sending for the men in white coats.' He laughs awkwardly.

At that moment, a noise comes from inside his room. It sounds like someone muttering to themselves.

'Who is that?' I ask.

'What? Oh, it's probably the radiator – you know how they get when they're warming up.'

I remember Saliha telling me that the staff floor doesn't have central heating.

'Anyways, I've got stuff to do,' he says. 'Sorry.' He shuts the door, leaving me to contemplate the space between us and all my unanswered questions.

I knock once more on the end door next to the tower, and again nobody answers. There's nothing more I can do for now, so I turn back and take the staff stairs down to the first-floor corridor, where I descend the main staircase.

When I reach the entrance hall, I take a moment's respite. That scene was so strange, I don't know what to make of it. Is Jamie keeping someone prisoner? But that seems so out of character with the generous young man I've observed. With a shiver, I think of Mr Rochester from *Jane Eyre*, and the wife he keeps locked in the attic. Jamie isn't Mr Rochester, I remind myself.

Glancing around the hall, I am distracted by the beauty of the place. All of the doors have similar frames to that of Lady Clara's study, with beautiful, elaborate carvings, each with its own theme. The walls feature wood panelling and carved picture rails, and the ceiling is hung with two large chandeliers.

I start when a familiar voice says, 'You'll ne'er catch a fishie standing there, lassie.'

'Sir Angus,' I say with a smile, turning to face him. He's sitting on a padded wooden chair, outside the Scottish Room. I don't know how I missed him.

'Just "Angus" will do, hen.'

He's so old, it seems disrespectful to use only his first name. 'What are you doing, sitting there?' I ask. 'Are you waiting for someone?'

'I'm always waiting. Sometimes it's for a person, other times it's for a drink.' He winks and beckons me closer, and I oblige. In a whisper, he says, 'And sometimes I'm thinking it might be for the man with the scythe.'

'Oh, dear! How old are you?' I ask. He doesn't seem like the type to get offended.

'Ninety-four,' he says. He thinks for a moment. 'Or happens as it's ninety-two. Or ninety-three. After a time, it seems less important to keep track.'

'I can imagine.'

'Did you find your weeds?' he asks me.

'I found plenty of them. And some beautiful plants, as well.'

'Aye, there's some grand old trees and bushes here at Ashford.'

'There certainly are.'

''Tis a pity about some of the humans,' he says, giving me a meaningful look.

'You mean William Blythe?'

'Aye, and one or two others I could name.'

I'm about to press him on this when the study door opens and Lady Clara pokes her head out. 'Uncle Angus? What are you doing, sitting out there in the draughty hall? Come into the study, where it's warm. I've got a fresh pot of tea and two cups.'

'Always the tea with this one,' he says, with a sigh, as I help him to his feet. I hand him his walking stick and he walks slowly towards the study. 'Dinnae forget what I was saying,' he says, opaquely.

Checking my watch, I discover I'm late to collect my lunch. I stride through the house to the dining room, at which point Jamie bursts out of the room, and we nearly collide. He's carrying a plate, laden with sandwiches, crisps, biscuits and fruit. There's a can of Coke protruding from one pocket.

'I hope I'm not too late for lunch,' I say.

'Nope you're good. Vix has made up a plate for you. It's on the table.'

'That's kind of her. I'm starving.'

I smile at him, but he's already walking away. He looks guilty, as if I've caught him in some shameful act. I wish I knew what was going on with him, and who is hiding out – or being kept – in the staff quarters.

I eat my lunch with Mouse in the living room. He's watching the garden from his favourite viewing spot. I'm just downing the last of a mug of coffee when he starts to bark. His tail's wagging, so it's definitely a happy, excited bark, rather than a warning about kittens needing saving.

'What is it, boy?' I walk over to look. 'Is Mirabelle back to visit?' He looks up at me, then back to the window, barking again. He's clearly eager for me to share in his excitement. But what has he seen? And then I spot her: a beautiful, grey, long-haired cat. She's stepping elegantly through the parterre, head high, queen of her domain.

'That must be Lilibeth,' I say.

Mouse runs to the top of the stairs, urging me to let him out. But I have no idea what Lilibeth will make of a large dog on her terrain. She might be hostile – or terrified.

Mouse starts to whine, and the sound is so pitiful, that I relent. I grab his lead. 'All right, let's go and see, boy. But you'll have to wear this.'

He runs downstairs to our front door, and stands eagerly while I follow him down and clip on his lead.

Outside, the dark sky has lightened to a pale, smoky grey. The rainbow's gone, as has the hail, but there's a cold wind that nips at my ears, making me wish I'd put on a woolly hat. Mouse tugs on the lead, pulling me towards the parterre. Every few paces, he stops to sniff, and his ears stick up in different directions, on the alert for feline sounds.

And then he spots her. She's standing very still, with her back to us. I don't know if she's marking a bird or rodent, or if she's just taking a break.

Mouse can't keep his excitement in any longer. He barks once, and the cat startles, turns to look at us, and runs away into the trees.

'Oh, well, maybe next time,' I tell Mouse. He looks dejected. I wonder if I could request another visit from Belle soon, to cheer him up.

That evening at dinner, Jamie's place is empty. I glance around the table, but there's no sign of him.

'Where's Jamie?' I ask Saliha.

'Headache. He gets dead bad ones.' Her sweet face is full of sympathy.

'Poor thing. Do they come on suddenly?'

'Yeah. I mean, he was fine at breakfast.'

I remember how on edge Jamie seemed, when I saw him coming out of the kitchen with his lunch – and that cut on his lip, and his evasive manner when I went up to his room.

'Is he OK otherwise?' I ask her.

'Jamie?' she asks. She smiles shyly. 'He's always all right.'

Mulling on the argument I overheard earlier, I wish I could be as sure as she is, that he is neither in harm's way, nor harming anyone else. But Saliha knows Jamie far better than I do. And he seems to have plenty of friends, which is a good sign.

My attention is caught by a conversation a few seats away, between Samuel and Olivia.

'Sorry, did you say someone's missing?' I ask.

'Lilibeth, Lady Clara's cat,' says Olivia.

'Oh! That must be the cat Mouse and I saw earlier in the garden – a beautiful, grey long-hair?'

'Did you tell Lady Clara?' asks Samuel.

I shake my head. 'I didn't know anyone was looking for her.'

'She's a house cat,' says Olivia. 'She's not supposed to go outside.'

'So, her pregnancy?'

Olivia shrugs. 'I said Lilibeth's not *supposed* to go outside. It doesn't mean she never does.'

It seems cruel to have all these fabulous grounds, yet keep a cat shut up indoors. 'Will she be all right?' I ask.

'She'll be just fine,' says Samuel. 'She's not the delicate specimen her ladyship believes.'

I look at Olivia. 'What happened with the kittens?' I ask her.

'The adoptive mother seemed delighted. When I left, she was giving them all a good wash.'

'Oh, that's great news.'

At the end of the meal, just as I'm leaving the dining room, Samuel walks over.

'I just wanted to apologise for earlier,' he says.

'What for? It wasn't your fault that Mr Blythe was drowning kittens – nor that Mouse rushed to their defence.'

'But you left your dog in my care. I should have been able to calm him.'

'Nonsense,' I say. 'I'm bringing him to you tomorrow, and you'll see that today was a glitch.' He tries to object, but I hold up a hand. 'I'm not listening. Mouse needs friends at Ashford.'

'You're very kind,' he says. When I look him in the eye, I see he's close to tears. I give him a pat on the back, and we walk out of the staff entrance together.

'Do you not live in the staff quarters?' I ask him.

He shakes his head. 'Lady Clara's late mother was very generous. When my Sally and I got married, her ladyship gave us a cottage in the grounds.' He points, beyond the kitchen garden, and I realise there are grounds I have yet to explore. He gives me a wave as he heads for his cottage, and I walk over to the tower. As I turn the key in the lock and step inside, I marvel yet again at my good fortune. The tower is like something out of a fairy tale (thankfully, minus the wicked witch).

Back in our living room, Mouse has fallen asleep in his bed. He's snuggled close to his rabbit toy, and I feel a pang for this loyal, loving dog, who just wants a playmate. Perhaps Lilibeth will return soon, and respond more positively to his overtures.

I close the heavy curtains, and sit with my current book, *The Gardener of Versailles*, by Alain Baraton, head gardener at the Park of Versailles. The pictures are glorious, and have me immersed in immaculate topiary and intricate parterres, until my eyes start to close, and I make my way up to bed.

Thankfully, there are no raised voices tonight, and I fall asleep quickly.

6

Jamie arrives late to breakfast on Thursday morning.

Michael calls out, 'Hey! Where've you been? I was just gonna eat your breakfast.'

Jamie grins. 'Hands off, man!' His hair is back to its coiffed state, but he's changed the style; it now hangs low over one eye. The cut on his lip is already healing, and is barely noticeable. It must have been shallow, at least.

'Looking very Louis Tomlinson this morning,' says Olivia. I don't know who this is. When I catch her eye, she says, 'Pop star? Was in One Direction?'

'It suits you,' blurts out Saliha, sitting beside me. She blushes, looking so vulnerable I'd like to give her a hug. She stands up abruptly. 'Back to the grindstone.'

There's the usual exodus. Jamie, though, remains at the table. As I glance towards him, I see there's a sluggish air to his movements. This is so unlike the exuberant Jamie I've seen so far, that I pick up my coffee cup and walk over, taking the vacated seat beside him.

'Hey,' I say.

He doesn't look up from his plate. 'Hey.'

'How's the headache today?'

'What? Oh, yeah. Better, ta.'

'That's good.' There's a long pause. He's sitting in a slumped position, as if gravity has become too strong for him. Observing him, I am no longer in any doubt: this is a young man in a corner, not a bully who is hurting someone else.

'Listen, Jamie,' I say gently. 'Are you OK?'

'I'm fine,' he says.

'You don't seem fine.'

He sighs, and turns towards me. And that's when I see the reason for today's hairstyle: he has a cut on his forehead, concealed from most angles beneath the fringe.

'Shit, Jamie! Who did that to you?'

He eyes me for a moment, before saying, 'You notice stuff other people don't.'

I say, 'Yeah, I guess you could say that. I like finding out answers to things.'

He nods, still eyeing me, as if weighing something up. 'So,' he says, with unexpected interest, 'what are your plans for the next couple of weeks? In the garden, I mean.'

I'm thrown by the change of subject. 'Just more of the same: surveying the parterre and the trees. And I've seen on the original plans that there's a second limestone fountain. I want to uncover that.'

He looks interested. 'Whereabouts?'

'Do you know the giant bramble patch, off near the garages?'

He nods. 'Is that where it is?'

'Yep. Those brambles are going down!'

He smiles. 'Got it. Good luck.'

He stands to leave, but I see his full plate and say, 'Hey, you've barely touched your breakfast.'

'I'm not hungry. Just . . . thanks for taking the time.'

I sit for a moment, after he's gone. I had some experience with a bullied teenager called Apple at my last workplace. I still feel bad for not intervening sooner. I wish I could get Jamie to open up to me.

My phone rings as I'm walking back to the tower to fetch Mouse. It's Caroline.

'What makes you think it's not him in the picture?' she asks, as soon as I answer the call.

I take a deep breath. 'To start with, it's a bit grainy, which makes it hard to identify anyone.'

'It's definitely Ben,' she says.

'Did you really study the man in the picture? You know how Jamie's got a straight nose? Well, this guy's turns up at the end.'

'I know my own boyfriend.'

'Then, why are you ringing?'

'I already cut up all his clothes.'

'You said you were doing that.'

'If he *hasn't* buggered off and left me, then he'll have nothing to wear when he comes back.' She sounds forlorn.

'Look, Caroline,' I say softly, 'take another look at the photo. If you're one hundred per cent sure it's Ben, then yes, he's off enjoying himself somewhere. But if you have any doubt, you need to tell the police.'

'It's been so long,' she says. She's silent for a moment, and I know we're both thinking the same thing: if he isn't living it up somewhere, he could be dead.

'What about his bank accounts?' I say. 'Surely he can be traced through those?'

'Well, duh,' she says, reminding me why I'm not keen on her. 'The police started there. But his accounts were in the minuses, and he hasn't touched them.'

There's another silence, filled with our mutual misgivings. But this is Ben: overconfident, charming, full-of-life Ben. He must be all right. I mean, he's *Ben*.

'Anyway, I have to go,' she says. 'I have yoga.' She hangs up.

I pull up the image on my phone. The more I study the man in the photograph, the more certain I am that he isn't my ex-husband.

I put away my mobile and go to fetch Mouse. He collects Mr Rabbit from his bed and trots downstairs with him. As soon as he sees we're heading to the courtyard, he races ahead, his toy swinging from side to side in his jaws. By the time I reach the door to the courtyard, my dog is enjoying a lively reunion with Samuel.

The older man gets to his feet with a groan, rubbing his back. 'Are you sure about this?'

'I can't think of anyone I'd trust more with him,' I say honestly.

He looks quite moved. 'Thank you.'

'I'll see you both later. Bye, Mouse. Be good.'

Mouse makes his rumble of assent, and I leave them to it.

Meanwhile, I take out my notebook and return to my survey of the parterre, where I continue my work, sketching out each bed, and adding it to the coded map showing its place in the scheme as a whole. It's engrossing work, and the morning passes quickly.

Olivia comes by at lunchtime, while I'm sitting on a tree stump in the wooded area, eating my lunch. The spot is sheltered, and I'm enjoying my picnic. Today's sandwiches are cream cheese and cucumber on homemade sourdough. Vicky makes delicious bread.

I have my mouth full as Olivia greets me, and I have to swallow before I respond, 'Hiya.'

She glances around. 'Have you got a minute?'

'Sure.' I stand and she gestures for us to walk together. We're close to the lake, but she points along a discreet path through the trees.

We walk side by side, without speaking for a moment, jewel-bright leaves crunching beneath our shoes. She's wearing a teal coat with the collar up; the rich colour complements her pale red hair. With her peaches-and-cream complexion and amber eyes, she's quite the beauty.

At last, she clears her throat and says, 'I need to talk to you about something.'

'OK.' For a hopeful moment, I wonder if it's about William Blythe. I'd love someone to reveal his kryptonite.

She's silent for another moment, and then says, 'That man you saw me with . . .'

'Oh don't!' I pull a face. 'I was mortified when you looked up and saw me watching. I'd honestly just gone to the window to get a view of the garden for my plans – I didn't mean to be spying on you!'

She smiles. 'It's fine – I know that. It's just . . . Would you mind keeping quiet about it? I'm not supposed to have . . . male visitors without prior approval.'

'That sounds a bit draconian.'

She smiles again. 'I think it's more about Ashford's being a family home – they want to keep tabs on who's visiting. It's fair enough, really.'

'Well, my lips are sealed,' I promise her.

'I appreciate that – thank you. And I'll make sure he gives me notice the next time. I told him off for just turning up like that.' From the smile on her face, I doubt that the reprimand was severe.

She walks me back to my lunch spot, where I collect my plate and mug, and we head in the direction of the house, at which point we separate, she towards the courtyard for a cigarette, and I to the staff entrance, to deposit my dirty crockery.

The kitchen looks empty, and I'm just setting my things on the work surface above the dishwasher, when I hear a whimpering sound. I look around, and see the top of a head, just visible on the other side of the butcher's block.

'Hello?'

I walk around the block, but take a step back when I set eyes on a young man of about fifteen or sixteen, who's sitting on the floor with his hands over his ears. His elbows are clamped on either side of his bent knees and, when he catches sight of me, he starts to rock, banging his head on the block behind him with each backward movement. He's saying one word, over and over: 'No, no, no, no, no, no, no', each utterance coinciding with the thud of his head.

I crouch down. 'Hey. Don't hurt yourself,' I say softly. But he starts rocking more frantically, staring past me.

'I'll go and find someone,' I say.

'I want Jamie,' he says, still rocking.

'I'm going to find Jamie, OK?'

He doesn't acknowledge my words. I run out of the kitchen and check the dining room, but there's no one there.

I start to open doors along the staff corridor. There's a scullery, with large butler's sinks, presumably originally for washing clothes, but there are now flanks of washing machines along another wall. The whole time, I can hear the thudding of the boy's head against the butcher's block.

I find a room that looks like an office of some kind, and another that looks like a storeroom.

I'm jogging along, towards the main part of the house, when I see Vicky coming towards me, carrying a tray of dirty crockery.

'Vicky! There's a young man in the kitchen . . .'

She frowns. 'Do you mean one of the staff? Is it Simon? Is he OK?'

'It's not Simon. It's someone I don't know. He's asking for Jamie,' I say.

'Jamie's running errands in town.'

'Shit. This boy seems really agitated.'

She abandons her tray on a hall table, and starts to run along the corridor. I follow close behind. We can hear the thudding sound as we approach the kitchen.

'What on earth?' says Vicky.

'He's banging his head,' I explain. 'We need to go in gently.'

She slows at the door to the kitchen. We can hear the regular 'No! No! No!', emphasised by each bang of the head.

'He's on the other side of the butcher's block,' I whisper. She takes a deep breath, before walking around the counter. I hang back.

I watch as she crouches down and says softly, 'You must be Benji.'

'I want Jamie,' says the young man, still banging his head.

'I didn't know you were here,' she says.

'I want Jamie.'

'I know, love. Jamie's just gone to the shops. How about I make you a hot chocolate, and we can wait together?'

'I want Jamie!' His voice is louder now, and he starts to bang his head harder and faster.

She stands up and turns to me. 'What should I do?'

'You know him?'

She shakes her head. 'No, but I've seen pictures and heard about him. He's Jamie's little brother, Benji. I don't know why Jamie didn't say he was visiting – I'd never have sent him into town if I'd known.'

I hear footsteps outside, and Jamie's friend Michael appears in the passageway. He's small and slight, with red hair that stands straight up from his head. If I hadn't known he and Jamie had been friends since sixth-form college, I would have thought he was far younger than twenty. He stands in the doorway, taking in the scene.

Vicky spots him. 'Michael! Thank goodness. Come and help us out. Do you know Jamie's brother, Benji?'

Michael nods and comes nearer, and Vicky steps back, so that Michael and Benji can see each other.

Michael kneels in front of the agitated boy, keeping his distance.

'Benji?' he says. 'Hey, Benji, it's me, Michael.' The banging slows. 'Let's go up to Jamie's room and wait for him there, mate. I've got pistachios.'

Benji stops rocking abruptly, looks at Michael, and says, 'In their shells?'

Michael says, 'Yeah, but I'll shell them for you, OK?'

'OK.' He gets to his feet, and he and Michael leave the room.

The kitchen feels strange after they've left – too quiet, as if all sound has been sucked out.

Vicky turns to me with a lost expression on her face. 'Thanks for—'

'Making things worse?' I suggest.

She smiles wanly. 'I didn't do any better. I don't know how Michael knew what to do.'

'I guess he knows Benji.'

'I guess he must. He and Jamie have been really close for a couple of years now.' She shrugs. 'Fancy a coffee?'

'I'd rather have a whisky, but a coffee will do for now, thanks.'

I take a seat on a stool at the butcher's block while she taps the old grounds out of the filter on a fancy coffee machine and starts making a fresh brew.

'Black, right?'

'Perfect.'

I mull over our encounter with Benji. At least I'm now pretty sure I know who's been shouting, late at night, in the end room. Could Jamie's injuries simply have been caused by his being a bystander during Benji's meltdowns? But would tending to his brother's needs really be enough to account for Jamie's withdrawn state?

She brings two steaming mugs over to the counter, and sits on a stool opposite me. As we cradle our mugs, I can tell we're both processing what just happened.

'How long do you think Benji's staying?' I ask her.

'He must just be here for the night, so he and Jamie can set off together in the morning for the birthday shindig.'

'That makes sense.' I don't tell her that I've been hearing Benji for several nights. It doesn't seem like my place to share Jamie and his brother's business.

We're silent for a moment, then she says, 'I feel sorry for the parents.'

I don't say that I feel even sorrier for Benji. The inside of his head seems like a frightening place to live, full of uncertainty and fear.

7

I spend the afternoon on my continued inspection of the parterre.

At one point, Dickie's son, Miles, appears without a sound, causing me to jump.

He puts up his hands: 'Sorry, sorry! Didn't mean to shock you, Ms Williams.'

Patting my chest, I laugh. 'That's OK. Was there something you wanted?'

I see him hesitate, and then he says, 'I saw you with Olivia earlier . . .'

When he doesn't continue, I say, 'And?'

He leans towards me and lowers his voice, 'My advice: don't get too friendly with that one. She wrecks everything she touches.'

I frown. 'What are you talking about, Miles?'

'I'm not at liberty to say more, but I just thought you'd want to know.' He strides off, before I can ask what he means.

I reflect that there must be something in the Spencer genes: Miles and his great-uncle Angus both possess an extraordinary ability to confound.

With a sigh, I get back to my work. After sketching and mapping each bed, I take pictures on my phone. Back in the tower, I compare the current planting to online images of other parterres designed by George London. The more I cross-reference with his other creations, the more certain I become that stone chippings would be a better choice for the outline than replacement hedging plants. There would be some occasional sweeping or raking to do, to retain the pattern's precise geometry, but maintenance would otherwise be pretty low, compared to the regular pruning of hundreds of shrubs. Given that Blythe has neglected this area, it seems unlikely he'd sign up to take it on now – especially when I, his nemesis, have created the work.

If I can get Lady Clara's approval quickly, I might even be able to call in contractors to dig up and remove all the box hedging in the next couple of weeks, allowing easier access to the flower beds for the Great Tidy-up. Any new planting within the flower beds will have to wait until spring, giving me time to choose the most appropriate plants for the job.

At three thirty, I knock on Lady Clara's study door.

'Come in,' she calls.

As I open the door and step inside, she smiles and says, 'Oh, Ms Williams, how is it going?'

She gestures to a chair and I sit opposite her. Today, she's wearing her blonde hair in a chignon at the nape of her neck. Her dress is a fitted woollen sheath, in a richly coloured print of peacock feathers, with a matching bolero. The fire is burning hard, and the room is stuffy again. I wish I could throw open a window.

She folds her hands on her desk in an attentive pose, as I start to talk. 'I mentioned before that it might be a good idea to replace the box hedging with hard landscaping. I'm now convinced this is the best option. It would be more in keeping with the age of the house, and would, of course, be entirely pest and disease resistant.'

'I must admit I had a little trouble visualising it, when you talked about it before.'

I nod and place my phone in front of her. 'I will find you some larger images, but I thought you might like to start with these, which show parterres at Versailles and a number of other important gardens. You can scroll through them.'

She studies my phone screen, swiping through the pictures, while I remove my jacket and sweatshirt in response to the heat. At last, she looks up, 'These are quite striking, aren't they?'

I nod. 'An edging made from a white limestone gravel would be wonderful in this setting.'

'And who's this?' She holds up my phone.

'Oh . . . that's a man who is supposed to be my ex-husband.'

She frowns. 'Supposed to be?'

I hesitate. But there's nothing private about Ben's disappearance: his face is on posters all over the country. 'He vanished, immediately after visiting me at Beaulieu, my last workplace.' I pronounce it the way the residents do: Bewley.

'Vanished?' She puts a hand to her forehead, in an elegant version of a face palm and says, 'Sorry – I don't meant to keep repeating your words. I'm just trying to understand—'

'I get it. It's fine. I don't really understand it all myself. Ben and I separated a couple of years back, after he'd squandered all our savings on bad choices, and I lost my business. He only came to see me to ask for money.'

Lady Clara looks enthralled by this sordid story. 'The gall of the man! What did you tell him?'

'I said that, thanks to his mistakes, I had nothing to lend to him or anyone else. I haven't seen him since. I wouldn't have thought anything of it if his girlfriend hadn't called me a day or two later, saying he'd never returned home.'

'Oh dear. Do you think the loan sharks got to him?'

'It's one thought I'm trying not to entertain.'

'Of course. I'm so sorry. How insensitive of me. Anyway, I expect he's simply hiding out.'

'I hope you're right.'

'And the man on your phone? You said he was "supposed to be" your ex . . .?'

'It's just a grainy photo of the wrong red-haired man. The police are so keen to close this case, they're jumping at anything that might be a match.'

'Do you know, I have some friends who are quite senior in the police force. Why don't you send me a picture of your ex-husband, and I'll ask them to put out some feelers?'

'That's a kind thought, but I don't think it's allowed.'

'Well, send it anyway. Let's see what we can do.'

'All right, thank you. Right, so I'll bring over some books for you to browse, so you can see some larger examples of parterres with the hard edging.'

'That sounds perfect.' She beams. 'Do you know, I'm getting quite excited about the change you're proposing? I think it could be rather spectacular.'

'I really think it might be,' I say, smiling back. 'And Mr Blythe would need to do very little to maintain it, compared with a living boundary.'

'Now I'm definitely sold!' We both laugh.

We say our goodbyes, and I head towards the courtyard, to collect Mouse from his play date with Samuel. When we get back inside the tower, Mouse settles on the window seat, watching the darkening scene. It's just past four and there's a spectacular sunset of orange stripes behind the tree-line.

Before dinner, I go through my stack of reference books and make a small pile of the ones that I want to lend to Lady Clara. These include *The Gardener of Versailles*, which I'm only part way through. I'll have to find something else to read in the meantime. It occurs to me that, among its many rooms, Ashford might boast a library. I'll have to ask.

I half expect Benji to come to dinner with Jamie that evening, but Jamie comes alone. I watch him, entertaining his friends, and I start to wonder if his big personality is a shield, covering up whatever's troubling him.

I remind myself that his injuries were quite possibly caused by one of Benji's meltdowns. I can only imagine how stressful it must be, having to do a full-time job while trying to care for someone who really needs constant supervision. At least it is hopefully only until tomorrow, when they're due to head off for the birthday party.

He glances over at me and smiles, mouthing 'Sorry!', and I smile back and shake my head, to show there's no need to apologise.

At the end of the meal, he comes over. 'I just wanted to say sorry for earlier – you know, when you came up to check on me and I behaved like a right dick.'

'It's fine, Jamie. I should have trusted you. I'm sorry. I didn't mean to interfere about Benji.'

His eyes widen. 'How'd you know about our kid?'

'Oh! I thought that's what we were talking about – when I came to see what the noise was?'

'Yeah, but . . .'

'Vicky and I found Benji in the kitchen earlier today, and Michael came to get him. I didn't realise no one had told you. I worked out that's who I'd been hearing through the wall.'

'Shit,' says Jamie. 'I told Benji not to leave his room. Did Lady C spot him?'

'No, just the three of us. Is he OK?'

'He seemed fine just now. Was he all right? He didn't melt down or nothing?'

'Well . . . I mean . . . He was rocking and banging his head, but he stopped when Michael came along.'

'Poor Benji. He must have been crapping himself.'

'Yeah. I don't think I helped – someone he didn't know asking him questions.'

'He's autistic.'

'I figured that was it.'

'He's lucky it was only you and Vicky that found him. I dunno what her ladyship would've had to say, like.'

'Or Mr Blythe,' I say drily.

His eyes widen again and he covers his mouth. 'Jesus, don't even go there!' We both burst out laughing. 'Seriously, though,' he says, 'your man's got issues. I have to work with him a fair bit, and I've only seen him smile once. Ever.' He pauses, then adds, with more venom than I thought him capable of, 'The man's an arse.'

Beside me, Saliha says, 'He's capable of smiling? I thought the muscles must be missing.'

This makes Jamie laugh, and she blushes with pleasure.

I ask, 'Now you've got to tell us, Jamie: what was it that made him smile?'

'When he got his bank statement. He opened it and his face just cracked into this giant beam.' We all laugh at this. 'Mind you, this place is his only job,' says Jamie. 'I can't see how he's earning enough to fill a bank account.'

'Maybe people pay him to leave them alone,' suggests Saliha. Jamie grins at her.

I make an excuse and leave the dining room, hoping Saliha will enjoy some quality time with Jamie – but, as I glance back on opening the outside door, I see he's leaving the room.

'Night!' he calls.

'Night,' I call back. I take a deep breath before stepping out into the bitter, dark night.

8

The next day is Friday, and Jamie and his brother have left for the boat party by the time the rest of us assemble in the dining room for breakfast. I pile the books for Lady Clara on the sideboard, before sitting down next to Saliha, who doesn't give me her usual lively greeting.

'You OK?' I ask, pouring myself a cup of coffee.

'I'm missing Jamie already,' she says, sorrowfully. 'I can't believe he's gone till, like, Monday. It's gonna be so boring here.'

She says 'Monday' as if it's a year away, rather than three days.

'It is pretty quiet in here without him,' I say.

Spotting my pile of books for Lady Clara over on the sideboard, I'm reminded that it contains my current reading matter. I ask Saliha, 'By the way, does Ashford have a library?'

'Oh my god, it's got this amazing one,' she says. 'I mean, floor-to-ceiling bookcases on all the walls. I reckon it's got more books than the library near where I grew up.'

'Are we allowed to borrow them?'

She thinks about this. 'I dunno. You'd have to ask Mr F or Lady C. I should think so, though. They're both pretty cool.'

'Where is it?'

'The far side of the Scottish Room. I mean, you can get there another way, but it's easier to just walk through there.' She hesitates. 'Though you might get caught by Sir Angus and have to listen to him talk about whisky for an hour.'

I laugh. 'I like Sir Angus.'

She smiles. 'Yeah, I'm being tight. He's actually dead cool. Sometimes I go in there just to chill, you know? He's a really good listener.' She pauses, then says, 'I like hearing him talk, too. He's got loads of stories about old times. He says he remembers when this place used to have gas lights on all the walls, instead of electric ones. And he described what it looked like when the ballroom was, like, full of guests, all dressed up in their ballgowns and stuff, with the flickering lighting from candles in the chandeliers.' She sighs. 'I wish I could have seen it.'

I pull a face. 'I'm sorry to tell you this, but I suspect our friend Angus of being a bit of a fibber.'

She frowns. 'How d'you mean?'

'It's just that electric lighting was introduced in the late-nineteenth century. Even if Ashford didn't get it till the early twentieth, Sir Angus would have to be over a hundred years old to have witnessed the house with the original gas lighting.'

She smacks her forehead. 'I should have guessed! This other time, he tried telling me there were these special newts in the lake with frills or something.'

'Actually, that might be true. If there are great crested newts, I should make sure they're recorded: they're a protected species.'

'He's a dead cheeky bugger, though. I'm gonna have words with him the next time I see him.' She has a grin on her face, so I can tell she isn't really cross with him.

I leave the room ahead of the exodus for once, collecting my books for Lady Clara en route.

Her ladyship is in her study when I knock, and I'm able to deliver the books and ask about the library.

'Oh, of course,' she says. 'I should have mentioned it. Everyone is welcome to use it. Every owner of Ashford has added to the collection, so it's quite extensive. We're looking into knocking through to the room beyond, so that we can extend the shelving. Anyway, yes, please do help yourself. Just pop a note in the record. It's on the main table.'

'That sounds great – thank you.'

After I've taken leave of her ladyship, I collect Mouse. I'm just locking the front door when a message arrives from Dad: Parsnip catastrophe! Call me!

I ring him as Mouse races off towards the trees.

'They're weird,' says Dad, on answering.

'Weird how?'

'Weird shapes. You know how parsnips in the shops are straight? These have legs or something.'

I laugh. 'Did you remove the stones from the soil, when you sowed them, like I told you?'

Long pause. 'You didn't say why I had to do it.'

I'm certain I did, but I just say, 'OK. Well, now you know that a parsnip root forks when its growth is impeded by a stone. So, next year, you can remove the stones before you sow them. And this year's crop will be perfectly edible – if a bit of a challenge to peel.' I decide not to tell him that parsnips are also prone to forking if they are damaged during planting, or if the soil is too heavy. Hopefully, just removing the stones will solve the problem next year.

After my call with Dad, I start to map out some of the planting that would work for the parterre. The deeper I go into researching George London, the more I'm becoming aware that most of the current plants will have to go. They must have been put in during the intervening centuries, when bare earth was no longer considered a desirable look.

I know, from my research, that there is another George London garden that has been restored, at Hanbury Hall in Worcestershire. There, they have planted cones of dwarf evergreen shrubs, alongside marigolds and white alyssum. These plants are widely spaced, and the design is repeated in each section of the parterre, to give a rhythmic cohesion to the overall design. This is where I intend to draw my inspiration. It will require more upkeep by Blythe – but I am going to suggest that Lady Clara hire an undergardener to help him, as she seems to have the funds.

By the end of the day, I have a pretty clear idea of which plants will work, though I still need to calculate quantities, and find a good nursery locally from which to source them.

In bed that night, I fall asleep easily without the sound of Benji shouting on the other side of the wall. I still have one strange dream, though, in which I get lost in the maze and come upon Olivia, kissing a man. His back looks familiar, but, however hard I try, I can't get him to turn round. If only I could place him, I know that I'd be able to find my way out. Olivia keeps laughing as I try to guess who he might be. I resort to shouting out names like 'Rumpelstiltskin!' and 'Pinocchio!' And, all the while, she laughs and laughs, until I wake in a cold sweat.

9

On Saturday afternoon, after a quiet, lazy morning, Mouse and I enjoy a lovely meander through Ashford's grounds, exploring past the kitchen garden and beyond. We see two cottages, one of which I presume to be Samuel's. It has a neat little fence, and a pretty, orderly garden. I expect that Blythe lives in the other, which has a tall, unwelcoming laurel hedge around it. I'd be surprised if he gets any light inside the house.

After our explorations, we head back home, where Mouse tries to squeeze next to me on the small sofa, squashing me against the arm rest, until I gently push him off.

'You can have your bed, the window seat or one of the chairs,' I tell him. He looks aggrieved.

I set up my laptop for a video call with my parents. This turns out to be largely dominated by Dad, wanting to interrogate about me about indoor heated propagators. Then I call my brother, Danny. This conversation is interrupted by Alice, who wants to talk to Mouse. The ensuing 'chat' mainly entails Alice saying the dog's name, and Mouse looking quizzically at me, unsure what's expected of him. 'OK, Alice, I think that's enough,' says my brother. 'Poor Mouse is looking very confused.'

'But I want him to talk to me,' says Alice.

'Mouse is better at cuddles,' I tell her.

'But I can't cuddle him if he's not here,' she points out.

'Don't you have a new baby brother to cuddle?'

Alice rolls her eyes. 'He's still crying *all* the time.'

'Oh, dear. Are you all managing to get any sleep?'

'The kids seem to be sleeping, thank goodness,' says Danny. 'But

Karen's up most of the night with him. She's like a zombie at the moment. I try to help, but I can't exactly breastfeed, and he's not taking her expressed milk . . .' He tails off, looking anxious and tired.

'It's so tough at this stage, isn't it? Just remember, you went through this when the other three were babies. This, too, shall pass.'

'I bloody hope you're right.'

'Daddy swore!' objects Alice.

'Oops!' says her father.

Vicky's visiting a friend locally overnight, so dinner is a pared-down affair. There's a cold buffet laid out for us. Everyone fills a plate, then takes it back to their own quarters.

Mouse and I watch an Attenborough programme on octopuses. We're both fascinated by these creatures, with their multiple brains, hearts and legs. I'm pretty sure they're more intelligent than the majority of people.

I end the day with another video call to Danny at ten o'clock. I could see he needed some moral support earlier, and know he'll still be up.

He takes a while to answer and, when he does, he has the baby in his arms.

'Hiya!' he whispers.

'Hi,' I say. 'Someone's up late.'

'Yes. Despite my best efforts, this one's wide awake. We've done rocking, we've been for a drive, we've walked around the block, but he's not letting go.' He holds the baby up towards his laptop; the little one blinks and reaches out a hand towards the screen.

'Is Karen in bed?' I ask.

'Yeah. I told her to get some kip while she could.' We chat about how they're all doing. While he talks, my youngest nephew's eyes become heavy and start to close. I can feel Danny's relief as he looks up from the baby's sleeping face and softly says, 'So, that's us. What's going on with you?'

I tell him about Jamie.

'What is it about you and tortured teenagers?' he asks.

'To be fair, Jamie's twenty.'

'Well, that makes all the difference.' He laughs.

'I just don't like seeing people unhappy.'

'And that's why we love you,' he says, before unexpectedly grimacing. 'Oh god. Got to go. Sounds like Luke's woken up.'

'Good luck!'

We say goodnight and hang up.

Later, I'm lying in the dark of my bedroom, when my mobile rings, giving me a start. The name that flashes up is Ben: my missing ex-husband.

I answer immediately.

'Hello? Ben, is that you?' I can hear something, but it's not a voice – more like a series of rustling sounds. Is this an accidental pocket dial? 'Hello?' I try again.

The call ends, and I'm left staring at a screen which bears the frustrating words: CALL ENDED.

I ring back at once, but it goes straight to the generic voicemail message.

I dial Caroline, my fingers fumbling with my phone.

She takes several rings to answer and, when she does, she sounds sleepy and cross. 'Louise, it's . . .' she must be consulting her clock because there's a pause and then she says, '. . . nearly eleven o'clock.'

'I just got a call from Ben's phone.'

A longer pause. 'Say that again,' she says slowly, and with a hint of something like menace.

'Ben rang. At least, I think he did. No one spoke. It might have been a misdial or something. Or someone else with his phone.'

'He rang *you*?'

Trust Ben's drama queen girlfriend to focus on the least important aspect of my message. 'Look, do you have a way to trace Ben's phone?'

'It's turned off, so the police can't trace it,' she says. 'They were able to find his last location, but he wasn't there any more. I can't believe he called you and not me. Though I guess I shouldn't be surprised—'

I interrupt, 'Ben's phone has just been used. You need to call the police *now* and tell them, in case there's some way they can track it again. It might have pinged a tower in the short time it was on?' I am a little vague as to the logistics of mobile-phone tracking.

'I've half a mind to leave him to stew,' she says.

Rosie Sandler

'Give me your police contact name and number and I'll call them,' I tell her.

She tuts loudly. 'No, I'll do it. I'm his girlfriend.' And she hangs up.

I wonder if she'll let me know what she finds out. After about an hour of lying in bed, wondering and worrying, I send her a text: Any news? Please let me know.

A message comes straight back: They're going to see if they can get a location from the phone company. Are you sure it was Ben?

I type a response: Depends what you mean. It was definitely his phone but might not have been Ben. As I said HE DIDN'T SPEAK.

I regret those capital letters the second after pressing 'send'. Caroline is sensitive, and will no doubt feel I was shouting at her.

No response comes. I wonder if there's anything I could have done, to keep the caller on the phone. But, I reason with myself, if it was a pocket dial, there was no one to hear me.

I can't help a little inner voice that keeps shouting to be heard: What if it was Ben, sending a distress message?

10

I check my phone the minute I wake up on Sunday morning. Miraculously, Caroline has deigned to keep me in the loop: Police say B's phone in v built-up area in Brum so unlikely to find but they will tell local cops to keep an eye.

I feel deflated. I roll out of bed and don my thick dressing gown and fluffy mule slippers. Sunday is our lazy day. It's also the one day of the week when breakfast isn't served at the big house, so I eat toast and cereal in the tower kitchen while Mouse empties his bowl. Then I leave him to gaze out of the front window while I walk over to choose a book from the library. I've decided to put the unsettling phone call to the back of my mind for now. If Ben's in trouble of some kind, there's nothing I can do, and at least I know that Caroline has informed the police.

There's no sign of Sir Angus when I walk through the Scottish Room. The door at the end opens on to the most beautiful library I've ever seen. The towering bookcases are all in oak, with their surrounds carved with images of quills, ink bottles, books and rolled parchment. Wooden ladders are set up along each long row of shelves. The windows are leaded, with stained panels, depicting books in different colours. There's a mezzanine level, housing several more bookcases, with a large, arched window. And, throughout, there are curved, padded chairs, in which to sit and read. Each chair has its own small table. The air is scented with a mix of lavender wood polish and the unmistakable smell of books. This place is a bibliophile's dream.

It takes me a few minutes to make sense of the library filing system, which at first seems arbitrary. At last, I work out that the books are probably arranged according to who acquired them.

The oldest books are on the shelves closest to the entrance. They get gradually more recent as one travels across the room to the far door. A recent inhabitant of Ashford Manor clearly had a thing for detective novels, and there's a large section dedicated to them. As an avid reader of crime myself, I scan the rows and spot Agatha Christie, Raymond Chandler, Ian Rankin and Ruth Rendell, among others. I'm surprised, among all these dead white novelists, to find a number of living black authors. I choose *Tell Me Your Secret* by Dorothy Koomson, and *Bluebird, Bluebird* by Attica Locke, both of which I've been meaning to read for some time. Then I look around for some appealing nonfiction.

After a couple of minutes, I locate a healthy collection of books on gardens and gardening. My eye is attracted to a volume on Victorian plant hunters, so I take that from the shelf as well. I enter my name, the date, and the book titles, into a huge, leather-bound volume, set on a wooden plinth near the door. Then, pleased with my small but hopefully stimulating haul, I head back to the tower.

Mouse and I set out for our run at nine, when the sun is fully up. It feels like a luxury not to have to wear my head torch. The temperature dropped below zero overnight, and the arable crops along the way glisten with water droplets from the melted ice. It's a glorious day.

After our run, I take a shower and we both have a drink before heading out to the grounds. Mouse settles for a nap at the base of a beautiful holm oak, a species that was introduced to the UK back in the sixteenth century. Unlike our native species, the holm oak is evergreen.

I, meanwhile, take a walk, purely for the sake of soaking up my new environs. I find that I view a place completely differently when I'm surveying it for a project, versus taking it in as a visitor. I imagine it's a little like being a proofreader, who can spot typographical errors and grammatical mistakes throughout a manuscript, but can't answer the question, 'Did you enjoy the story?' It's important that I get an overview of the landscape as a whole.

I'm not sure which of the staff work on Sundays, but I don't see anyone all morning. Even when I go in for lunch, there's no one in either the dining room or kitchen. A note on the side informs me that my lunch is in the fridge, and I locate a covered plate bearing my name on the top shelf of the huge industrial fridge.

In the afternoon, Mouse and I take a walk together to the lake, where he has a swim and I keep a towel to hand for rubbing him down when he comes out of the water coated in mud.

On our way back to the tower, as we're passing through the parterre, we see someone in the distance, coming through the door from the courtyard. The figure is tall, wearing a Barbour jacket with a hunting cap: Mr Fanshawe. He doesn't see us as he looks around, before striding purposefully along the path that leads to the front door of the house. I think little of it, until the courtyard door opens a second time, and Olivia appears. She also glances around, before running towards the back of the house.

Remembering the sight of her meeting with a man whom she pulled out of sight, I wonder for a moment if Olivia is having an affair with Mr Fanshawe. After all, Miles did say she 'wrecks everything she touches'. But this seems ridiculous: I can't imagine that our employer's old-fashioned manners would appeal to straight-talking Olivia. And he seems besotted with his wife. Perhaps the two of them coming through that door in quick succession is just coincidence. But the little part of my brain that is always alert to signs and clues is pretty sure Olivia and Mr Fanshawe are meeting in private. The only thing my brain and I can't work out is why.

11

Mouse wakes me at five on Monday morning, running into my room and barking repeatedly.

I sit up, my heart racing, and turn on the bedside lamp. 'What is it, boy?'

As my eyes get used to the light, I see that his tail is wagging. I take a breath of relief before clambering out of bed. As soon as I'm on my feet, he races to the top of the stairs, making the yapping noise which is his main way of summoning me. It roughly translates as, 'Get over here *now*, human.'

I follow Mouse out to the stairs, where he leads me down to our front door. His tail is wagging frantically, and he's whining. As soon as I open the door, a large canine figure pushes her way into the tiny hall: Mirabelle. They put their noses together, and she licks his face before he leads her upstairs. I'm left standing by the open door, wondering what on earth she's doing out and about on her own at five o'clock in the morning.

I run upstairs for my head torch, then return to the first floor, where I put on my jacket and wellies. I poke my head inside the living room, but neither of them looks up from their position on the rug, where they're rolling and playing together.

I leave the tower and walk around to the back of the house, where I'm surprised to find the staff door wide open. This must be how Belle got out. Passing through, I close it behind me, before walking along the staff corridor, past the kitchen and dining room. All of these rooms are in darkness, so I continue into the family's part of the house, where I'm relieved to see a light shining from beneath Lady Clara's study door. I knock.

Her ladyship comes to open the door, saying, 'Oh! What are you doing here?' when she sees me on the other side. She checks her watch, as if she might have lost a couple of hours. She's in a deep-blue and purple paisley dressing gown, her fair hair loose, making her appear younger than usual.

'Sorry to call so early,' I say, 'but Belle has just made an appearance at my place, and I didn't want anyone to be looking for her.'

She looks surprised. 'Mirabelle is here?'

'Yes. You didn't know?'

'I suppose my brother must have dropped her off with one of the staff last night. Perhaps he has a business commitment early this morning. I wonder how she got out . . .'

'The staff entrance was open.'

'Open? For goodness' sake!' She shakes her head. 'I'll have to have words. I'm so sorry you've been disturbed. I'll send someone over to fetch her.'

'She's welcome to spend the day—'

She takes my hand in a surprisingly warm gesture. 'Are you sure? Because that would be wonderful. Thank you. Would you mind holding on, just for a moment?' She walks over to a bell on the wall and presses it. We wait, standing in an awkward silence. 'Damn that boy,' she says, pressing the bell a second time.

At last, Simon appears, hair clearly styled by the pillow, shirt inside out.

Lady Clara addresses him, 'Simon, would you mind telling me how the staff entrance door came to be open again this morning? Mirabelle got out.'

'It wasn't me, Lady Clara,' he says. 'I locked it when I went to bed at ten. Wait, who's Mirabelle?'

She sighs quietly and says, 'The wolfhound?' in a world-weary tone.

'Oh, yeah, of course.'

'You really have no idea how the door came to be open? You are absolutely sure you shut and locked it last night?'

'Yeah, ma'am. I remember, cos I wanted a piece of toast, so I locked it on my way back from the kitchen.' He yawns, and sways slightly. I'm worried he might fall asleep on his feet.

'And was it you who received Mirabelle?' she asks. He frowns with incomprehension, and she explains, 'Did my brother entrust the dog to your charge?'

He shakes his head. 'I didn't even know it was here, ma'am.'

With a shake of the head, she says, 'Thank you, Simon. That will be all.'

As soon as he's left the room, she says, in a low voice, 'That boy ... He was one of my husband's hires, and I think it was more of a pity thing.'

'I'm sure he can be trained up,' I say hopefully, but she shakes her head.

'Sometimes staff just don't work out.' There's a brief pause, during which I try to think of a suitable response, but she gestures for me to leave the study with her. 'Thank you so much for coming over,' she says, when we reach the front door. 'We would have been simply frantic, once we realised Belle was missing. She's very well loved, as you might imagine.'

'She's a darling,' I say. 'She and Mouse are enjoying a massive cuddle at the moment.'

'How lovely!' She opens the door. 'Anyway, you must want to get back to your quarters.'

I'm always amused by the way my clients summarily dismiss me.

'Goodbye then,' I say, suppressing a laugh as I step back out into the cold, dark morning.

When I reach the living room, Mouse and Belle have moved to the sofa, where they have fallen asleep, wrapped back around each other.

I leave them to it, and return to bed myself. When I awaken a second time, it's seven thirty, too late for my usual Monday morning run. Instead, I take a hot shower and pull on a clean pair of thick trousers with woollen socks, and a T-shirt and sweatshirt, ready for my day in the garden.

The dogs are still asleep in the living room, both snouts resting on Mr Rabbit, so I grab my jacket and boots, and shut the door quietly on my way to breakfast.

When I walk into the dining room at eight o'clock, I find the other staff already in their seats – apart from Michael, who's clearly meant to be serving, but instead is standing beside the table, holding out his phone to show something to the others. They're all laughing.

'What's going on?' I ask Saliha, as I take a seat beside her.

She grins. 'Pics of Jamie from the boat party. Michael arranged with one of Jamie's brothers to send him photos after Jamie got lashed.'

I look over at Michael. 'What have you got?'

He comes over to show me, holding out his phone. I take it from him and see a photo of Jamie, slumped on a bench-style sofa. Someone has removed his top, and doodled in what looks like black marker pen all over his torso. A line of drool hangs from Jamie's chin.

Feeling uncomfortable, I hand the phone back. 'Isn't that a bit cruel?'

Michael shrugs. 'It's only what he'd do to the rest of us.'

'Fair enough,' I say. 'Where is he, anyway?'

'He didn't make it back yet. Must be too hungover,' says Michael, with obvious glee. 'His brother says they were doing tequila shots.'

'Ouch,' I say, at the thought of the thumping headache Jamie must have today.

Vicky appears in the doorway. 'Michael, leave it alone about Jamie and get on with the breakfast service. You know the family want brunch at eleven thirty.'

He salutes. 'Yes, ma'am!' He turns sharply and marches out of the room, arms swinging like a soldier.

Vicky rolls her eyes. Seeing me, she says, 'Did he take your order, at least?'

I shake my head, laughing. 'Can I have the full cooked, please?'

'Toast?'

'Yes, please.'

She nods and leaves the room. I help myself to coffee and admire the jam jars full of flowers and seed heads while I wait for my food. There are pink viburnum flowers, which I sniff. They give off a lovely scent.

After breakfast, I fetch Mouse and Belle from the tower, and they race off to play while I set to work. I spend the morning in the parterre, checking my measurements of each bed, and working out how much bare earth is needed between the plants, to give the impact George London would have wanted.

Just before lunchtime, I take the dogs back to the tower for a nap. I want to schedule another meeting with Lady Clara, to discuss our next steps for the parterre.

I enter via the staff entrance, and walk through to the front hall. When I knock on the study door, she calls, 'Just a moment.' I wait for a minute or two, but I can hear her voice from inside, in conversation with someone. Remembering how long she kept me waiting on the day I arrived, I decide to come back later.

As I turn to leave, the diminutive figure of Sir Angus beckons to me from the entrance to the Scottish Room.

'Hello,' I call, but he places a finger to his lips. I tiptoe over to him, and he gestures for me to enter the room ahead of him. I wonder what his latest secret is, and whether I will be able to interpret it.

When we reach his blue-and-green-check chair, he points to another, opposite it, in bright red and navy. 'Take a seat, lassie.'

'Thank you.' My stomach growls in anticipation of lunch, but I like Sir Angus, and I'm intrigued to hear what he has to say.

He sits in his own chair, and fishes down the side of the seat cushion, drawing out a small silver flask, which he opens and holds out to me. 'Can I tempt you with a wee snifter?' Even without taking the flask, I can smell the strong whisky.

'No, thanks. I don't think I'd get much done.'

'Aye, fair enough.' He nods and takes a swig himself, before stashing the flask away. 'Now, what I can do for you?'

'I think you wanted to talk to me?'

'Oh, right you are, hen, right you are! Now, let's think . . .' He gazes into space for a moment, before putting up a finger to show he's remembered. 'It was about . . . the stuff that's going on hereabouts.'

'The stuff . . .?'

He nods again and leans forwards. But, at that moment, Mr Fanshawe strides into the room.

'Oh, there you are, Uncle A. I've been looking everywhere for you.'

Angus winks at me and whispers, 'I keep telling him as I'm not his uncle.' He taps his temple with one finger. 'I don't think all the tools in the box are too sharp, if you catch my drift.' He raises his voice to reach Mr Fanshawe and says, 'I don't know why you'd be looking all over, seeing as I'm always to be found in the same chair in the same room, in the same house, in the same—'

But, at that moment, Mr Fanshawe catches my eye and says, 'Ms Williams, do forgive the intrusion. My uncle here is due his afternoon nap.'

Angus raises an eyebrow at me. 'As if I were a wee bairn,' he complains.

'Let's get you up,' says his lordship, placing a hand at Angus's elbow. Once the old man is upright, Mr Fanshawe passes him the walking stick, before saying to me, 'I think my wife was hoping to speak to you.'

'Oh, right, thank you. I wanted to talk to her, actually.' I get up, and they let me pass.

This time, when I knock on the study door, I receive an instruction to, 'Come in.'

I step inside, and Lady Clara says, 'Thank you for coming over, Ms Williams. Do take a seat.'

I take my seat and she asks her standard, 'How are you getting on?'

'Good so far, thanks. I'm really starting to be able to picture how the parterre could look. Have you had a chance to browse through the books I left with you?'

She sits forward eagerly. 'Yes, that's why I wanted to talk to you. There are some wonderful examples of what you're proposing. I'm feeling quite inspired. Could we introduce some new greenery, do you think?'

'Definitely. The beds are a bit sparse at the moment, and most of what's there is inappropriate planting. I've been researching what we could use, to give that green structure inside each one. We'll also need some flowering plants. Did you see the photos from Hanbury Hall?'

'I did. Intriguing! I had no idea there should be quite so much blank space. It's striking though, isn't it?' She smiles. 'So, where do we go from here?'

'First, I need to get some quotes for having all the box removed, and then look into costs for the limestone chippings. What we're basically talking about is gravel, made by grinding local stone. I'd like to bring in a landscaping firm for everything to do with preparing the ground and laying the gravel, if that works for you? We'll need them to dig down quite far, and backfill the trench with aggregate, to suppress weed growth, and then lay the gravel on top. It's a big job.'

'That should be fine. Just let me have the figures before we commit to anything.' She continues, 'Do you know, for a long time I really didn't think we'd be able to do any restoration work on the house or the grounds. We're so fortunate that we came into some funds rather unexpectedly recently. I can't tell you how excited I am, to know that the grounds are going to be returned to their former glory.'

I smile.

'Did you find a book to read?' she goes on.

'Yes, thank you. I found three, actually – two crime novels, plus a book on plant hunters.'

'You like crime, I take it?'

I nod. 'In fiction,' I clarify, and she laughs.

'Glad to hear you don't pursue it as a hobby. The crime books all belonged to my mother. She loved nothing better than a truly gory murder to solve. What about the plant hunters? Is that another special interest of yours?'

I smile. 'Anything to do with plants and gardens is a special interest of mine.'

'Ah. Well, in that case, you should find plenty to entertain you on those bookshelves. My great-grandparents were avid collectors of all sorts of specimens. When they died, a lot of the fauna – most of it in the form of taxidermy or those gruesome, mounted displays of bugs – went to the Natural History Museum. But much of the flora, in particular the older trees we have here, were planted from seed they acquired. And they were voracious readers of writings on the natural world, so there are plenty of volumes like that plant hunter one. Do let me know if you'd like me to show you where to look.'

'Thank you.'

I get up to leave. I've just reached the door, when she says, 'By the way, do take everything my uncle says with a pinch of salt. I'm afraid he's rather rambling these days.'

I turn back. 'Sir Angus?'

She nods. 'He has his lucid moments, but he's largely delusional now. It's terribly sad.'

'I'm sorry to hear that,' I say.

'Thank you. It is hard to see a loved one lose their clarity of mind.'

I step outside and close the door. I remain on the spot for a moment, reflecting on Lady Clara's words. Sir Angus doesn't give the impression to me of being delusional. And it occurs to me that he has been interrupted by Lady Clara or her husband every time he's tried to confide in me. I go a little cold at this thought. I shake myself and begin to walk towards the dining room. Hopefully, my imagination is just getting the better of me.

As soon as I open the door to the staff corridor, I'm greeted by the delicious smell of freshly baked bread. I follow it to the empty dining room, where I'm pulled up short by an observation. At breakfast, I'd noticed that the jam jars had been filled with a fresh selection of flowers, but I'd failed to make the connection to Jamie, the resident flower arranger. So, he must be back from the party, after all. I wonder if he's made an appearance yet.

I step back into the corridor and push open the kitchen door, where Vicky and Becky are clearing up after the family's brunch. Vicky glances over at me as I walk inside.

'Hiya,' she says. 'Did you want something?'

'I was wondering if anyone had seen Jamie yet?'

She's in the process of stretching cling film over plates of leftover food. 'No,' she says, over her shoulder. 'Lazy beggar's still sleeping it off at his brother's, I reckon.'

'It's just . . .' I step closer, and she stops what she's doing.

'What is it?'

'Only that I think he must be here. He's done fresh flowers this morning.'

'Are you sure?' She wipes her hands on her white cloth apron and strides out of the room, across to the dining room. I follow, and we stand in front of the table. She gestures to the jam jars. 'What makes you think these have been done fresh?'

I'm surprised she can't see it. 'There are new additions, and the water's been refreshed. Might someone else have done it?'

'Not a chance. It's only Jamie who ever touches those. Right . . . So, sounds like he got up, did the flowers, then decided he felt too rough and went back to bed. I'll send Michael up to check on him. Thanks for letting me know.'

'Sure. This looks good.' I gesture to the large wooden board which bears a couple of loaves of homemade olive bread.

She nods. 'I always make the bread fresh. The secret's in the dough, mind.' She gives me a wink and a wave, and heads back to the kitchen.

A minute or two later, Michael spots me from the corridor and comes into the room, while I'm piling my plate high with slices of cheese, hard-boiled eggs, cherry tomatoes, thick pieces of olive bread and a spoonful of homemade green tomato chutney.

'Hiya. Vicky says you reckon Jamie's back? I'm just going to check on him.'

'Tell him I've got paracetamol in the tower, if he needs some. I'll hang around for a few minutes, in case.'

'Cool. I'll tell him.'

I pour myself a large mug of coffee and take a seat on the side of the table nearest to the door. I'm about to bite into a slice of buttered bread, when I hear a loud, almost unearthly wail.

I drop the bread, jump to my feet and run to the door. Vicky and Becky come out of the kitchen at the same time as I exit the dining room – and Michael comes reeling through the swing door towards us. As soon as he gets inside the staff corridor, he sinks to all fours and vomits.

Vicky strides to his side, placing a hand on his shoulder. 'Michael, what is it?' she asks. But he's in no state to respond. He shakes his head and Vicky has to jump back as he vomits a second time. He points up and just manages to say, 'Jamie . . .'

'Becky, stay here with Michael,' Vicky says firmly, before taking off at a run, with me right behind her.

She passes through the door to the office corridor, then leads me up a staircase I failed to notice the last time I was here. We race up to the first floor, and then across a small landing, before starting up the next flight. Vicky stops, panting hard, and gestures for me to go ahead. At the top, I pass through the door to the staff quarters. The staircase has brought me out close to Jamie's bedroom. His door is ajar, and I push it open.

And then I stop.

Jamie is in the centre of the room, hanging from a noose.

12

I back away, and Vicky runs into my back.

'What? What is it?' Her voice is breathy and anxious.

'Don't come any further!' I say, turning with my arms outstretched to block her view.

But she pushes past me. Then she lets out a gasp at the sight of Jamie hanging there. She walks towards him, emitting a moan.

'Don't touch him,' I say. 'The police will need to be called. They'll have to examine everything.'

'But, what if he's not dead?' she says, in a panicked voice. 'We need to cut him down.'

His face, hands and bare feet are a strange, waxen colour. 'I don't think this has just happened,' I tell her gently. 'I think he's been dead for a while.' I compose myself enough to quickly take in the scene. The noose has been made from knotted bed linen, and a chair has been toppled beneath him. It looks like a suicide, but I instinctively don't believe it. I think this is a carefully staged murder.

I want to weep for Jamie, but I'm aware I need to hold it together for Vicky. I would also like to look around the room, in case there are any clues – but, at that moment, Vicky's legs give way, and she sinks to the floor. I have to crouch to support her while dialling the emergency services.

'Police, please,' I tell the operator.

As soon as I get through, I explain the situation.

'Is he breathing?' the voice asks.

'No. He's really pale. I think he's been hanging for a while.'

Vicky begins to wail, so that I can hardly hear the voice on the other end, and I finish the call as quickly as possible, after making sure they have the address and are sending someone to the scene.

'Come on, we need to get out of here,' I say. But Vicky doesn't register that I've spoken. I call Lady Clara on her direct line, against the sound of Vicky's cries.

'Jamie is dead,' I tell her quietly, as soon as she answers.

'What's that awful noise?' she asks me. 'You'll have to speak up.'

I give up, and end the call. No doubt someone will inform her soon.

'Come on. Let's get out of here,' I tell Vicky, trying to get her up.

But she remains on the floor. 'No!' she says. 'I'm not leaving him on his own!'

'OK.' I put my arms back around her rigid body and hold her. And we wait for the police.

I only realise they've arrived when a stern female voice says, 'You shouldn't be in here.'

I glance up. Vicky is quiet now, but she's clinging to me as if she's the only survivor of a shipwreck, and I'm the piece of driftwood keeping her afloat.

'My friend knew the victim very well,' I say.

The police officer – a small, stocky white woman – says, 'Still, you need to take your friend somewhere else. We have to examine the scene.'

Her companion – a black male officer, who is clearly her senior – says something softly to her that I can't hear. It must be a reprimand, as she sighs and looks back at us. 'I'm very sorry for your loss,' she says, in a tone that suggests she's been coerced to learn this phrase by rote.

I'm helping Vicky to her feet when the male officer addresses me, 'I'm Detective Sergeant Vincent McLeod and this is my colleague, Detective Constable Mandy Chambers. We'll need to speak with you both, but this isn't the best place for your friend right now. She could probably do with something for the shock. She didn't witness him in the act?'

I shake my head.

'Did anyone see him?' asks the woman.

'Not that I know of.'

'But you two found the bod . . . deceased?' she corrects herself.

'No. Michael – our colleague – he found Jamie.'

She's writing in a small notebook. 'Where is Michael now?'

'Downstairs. We left him with Becky, another colleague.'

'We'll need to talk to Michael after this,' she says.

'I'll do that,' says the male officer. He's tall and broad shouldered, with an air of long suffering that I imagine is borne of having to babysit a colleague with no bedside manner.

'I can do the questioning,' she says.

'We'll discuss it in a few minutes, Mandy,' he tells her quietly. 'Are CSI on the way? Remember, we mustn't disturb anything till they get here.'

She sighs. 'Look, sarge, it's clearly a suicide. We might as well get on and do our jobs.'

'We talked about this, Mandy,' he says firmly. 'We can observe and take some photographs for the coroner, but don't touch anything until they get here.'

I look at Vicky. 'You OK to stand?' She nods, and the sergeant and I help her to her feet, then I support her out of the room.

He follows us into the corridor. 'I can't imagine what you're going through,' he says gently to Vicky. 'Make sure to get some sugar for the shock – sweet tea and maybe a couple of biscuits.' He hands me a card, bearing his name. 'Can I talk to you both a bit later?'

I look at Vicky, who nods again. 'Yes,' I say. DS McLeod asks our names and jots them down in his notebook.

'I'm so sorry for your loss,' he says. And, from the sympathetic expression on his face and in his tone, I'd say he means it.

After he's gone back into Jamie's room, I ask Vicky, 'Kitchen or bedroom?'

'I need to go back down,' she says. 'I have to check on Michael and Becky.'

'OK.'

The main staircase is wider than the one we came up, so I opt to take that route down, supporting her all the way to the ground floor, where Lady Clara is standing in the hall, waiting by the open front door. When I glance out, I see there are already police cars and a van outside, the latter bearing the words, 'Forensic Investigation'.

'What a frightful business,' she says. She walks over to us. 'Vicky,' she says in a gentle tone, 'shouldn't you be resting? You must have had an awful shock.'

'I want to be with the others,' she says.

'Very well.' Lady Clara looks at me with concern, and I nod, to reassure her I'm doing all right.

I escort Vicky to the staff dining room, where people are sitting around the table, in a state of shock. Mr Fanshawe has arrived on the scene. He's passing around a plate of biscuits, while Simon pours cups of tea.

Michael practically throws himself at Vicky, who draws him close for a hug, releasing one arm for Becky to join them, which she does, sobbing loudly. No one speaks, and several are in tears. Saliha, Olivia, Simon and Samuel are all there, looking pale and shocked. I realise that William Blythe is missing, as usual. I wonder if he's even heard about Jamie yet.

At last, Michael pulls away from Vicky and says, 'I just don't get it. Why'd he do it?'

She shakes her head, tears streaming down her face. 'I don't know. It makes no sense. Maybe the police'll find a letter or something.'

Mr Fanshawe hands me a cup of tea and offers me the plate of biscuits, from which I select a shortbread finger before sitting down next to Samuel. I'm aware that I can't relax for long, though, if I want to direct the police towards investigating a murder, rather than accepting Jamie's death as suicide.

Saliha is sitting on Samuel's other side, sobbing on his shoulder. Samuel himself is wearing a lost expression. 'He was only a youngster,' he says to me. 'He had his whole life ahead of him. I can't understand it.'

'Let's hope we get some answers,' I say, swallowing the last of the shortbread and taking a couple of sips of the tea before readying myself to find DS McLeod.

A loud shriek from somewhere above our heads, followed by a repetitive thudding, has us all go quiet, listening.

'What is that?' asks Saliha, looking scared.

Michael stands up suddenly. 'Fuck!' he says. 'Benji must be back! I didn't realise.' He runs from the room.

'Who's Benji?' asks Samuel.

'Jamie's little brother,' I say. 'He was staying with Jamie before the party weekend.'

'And he's back here now?'

'It sounds like it.'

We sit in silence for a few minutes. I cover my eyes with one hand, wishing I could wipe from my mind the scene that Vicky and I just endured – Jamie hanging like a life-size wax doll.

I only take my hand away from my eyes when I hear Michael return and say, in a panicked voice, 'I can't find Benji. I thought he'd be in the end room, where he was staying last week, but he's not there, and the place is in a right state. I reckon he's had a meltdown and gone AWOL.'

I don't speak my thoughts: that I hope Benji didn't push open his brother's bedroom door.

'Is Benji a dog?' asks Mr Fanshawe. Michael stares at him.

'He's Jamie's little brother. He's only fifteen and he won't be coping on his own. I didn't even realise he was here till just now.'

Vicky looks at him with a confused expression. 'Did he not go with Jamie on the boat?'

'He did,' says Michael. 'But he must have come back with him as well. I didn't know . . .' His voice breaks.

Vicky nods and walks over to squeeze his hand. 'We'll find him. Don't worry.'

I get to my feet. 'Who's up to helping me look for Benji?' Mr Fanshawe puts down the biscuits and dusts off his hands, ready for action. I catch Samuel's eye. He nods and eases Saliha off his shoulder before getting up. Simon stands, too, and walks over to pat Michael on the back. 'We'll find him, mate.'

'I'll start in the kitchen,' I say, remembering that it was where Benji hid the last time.

'And I'll take the second floor,' says Mr Fanshawe. 'Mr Finch and Simon, would you search the grounds?'

It doesn't take long to establish that the kitchen's empty. I check behind the butcher's block and inside the large, walk-in pantry, but there's no sign of the missing teenager.

I explore the rooms along the corridor towards the family's section of the house, until I reach the main entrance hall, where the front door is still wide open. The police vehicles have been joined by another van, beside which two figures in black coats are lifting a long object into the back of the vehicle. With a jolt, I realise I'm watching the undertakers move Jamie's body into a private ambulance, for transportation to the mortuary.

I'm about to head out myself, to help search the grounds, when a male voice says, 'You're not leaving, are you?'

I turn and see the detective sergeant from earlier. 'Jamie's brother's missing,' I tell him. 'I was going to join the others, who are searching outside.'

He looks concerned. 'How old is he?'

'Fifteen, I think.'

'Do you think he saw . . . ?'

'I really hope not. He has additional needs.'

The police officer speaks into his radio. 'We're missing a vulnerable adolescent, brother of the deceased.'

'I think I just found him,' comes a crackly response.

'They shouldn't approach him,' I say quickly. Realising I've made Benji sound like an armed convict, I add, 'He's highly anxious and will get agitated. Where is he?'

The officer talks into his radio again, and the answer comes: 'A storeroom on the second floor.'

'I'll send someone up,' I say, running towards the dining room. 'Michael!' I say, on entering, 'Benji's in a second-floor storeroom.'

'Thank fuck.' He runs out of the room, leaving me free to return to DS McLeod. I'm keen to discuss my own observations regarding Jamie's death, before it gets put down to suicide. I know he'll also want to interview Vicky. I wish I could take on this gruelling task for her.

'I'm going to talk to that police officer,' I tell her, and she turns her eyes towards me and nods. Her expression is one of utter bewilderment. It almost breaks me.

'I'll come when they want me,' she says.

Squeezing her arm, I say simply, 'OK, I'll let you know.'

I head back to the main entrance hall, where there's now no sign of the sergeant. Unsure where to go, I hesitate. At that moment, the door to the Scottish Room opens and Sir Angus beckons to me. From his grave, urgent demeanour, I'm sure he's heard about Jamie.

I walk over and he gestures for me to go ahead of him into the room. I hesitate, then say, 'I can't stay long – I'm meant to be talking to the police.' I walk inside the room, take the same seat as per my previous visit, and wait for him to make his laborious way over. After sitting down with a groan, he takes a few seconds to catch his breath before saying, ''Tis a terrible business.'

'It really is.'

'Such a wee, young lad.'

It would seem petty to point out that Jamie was quite a big lad – or tall, at least.

'Did you know him well?' I ask.

'Aye,' he says, then seems to reconsider, 'and nae. I had no idea the young'un would do a thing so desperate as to take his own life.'

'But you knew he was unhappy?'

'I'd say he was feart more than unhappy.'

'Afraid?' I check, and he nods.

'Aye.'

'Do you know who or what he was scared of?'

He leans closer, and I hold my breath as I wait for a revelation, but all he says is, 'I dinnae rightly ken. But he always seemed to be checking over his shoulder.'

'There you are, Great-uncle Angus!' Julian has walked into the room without our noticing. The family really do seem determined to keep me from conversing with Sir Angus. At least I've had time to establish that he doesn't have anything specific to tell me. Julian continues, 'Mother says you're invited to join her for afternoon tea in her study.'

Angus eyes his great nephew. 'Not today, lad.'

Julian is visibly taken aback. 'What? Why ever not?'

'That weak liquid won't cut it today,' says Angus.

'Ah!' says Julian. 'In that case, can I interest you in some rather fine malt, which I filched from Father?'

Sir Angus looks at him appreciatively. 'I taught you well, laddie.' He looks at me, 'Will you join us in a wee dram?'

I shake my head. 'I'd better go and find the detective. I was one of the first people in the room . . .'

Angus reaches over and places his hand over mine. It feels warmer than I'd expected, but it trembles with age and effort. I'm touched by the gesture.

''Tis a sad affair,' he says. 'You know where to find me.'

I do my best to smile. 'Thank you.'

When I get back to the hall, I find DS McLeod and his colleague standing together, talking in hushed tones and comparing notes. They look up at my approach.

'Are you free to talk now?' asks McLeod. I nod. 'Lady Clara is letting us use a study.' His accent is local, but he doesn't leave off the ends of some words the way Vicky and Samuel both do.

He leads the way past the Scottish Room, to an open door. Inside, a log fire is burning brightly behind a large, carved, mahogany desk. He shuts the door, then gestures for me to take a seat in one of two small, upholstered chairs in front of the desk, while he sits in the desk chair.

'That must have been a nasty shock you had earlier. How are you doing?' His manner is warm and kind.

'It was worse for Vicky,' I say. 'She's known Jamie far longer – they're like family.' I can't bring myself to use the past tense.

'Still,' he says, 'it's never easy coming upon a dead body. Don't underestimate the effect it might have on you. Down the line, if you find you need to talk it through with someone, we can refer you, or you can speak to your GP.'

'Thank you.' I breathe in and out slowly, readying myself for the difficult conversation ahead. 'Right, let's do this. I also have some things I want to discuss with you, if that's all right.'

He nods. 'Of course. Well, first of all, I appreciate you taking the time to talk to me. As you know, I'm Detective Sergeant Vincent

McLeod. And I believe you are . . .' He consults his notes, 'Steph Williams?'

'That's right. I'm a gardening consultant, brought in to overhaul the gardens. I've only been here just over a week – I arrived last Sunday.'

'Where were you based before?'

'North of London, a place called Beaulieu Heights.'

'So, what brought you here?'

The conversation continues in this vein, until he's happy he has enough background for his notes, and turns the topic to Jamie.

'It wasn't suicide,' I say, watching his face. But his expression remains politely attentive and sympathetic.

'What makes you say that?'

'Someone was hurting him. And he kept having these arguments. I did try to get him to open up around those, and about his injuries, but he wouldn't tell me anything.'

The DS's face reacts visibly. 'He had injuries?'

'Yeah. He had a cut on his lip on . . .' I work out the days, 'It must have been Wednesday afternoon, because a hail storm kept me indoors. And then he had his hair pulled down over his forehead on Thursday at breakfast, and I saw it was covering another cut, a bigger one.'

He notes all this down. Then he looks up, pen in mid air, and says, 'You mentioned his brother shouldn't be approached?'

'Yes. I did think that maybe Benji had had a meltdown – he's on the spectrum – and it's possible Jamie got caught in the crossfire, if Benji was throwing things or something. It's just that Jamie looked so . . . *down* and kind of introverted. He really didn't want to talk about how he'd got the cuts.' I take a deep breath, while I consider. 'Michael might know more, though, about how Jamie got hurt.'

He nods and puts down his pen. 'Thank you for sharing this. It could be important, even if just in discovering a motive for suicide. If Jamie was being bullied, for instance . . .' There's a pause, then he says, 'Julian Fanshawe seems quite badly hurt. The bruises were several days old, but—'

'Oh, that was his cousin, Miles,' I say. 'They had a fight.'

He takes up his pen again. 'A fight? About what?'

'I don't know. In fact, no one seems to know. Apart from the two of them, I mean. Apparently, it's rare for them to fall out.'

'We've been hoping to talk to Michael, but we're having trouble tracking him down.'

'Oh, right. He's looking after Benji. He'll be calming him down right now.'

'And you said you don't believe Benji saw his brother, after . . .?' This question – which I'd pushed aside before – now lands like the lob of a grenade straight into my internal panic room. Did Benji see Jamie hanging there? Or, even worse, did he see someone string Jamie from the beam? This doesn't bear thinking about.

'It would be hard enough for anyone, but Benji . . .' I say weakly.

McLeod makes a note. 'We'll need to talk to Benji.'

I start to object, but he looks up from his notes. 'Don't worry – we have people specially trained to interview vulnerable people, and those with additional needs. It's important to find out anything we can from Benji. He might have talked to his brother beforehand, or maybe he saw something that could be useful.'

He meets my eye and says gently, 'I will look into all this, of course. But I'm sorry, it really does look like Jamie took his own life, as there is no sign of a struggle. I know that's hard to process, for those close to him.'

'I wasn't close to him,' I say simply. 'I just liked him.'

He nods. 'Right, I think we're done for now. Unless you have any other concerns?'

I've just got to my feet when I remember the jam jars. 'Oh!' I say. 'Jamie does these flower arrangements – little posies for the table.'

DS McLeod nods in a polite, noncommittal way, which suggests he thinks I'm about to launch into some monologue on the art of flower arranging.

'It's just, he did them today. Before allegedly killing himself. He went out into the garden – possibly even in the dark, with a torch – and cut seed heads and flowers, and arranged them in jam jars for the table. Doesn't that seem a bit odd to you?' Another thought occurs to me. 'I wonder if it was him who left the door open.'

'What door?'

'The staff entrance door, at the back of the house, by the staff kitchen. It was open around five this morning, and the dog got out.'

He makes a note, then looks up from his notebook. 'Why are the posies odd, if Jamie always did them?'

'Well, why would he go to all that trouble over something as banal as flower arranging, if he was planning on hanging himself?'

'Would you like to sit down again?' he asks.

I shake my head. 'I'm fine standing.'

He continues: 'Right, well, about the flower arrangements . . .' He's clearly searching for tactful language. He continues softly: 'We tend to find that, after a suicide, those closest to the deceased often search for proof that they didn't intend to kill themselves.'

'Like I said, I wasn't close to him. I just know enough to be sure this was a murder.' Out loud, the word sounds shocking.

There's a long pause, then the DS pronounces, slowly and calmly, 'As I said, we will make sure we examine all the evidence dispassionately. But you should know that I intend to notify the coroner that it looks as though Jamie has almost certainly taken his own life.'

'So that's it?' I ask him.

He smiles kindly. 'We will, of course, consider any new evidence that comes to light.'

I take my leave, more determined than ever to get to the bottom of what actually happened to Jamie.

As I pass the Scottish Room on my way to the front door, I notice the door is closed, and I wonder if Julian and Angus are still working their way through the stolen malt.

I fetch Mouse and Belle from the tower, feeling bad that they've been cooped up all morning. A cold wind has picked up, but the sky is a bright blue. I watch them race off towards the lake. I hope they're not going to come back muddy and stinking again. I take my orange woolly hat out of my pocket and pull it on, tugging it down over my thick curls, before taking out my notebook, and squatting down beside an area of parterre. To a casual observer, I might seem unaffected by the horrors of the death scene. But this is how I process grief and trauma: through the calm, quiet language of plants and soil.

* * *

At around 4 p.m., while the dogs are snoozing beneath the holm oak and I'm packing up for the day, Lady Clara calls Mirabelle's name from the house. Mouse barks his views on losing his friend, but Belle gives him a goodbye lick and obediently runs to her ladyship's summons.

'I'm sure she'll be back soon, boy,' I tell him. I feel as if I'm forever having to offer him the same platitude. He stands, staring towards the house, looking bewildered, as if he can't believe Belle would forsake him.

'Let's go,' I say. 'It's nearly dark.' The way he trails mournfully behind me captures my own mood exactly.

13

On my short walk from the tower door to the staff entrance for dinner, I wonder what to expect. It seems unlikely that Vicky, Michael and Becky will have done any cooking. Will we be allowed to raid the kitchen, or will someone have managed to prepare a meal for us?

The answer is provided when I arrive in the dining room. Mr Fanshawe is present again, this time wearing a striped half-apron and supervising Simon and Becky in the unloading of various paper carrier bags.

He catches my eye. 'Indian takeaway suit you?'

'Sounds lovely,' I say. 'Where did you get it? I can't imagine there's a takeaway place in Larkham.'

'No, indeed!' he agrees. 'We had to go all the way to Highfield for this, didn't we, folks?'

Becky nods. She looks close to tears. 'P-please can I go now, Mr Fanshawe?' she stammers.

'Won't you eat something first, Becky?' She shakes her head. 'Well, at least take something with you.' He peers inside one of the paper takeaway bags on the table. 'Here – this one still has a container of rice and a lamb korma.' But she shakes her head again. 'I don't like to think of you starving up there in your garret room—'

I imagine his choice of words makes us all think of Jamie in his own garret room, hanging from the beam. Becky starts to cry. It's a staccato, hiccoughing sound, and Mr Fanshawe says quickly, 'Do whatever you need. You can always help yourself to leftovers later.'

She runs from the room.

Saliha enters and I catch her eye. Although she's dry eyed at present, her face is red and blotchy, as if she's been crying for hours and has only just stopped. I walk over and give her a hug.

Then I turn to Mr Fanshawe. 'What can I do?' I ask.

'Fill the water jugs?' he suggests.

I nod and pick up the empty jugs from the sideboard. I wonder how many staff members will come to dinner. Perhaps I should be offering room service.

But everyone except for Vicky and Becky appears for their food, all accepting the unusual dinner arrangements without much comment. We pass around the rice, and share the various main courses and side dishes.

Once we all have food on our plates, Mr Fanshawe clears his throat.

'As my wife has already told some of you, we don't expect you to work for the next two days. You've all had a nasty shock, and lost not just a colleague but, for many of you, a dear friend as well. Please accept our sincere condolences and know that both my wife and I will be on hand, should you need support. Our doors are open. We would appreciate it, if you could return to your duties on Thursday morning, in time for the weekend, but we will understand if any of you do not feel up to it. Thank you.'

He then takes his leave, saying, 'Now, if you'll excuse me, I have my own dinner to attend. I believe my wife and her brother have been whipping up something in the family kitchen.'

After he's gone, we sit in silence. I look down at the food, already congealing on my plate. It must not have been reheated after being brought here from Highfield. There's a layer of oil, which has separated from the sauce. I put down my fork. I know I should eat, but I can't bring myself to put anything in my mouth and chew. Glancing around, I see Michael, Samuel and Saliha all poking at the food on their plates.

'I can't believe he's gone,' Saliha suddenly says quietly to me.

I turn to face her. 'I get that,' I say. 'I only knew him a week, but he seemed so *alive*.'

I pull a face at my clumsy expression, but she nods, her big eyes solemn.

'Exactly,' she says. A few minutes later, she asks, 'D'you think you'll stay on here?'

I'm taken aback by the question. 'Yes. Won't you?'

She shrugs. 'My mum's freaking out. She wants me back home. She thinks it's not safe. Even though Jamie . . . even though he . . .'

I don't make her say the words. 'So, what do you want to do? Do you want to go back home?'

'I don't know.' She starts to cry. 'Everything's crap.'

I put down my fork and place an arm around her shoulders, and she leans against me and sobs. After only about a minute, though, she sits up and wipes her eyes on her hand. Strands of her dark hair are stuck across her cheek. I gently lift them free.

'I'll miss you,' I say. 'If you go home, I mean.'

She pulls a face. 'Yeah. And it's not like I've got anything lined up.'

'Maybe the Royal Academy will come knocking.'

She laughs. 'Yeah. After Charles Saatchi buys some of my stuff.'

'It might happen.' I glance at her plate. 'You've not eaten much.'

'I'm not hungry.'

'Grief and shock can do that. But it's important to fuel your body, even if you don't really feel like it.' Realising I'm being a hypocrite, I force myself to take up my fork and eat a mouthful of chicken. It feels thick and slimy.

She, in turn, forks a small amount of chickpea and potato into her mouth.

'Good girl,' I say. Then I grimace. 'God, that sounded patronising!'

'More like maternal,' she says. 'You know, like my mum. She loves feeding me.'

The word 'maternal' sends my thoughts into disparate corners, where my adoptive mother is ever ready with a hug, while my birth mother is still waiting for a response to that alert she sent.

I'm pulled back to the present by Michael, holding up a bottle of Prosecco. 'Shall we toast Jamie?' he asks.

There's a chorus of assent. 'All right,' he says, placing glasses on the table. 'Let's start by passing the bottle round the table. When it gets to you, you have to tell us about one time that Jamie made you laugh.'

Everyone smiles. I sit and listen to stories of Jamie swimming naked in a lake in December and getting so cold, he had to be rescued by two of his brothers in a dinghy; of his gift for mimicry, to the point where Lady Clara actually believed him to be her husband when he called her from the landline; of his love of practical jokes, but the way his pranks were never cruel.

I move to pass the bottle straight to Saliha when it reaches me, but Michael surprises me by saying, 'Come on. I know you didn't know him long, but I bet you've got something.'

I think for a moment. 'Only that he was kind,' I say. Everyone nods. 'He didn't know me, but he went out of his way to make me feel welcome.'

'That was Jamie,' agrees Samuel. 'Always making sure no one was left out.'

Michael starts to cry. 'Sorry,' he says to the room. 'I just . . . I can't get that he's gone, you know?'

There are murmurs of agreement. Then Michael addresses me again: 'I've been meaning to ask: how did you know he was here? The flowers all looked the same to me this morning.'

I glance around the table, but they're all wearing expectant expressions. I clear my throat, feeling like Hercule Poirot, about to make a pronouncement. 'There are three changes since Friday,' I say. I put down the wine bottle, pick up the nearest jar, and draw out a stem bearing a small pink flower and a delicately divided leaf. I hold it up to the group. 'I have no idea how Jamie found these so late in the year, but this is the wildflower, *Geranium robertianum*, also known as Herb Robert. They were not in Friday's arrangement.' I lay the flower on the table and remove another stem from the jar, this one bearing red rose hips. 'Seed pods, also known as "hips" from a wild rose: again, a new introduction to the arrangement.' I draw out a stem of flat white seed pods. 'And this is honesty. Definitely not present on Friday.'

I take a deep breath before continuing, 'In fact, I know I said there were three things, but there is a fourth – if you look at the water, you'll see it's clear. This is not water that has sat around for three days, while plant material decayed into it. It's obviously been refreshed.'

There's a long silence.

'Sorry,' I say. 'I notice these things.'

'Thank god you do,' says Olivia. 'Otherwise, god only knows how long . . .' She doesn't finish the sentence.

Keen to move the conversation on, I pass the Prosecco bottle to Saliha. 'Your turn,' I say.

I think everyone's relieved when she begins an anecdote, featuring a scantily clad Jamie (just back from a swim in the lake), a lettuce leaf and an improvised dance involving said lettuce leaf. Several people call on her to demonstrate the dance, but she shakes her head shyly and passes the bottle on.

About twenty minutes later, after everyone has shared their story, I slip away gratefully to the peaceful solace of my limestone tower and beloved dog.

While Mouse and I enjoy a big cuddle on the sofa, I think about how sure DS McLeod seemed, that Jamie's death was suicide – and how I am equally certain it was not. I mull on the factors, from Jamie's introverted emotional state and the bruising and cuts he'd sustained, to the fact that he'd gone out and picked flowers that morning. Also – while I know that many people do give up on life when caring for a loved one – this seems too sudden after his return with Benji. If he'd been feeling that desperate, wouldn't he have left his little brother with another family member?

Shortly before nine, when I've finally managed to immerse myself in the racially charged tension of Attica Locke's *Bluebird, Bluebird*, Mouse jumps up and starts barking. 'What is it, boy?' I ask. He barks again, and I follow him upstairs to my bedroom, where he begins to pace, making strange, unsettled noises, his ears pricked like antennae tuned to a signal.

And then I hear it, too: a shout followed by a crash, followed by more shouting. Jamie might be dead, but the argument is still going on.

I run downstairs, where I pull on my trainers and jacket. I consider leaving Mouse behind, but I'm feeling unsettled after today's traumatic event, so I decide to keep him with me.

'Mouse, boy!' I call. He comes running down to join me on the first floor, alert and expectant. 'Let's go and investigate, shall we?' He makes his rumbling assent.

I clip on his lead as we leave the tower and walk around to the staff entrance, stopping for him to do a quick wee on the way. The door is unlocked, so we pass through, along the staff corridor, and through the doorway to the staff staircase.

I'd heard there had been police tape across Jamie's door earlier. When we reach the second floor, I see the blue-and-white plastic strips are still in place.

We stand outside the end room, and listen for a moment to the shouts and crashes from inside. I knock and call out, 'Are you OK in there?'

'Keep out!' shouts Michael's voice, almost immediately followed by another smash. 'Ow, shit! Benji!'

Benji's voice comes, a noise like, 'Errrrrghhhhhhhhh!'

I glance down at Mouse. 'Stay here, boy,' I tell him. I call through the door, 'I'm coming in. Please don't throw anything.'

Taking a deep breath, I open the door slowly, trying to keep Mouse safely out of the line of fire. But my normally obedient dog pushes past me.

Benji is standing in the far left corner of the room, his hands raised above his head, holding a large porcelain table lamp. He cranes his neck as we enter. 'Dog!' he says.

'This is Mouse,' I tell him.

Benji puts down the lamp without looking, right on the edge of a table. It topples, and I see Michael leap like a goalkeeper, landing on his back and catching the lamp, holding it aloft in triumph – or possibly relief.

'I stroke?' asks Benji.

I let go of the lead, and Mouse trots over, pushing his nose into his hands. Benji laughs with pleasure.

Without getting up from the floor, Michael leans over to replace the lamp on the table, then sinks back down. He catches my eye and mouths, 'Thank you.'

'Can we talk outside?' I ask him.

He glances warily towards Benji, but he's lying on the floor, hugging Mouse. I've known my dog for nearly four years, but he never ceases to amaze me.

Michael and I step out into the corridor. He's rubbing his head.

'Are you OK?'

'Benji hit me with the corner of a book he threw. He didn't mean to.'

'Do you want me to take a look?'

He shakes his head. 'I've had worse.' He smiles, but he looks exhausted and troubled. I reflect on the awful day he's had, and have to resist the urge to offer him a hug.

'Doesn't Benji have any parents?' I ask.

Michael pulls a face. 'Their dad's been a right shit to Benji since their mum died. Jamie brought him here to live for a few days, until his brother Oli could get over from Wales to fetch him. He was meant to come for the big party on the boat, but his car broke down the day before, so he's had to stay home till it's fixed.'

'So, you're left to look after Benji?'

Michael shrugs. 'It's not always as bad as this. He's missing Jamie today. He can't understand why he's not here. I mean, I did tell him Jamie had . . . you know, passed, but I don't think he believed me.'

'Do you think Benji saw what happened?'

He rubs his face and looks at me with big eyes that seem full of shadow. 'I dunno. I hope not. He doesn't always tell me stuff, you know?'

'What can I do to help?'

'Lend us your dog?' He laughs, but it's a sad sound.

'I can do that.'

'Seriously?'

'Of course – just till Jamie's brother can get here. I can come by to feed Mouse. And he'll need exercising. Do you think Benji would like to help with that?'

'Maybe. We can ask him.'

We step back into the room and discover that Benji has fallen asleep, his arms wrapped around Mouse, his face tear streaked, and the floor strewn with broken mugs, splayed books, ring binders and stationery. It's like the aftermath of some strange battle between rival office suppliers.

I notice now that there's a single mattress on the floor on the far side of the table. That must be where Benji has been sleeping.

Mouse is awake, and his gaze follows me as I help Michael to tidy the room, but he makes no attempt to leave his station. I see his lead is still attached to his collar, and I unclip it and stroke his head.

'Your dog's a miracle worker,' whispers Michael.

'He really is.'

Once the room is pretty much straight, Michael whispers, 'Wait there.'

I take a seat at the desk, and he returns a minute or two later with a bottle of red wine and two mugs. He pours wine into each one and hands one to me.

I touch my mug gently to his. 'To Jamie,' I say quietly.

'To Jamie,' he agrees. 'And Mouse the wonder dog.'

'I'll definitely drink to that.'

'You heading back after this?'

I shake my head. 'No – actually, I think I'll sleep here.'

'You can't use the mattress,' he says bluntly. He closes his eyes briefly. 'I'm sorry – that came out wrong. It's just, Benji can't cope with people using his stuff.'

'No, it's fine. There's the sofa by the window. I'll sleep on that. You can go to your own bed, if you like.' He looks dubiously towards Benji. 'Mouse seems to have it covered,' I say. 'Any problems, I'll come and get you.'

'Promise?' I nod. 'OK. Mine's the room the other side of Jamie's. I'll bring you a duvet and pillow.'

'That would be great, thanks.'

He leaves the room and returns a few minutes later with my bedding, which he places on the sofa. He locates Benji's duvet in one corner, and drapes it over Benji and Mouse. As I get to my feet, Michael throws his arms around me and gives me the briefest of hugs before leaving. I have to hold back the urge to cry.

I send Danny a goodnight message, in case he tries to reach me. Then I turn off the notifications on my phone, so they won't disturb Benji.

There's a basin in the room, where I quietly rinse out my mouth and wash my face before switching off the light and lying down on the sofa. It's too short for me, so it takes a while to find a comfortable position. When I do, I wait for sleep to claim me. It's only ten, but I'm wrung out. But, almost as soon as my body calms, my brain awakens, conjuring a slide show of the day's events that keeps me awake for hours. The night is thick treacle and I am suspended within it. I lie very still and let tears trickle down my face until exhaustion finally overtakes me in the early hours, and I'm dragged down into darkness.

14

I wake abruptly, convinced I heard a thud from Jamie's room next door. I lie for a moment, reminding myself that Jamie is dead. The image of his hanging body forces its way back into my mind, like a zombie in a horror movie. I check my phone, and see it's 3 a.m. I've been asleep for two hours at most. I want to go straight back to sleep, but what if there really is someone in Jamie's room?

In the end, I drag myself off the sofa, creep out of the room, closing the door quietly, and go to stand in the dark outside Jamie's room. There's no light coming under the door. I put my ear to it, but can't hear anything. I shine my phone torch on to the police tape, and see it's still in place. Reassured, I return to my sofa to sleep for a few more hours. When I wake again at six, my body is stiff from being crammed on to the short sofa, and my head is foggy from the lack of sleep. Benji is snoring loudly. It's still too dark to see Mouse, but I'm pretty sure, from his regular breathing, that he's also asleep.

I get to my feet, then bend to touch my toes. I stay in that position for a while, luxuriating in the stretch along my vertebrae.

I'm working on loosening my arms and shoulders when I hear claws tapping on the wooden floor, and Mouse nudges my leg.

'Hey, boy,' I whisper. 'You did great.' I stroke the top of his soft head, and he licks my hand.

A little grunt from Benji suggests he, too, is waking up. I tense, wondering if I should have Michael on standby. But Mouse is straight back to his duties as carer. I hear the sound of his claws again as he trots over to greet Benji.

'Hello, dog,' says Benji. 'It's dark.'

'Hi, Benji,' I say. 'It's Steph, remember, from last night? Shall I put the light on?'

'Yes.'

I walk to the door and feel along the wall until my hand encounters the switch. The bulb is weak, but it casts enough light to illuminate the centre of the room, where Mouse is standing to attention, awaiting Benji's instruction. The boy is still lying on the hard floor, curled like a shrimp. His eyes are screwed up against the light.

'I think Mouse probably needs to go outside for a wee,' I say. 'Would you like to take him with me?'

'No. Too dark,' he says.

'Ah, but I have a magic lamp,' I say.

Benji sits up, his eyes wide. 'Really?'

I switch on the torch on my mobile. 'Not really. It's just the light on my phone.'

'Can I hold it?'

'I don't see why not. But first, we need to go downstairs.' I retrieve Mouse's lead from the table, where I left it the night before, and clip it to his collar. 'Would you like to hold the lead?'

Benji nods excitedly, so I reach out to pass it to him. Our hands touch momentarily and he jumps back as if he's received an electric shock, then wipes his hand on his trouser leg, back and forth, several times. 'Now,' he says. 'But no touch.'

'OK, got it.' I hold the lead further from the end, so that he can take the loop without any risk of repeat contact.

When we leave the room, Mouse walks so well to heel with Benji, it's as if he's been trained as a support dog. I have no idea how he understands this human's needs so well.

When we reach the staff entrance, there's a key in the door, so I unlock it and hold it open. Benji stops on the threshold, thrown by the darkness outside. I hold out my phone.

'Here's the magic lamp,' I say.

Benji laughs. 'Magic lamp,' he says.

He shines the torch on Mouse, until I say, 'Not in his eyes,' and he redirects it to the ground.

'Sorry, dog,' he says.

'He's called Mouse,' I say.

Benji laughs again. 'Not mouse. Dog.' I can't argue with this logic.

We step outside, walking until we're just past the vegetable garden. I can't see much, as Benji is a bit erratic in his handling of the lamp, but I have some idea of where we are, thanks to my inner compass.

'We can let Mouse off the lead now,' I say, 'and he'll come back when he's done his wee.' I unclip the lead from Mouse's collar, and we wait while Mouse moves away to find a suitable spot to perform his business.

But we wait longer than expected, and then Mouse starts barking and growling.

'Why bark?' asks Benji.

'I don't know. I'm going to look. Are you OK here?'

'No! Don't go!'

'We'll go together,' I say in a soothing tone, which belies my concern for Mouse's situation.

We walk towards Mouse. I have to walk more slowly than I'd like, for Benji's sake. He is not a fast walker. As we get nearer, I can hear a man's voice, low and urgent, against the backdrop of Mouse's growls and barks.

'Can you shine your torch where Mouse is?' I ask Benji.

'Not eyes.'

'No, not in his eyes, but maybe nearby?'

He lifts the beam and points it in Mouse's direction. It picks up a man's feet.

'Shine it on the man's face,' I direct firmly, and Benji obediently lifts the beam.

William Blythe puts a hand up to shield his eyes. 'What the hell?'

Mouse is now growling loudly.

'Get away from my dog,' I say.

'He's the one coming for me,' says Blythe.

'Mouse,' I call. 'Here, boy.'

With a last bark at Blythe, Mouse comes over and lets me clip on his lead. He's still growling, though more quietly. I stroke his head.

'Don't like man,' says Benji, in a frightened tone.

Nobody does, I think. 'It's OK. We have our big, strong dog here,' I say. 'Can you hold his lead?' Benji doesn't respond. 'Is that OK?'

'I nod.' He sounds aggrieved.

'Oh! Sorry, Benji – I couldn't see you nodding in the dark.'

We repeat the delicate transfer of the lead, from my hand to the boy's. 'Please can you keep the torch shining on the man?' I walk over to Blythe. 'Why was Mouse growling at you?' I ask him.

'Because your dog hates me. Do you not remember the last time?'

'Last time, you had a bucket full of kittens. What's going on this time?'

He sighs. 'I may have accidentally kicked it.'

I feel a fist of tension clench in my belly. 'You kicked Mouse?'

'It's not my fault that he's a black dog on a dark morning,' he says defensively. 'I tripped over him. It's lucky I didn't suffer a nasty fall.'

I glance behind him and see the wheelbarrow. Once again, it has a tarpaulin, covering the contents. 'What's in the barrow?' I ask.

'None of your bloody business. You're not my boss. You do know that, right? I am head gardener here at Ashford.'

I realise he has a point. Suspicious though his behaviour seems, I can hardly insist he reveal the contents of his wheelbarrow.

'Right, well, we'll leave you to it,' I say.

'Do I not even get an apology for nearly being savaged?' He sounds incredulous.

I suppress a sigh. 'Sorry about Mouse. He didn't mean to get kicked.' I know I'm being passive aggressive, but Blythe brings out the worst in me.

He swears under his breath before collecting his wheelbarrow and pushing off, past the back door and away into the darkness.

A whimper from Benji brings me back to the matter in hand. Running over to him, I say,

'Well done, Benji. You did a great job! Now, shall we go inside?'

'Hungry.'

'Ah. I wonder if the kitchen's open yet.'

'Hungry,' he says again, but this time with another whimper.

'OK. Let's see what we can do about that.'

There's no one in the kitchen when we get there, but the door's unlocked, so I rustle up some toast and cereal. I find out that Benji likes his toast with lots of butter and the crusts removed. I make a coffee for myself, and a hot chocolate for Benji.

Michael appears while we're sitting on stools at the butcher's block, as Benji eats breakfast. Michael has dark circles under his eyes.

'Did you sleep at all?' I ask him.

'Not much.'

I think again about how he's just lost his best friend, and has been plunged straight into the duty of caring for the friend's brother. But I can't talk to him about any of that now.

Instead, I say brightly, 'Benji, Mouse and I have been outside this morning.'

Benji looks up from his toast. 'Dark ou'side.'

'I bet it was, mate,' says Michael. He notices Mouse, seated at Benji's feet like a guard dog. 'The dog can't be in here.'

'God, I hadn't even given it a thought,' I admit.

'It's a complete breach of the hygiene regs.'

'Sorry. I'll take him out. Come on, Mouse.' The dog trots over to me. I look at Benji. 'Are you coming, too, Benji?'

But he doesn't move and says, 'No. Dog stay.'

'He can't, mate,' says Michael. 'Dogs aren't allowed in the kitchen.'

'Not dog. Mouse.' Benji smiles cheekily.

'Nice try, but mice aren't allowed, either,' says Michael.

Benji's face clouds over, and I realise we might be about to enter meltdown territory.

'How would you like to come inside a real tower, and give Mouse his breakfast?' I ask.

Benji's eyes widen. 'Tower?' I nod. He gets up immediately, sliding off his stool and stuffing almost an entire piece of toast into his mouth. 'Go now,' he says, though it comes out more like, 'Gunno,' thanks to his overfull mouth.

'Should I come, too?' Michael asks me.

'No, you just take some time to yourself.'

He looks so grateful, it almost hurts.

When we get inside the tower, Benji takes the steps up to the first floor slowly and with great concentration. I admire his quiet determination. Mouse marks him patiently, like a parent with a child. I take the rear.

Once we reach the first floor, I open the living-room curtains. The sun isn't fully up yet, but it has begun to raise its glowing head behind the tops of the trees. Benji is impressed.

'Wow,' he says, looking out at the dramatic silhouette. 'Wow.' He moves away from the window and performs a slow turn. 'Circle.'

'Yeah, the room's round. Cool isn't it?'

He nods and keeps nodding. 'Very cool. Very, very cool.'

It turns out that Benji isn't interested in helping to feed Mouse, so I set out the dog food while Benji explores, opening the kitchen cupboards and even the oven and microwave. At last, he says, 'Up?'

'Sure. It's just my bedroom and bathroom, but you're welcome to explore.'

He nods. Mouse runs ahead and waits for him at the top, and again I follow them up, keeping an eye on Benji's footing on the steep stone stairs. He makes it to the top without even a stumble.

Almost as soon as we reach my bedroom, Mouse starts barking, heralding the arrival of a visitor. I'm nervous about leaving Benji on the second floor unsupervised.

After a moment's hesitation, I say, 'Mouse, boy, can you stay here with Benji?' Mouse makes his rumble of agreement. Then I look at the teenager and say, 'Benji, please can you stay here in the bedroom and look after Mouse for me, until I come back up?'

'K.'

'Thank you.' I run down to the ground floor and open the door. I don't know who I was expecting, but it wasn't Jamie, standing on my doorstep like he's risen from the dead.

My brain falters for a moment. And then the young man says, 'Hi. I'm Jamie's brother, Oli. Is Benji here?' His accent is less overtly Liverpudlian, and his voice is also deeper than his brother's.

'God, of course.' I step back so he can enter. 'Come in. I'm sorry – you just look so like . . .'

He nods. 'We get that a lot. I didn't mean to shock you.'

He looks exhausted. 'I can't imagine what you're going through,' I say. 'Jamie was lovely. I'm so sorry.'

He runs a hand through his thick, blond hair. 'Did you know him well?'

I shake my head. 'I've only been here a little over a week. He was so friendly and kind to me, though.'

He nods again. 'Yeah. We're all reeling, to be honest. I'm kind of glad our mam's already gone. She'd never have got over this.' He meets my eye. 'Does that sound really bad?'

I shake my head. 'No. It makes sense.' We look at each other, and his lost expression makes me wish I could protect him and his siblings – I remember Saliha saying Jamie had four brothers. But the only way out for them all now is through the grief. At least they have each other.

'Shall I take you up to Benji?'

'Yes, please.' He follows me up the stairs. 'This is a proper tower, isn't it?' he says, as we reach the first-floor landing, cross it, and start up the next flight to the second floor.

'Yes, it's something else.'

When we reach my door, we find Benji sitting on the bed, with Mouse at his feet.

'Well, look how well you've looked after Mouse,' I say.

'Oli!' shouts Benji, jumping up and nearly standing on Mouse's tail. 'Oliiiii!' He runs over to his brother and they have a big hug.

'Hey, Benji Bear. How's you?'

'Good. You K?'

'I've been better.'

Benji lets go of his brother and says, with a concerned look, 'What matter, Oli?'

There's a chair in my room, and Oli sits down, leaning forward, his forearms resting on his knees. His eyes flick to mine, then back to Benji. 'Did no one tell you about Jamie?'

'Jamie gone shops.' He sounds so sure, Oli looks almost hopeful for a moment. Then his eyes tear up, and he shakes his head.

'No, little bear. Jamie's dead.'

Benji shakes his own head. 'Not dead. Gone shops.'

Oli starts to cry, and I decide they need some space. 'Come, Mouse,' I say softly.

Down in the living room, I pace anxiously while Mouse sits on the floor, licking my hand whenever I pass close by. I can only imagine how hard it must be for Oli, to have to convince his vulnerable brother that a much-loved sibling is dead.

And then Benji starts shouting, 'No! No! No! No!' An accompanying banging announces that he's hitting his head against something wooden. Mouse makes a concerned sound in his throat, and runs out to the landing.

'I don't know, boy,' I say. 'Maybe we need to leave them to sort this out.' He whimpers, and I feel at a loss. 'You go if you think you can help,' I say at last. 'Go on – see Benji.'

At the word 'Benji', he takes off. I walk to the bottom of the stairs and listen, checking Mouse's arrival doesn't cause more upset. However, the shouting starts to ease almost immediately, and the banging slows soon after that. I can hear Oli murmuring to Benji. Not wanting to eavesdrop, I go back to the living room, where I perch on the sofa and wait.

After another few minutes, noises on the stairs announce the arrival of Mouse and our visitors. Mouse runs into the room first. A few seconds later, Oli and Benji appear in the doorway.

'Sorry about that,' says Oli.

I get up. 'There's absolutely nothing to be sorry about.'

'We're going to head off,' he says.

'Mouse dog come, too?' asks Benji hopefully.

'What would Steph do without her dog?' asks Oli.

'New dog?'

'I don't think that would be very kind, do you?' says Oli.

'I want Mouse dog come.'

'Hey, Bear,' says Oli, squatting until he's eye to eye with Benji. 'Do you remember those puppies at my place?'

Benji's face lights up. 'Golden puppies.'

'That's right – Auntie Ellen's golden puppies. Well, I was going to keep this as a surprise, but she wants you to have one. Would you like that?'

Benji nods enthusiastically. 'Jamie share, too.'

I see Oli's eyes shut momentarily before he says, 'Say thank you to Steph.'

'Thank you, Steph,' says Benji robotically.

I smile. 'That's all right, Benji. It's been lovely to have you.'

'Goodbye, Mouse dog,' says Benji. Mouse nudges one of the boy's hands with his nose, and Benji giggles. 'Mouse dog.'

While Benji and Mouse take a minute to say their goodbyes, Oli surprises me by taking my hand and pulling me off to one side.

'He didn't do it,' he says, in an urgent whisper.

I'm confused, until he says, 'Jamie didn't kill himself. I could see something was off all weekend. But all he'd tell me was that he'd got himself into trouble and he was going to sort it.'

I must look like a rabbit caught in headlights, because he says, 'Sorry. I just . . . I need to know what happened. I can't worry Vicky and Michael, but maybe you could keep an eye out – is that a ridiculous thing to ask? I can't tell what's mad any more . . .' He breaks off and runs a hand through his hair, breathing hard. I can see he's trying not to cry. 'I mean, I know you didn't know him well, but . . .'

It's my turn to take his hand. I squeeze it and say, 'I agree: he didn't kill himself. I'll do everything I can to find out what really happened, OK? You just look after yourself and Benji.'

He squeezes back. 'I will. Thanks.'

We nod to one another, then he calls to Benji: 'Right, that's enough cuddles, you two. Time to go.'

I escort them downstairs and watch them walking away, towards the front of the house. I hear Oli say, 'What are you going to call your dog then, mate?' and Benji reply, 'Dog.'

'Good name,' says Oli.

15

After Oli and Benji's departure, I take Mouse out for our run. The temperature hasn't risen above the minuses, and there's a dewy frost on the ground, which creates a magical landscape within the beam of my head torch – but also makes the earth slippery underfoot, so that I'm glad of the grips on my trainers. The cold feels like a blade on the exposed skin of my face, and I pull my woolly hat down as low as I can.

Mouse keeps to heel, and we get a rhythm up, regular and pulsing, which clears the fog in my head and gives me some respite from the flashbacks. By the time we turn for home, it's light enough to turn off my torch. I pick up speed towards the end, sprinting as if I can outrun my demons, and Mouse races alongside me. The air is fresh and clear, and the hills glow amber in the morning light. It's a glorious setting, but it's been tarnished for me by Jamie's death.

Back at home, I take a quick shower, then leave Mouse dozing in his bed with Mr Rabbit, and head over to the house for breakfast.

There are several staff members in the dining room when I get there. Michael enters right behind me, bearing a pot of coffee. He's pale and drawn, but he manages a small smile when he sees me. 'Hiya. Did Oli pick Benji up OK?'

I nod. 'It didn't go entirely smoothly, but Oli's a pro.'

'Yeah. He's great with Benji.'

'I don't think Benji's really taken in that Jamie's gone for good.'

'Shit. I was worried about that. He seemed to keep thinking he'd just gone to the shops or something. I gave up trying to tell him in the end.'

'Oli had to break it to him again, but Benji was still in denial when they left.'

Michael sighs. 'Thanks for all your help, anyways.'

'My pleasure. It was the least I could do. You've been amazing, holding it together like that for Benji.'

Michael smiles sadly. 'Thanks. It's all so shit.' He takes a deep breath, 'But we're all still here, so what d'you want for breakfast?'

'Aren't you all meant to be taking today off?'

He shrugs. 'Vicky says she's got to keep busy or she'll go off her head. And I can't leave her to do it all on her own.'

'Can I do anything to help?'

He shakes his head. 'Just tell me what you want.'

'OK, in that case, I'll have fried eggs with sausages, mushrooms and tomatoes, please.'

He nods. 'On it.'

After he leaves, Saliha says, 'Did you hear Jamie didn't leave a note?'

I turn to look at her. 'No, I didn't hear that. Though I did glance around his room, and I couldn't see one. I figured the police would find it, if he'd written one.' I hesitate before saying, 'Sorry to ask, but did Jamie suffer from depression?'

'I don't think so.'

Samuel, on my other side, says quietly, 'I stumbled on him, sitting in the maze last week, when I went in to check a drainage problem. He was crying, poor lad. The minute he clapped eyes on me, he made out like he was fine, and scarpered. He always seemed so happy and smiling – it was a shock to see him upset like that. I should've tried harder to find out what was wrong.'

'I don't know if he'd have told you,' I say. 'I pushed him pretty hard about where he'd got those cuts – I don't know if you saw them, on his lip and forehead? – but he wouldn't tell me. I keep trying to work out if they could have been accidental, during one of Benji's meltdowns. Did anyone apart from Michael know Benji was staying?'

Saliha shakes her head. 'It's just, we're not allowed visitors without permission, and I'm pretty sure Lady Clara wouldn't have let him have Benji here if she'd known. She'd have thought he was, like, a liability or something. You know, 'cos he's got additional needs.'

'So, that's why Jamie had to keep him hidden away,' I say,

remembering how startled Jamie had seemed at lunchtime on Wednesday, when I'd 'caught' him with the plate of food.

'Poor Jamie,' says Saliha.

'Poor Jamie,' I echo.

I glance sideways at Samuel, and see he's looking understandably dejected. 'Would you like a visit from Mouse today?' I ask him.

He manages a small smile. 'Oh, I would at that. Are you sure you can spare him?'

I nod. 'He's sleeping at the moment, after a good run, but I'll bring him to you early afternoon, if that works?'

'I'll look forward to it,' he says.

'He'll be thrilled. He adores you.'

Michael brings my breakfast, and I tuck in. Meanwhile, the dining room begins to empty around me, until there are only Olivia and I left at the table. She gets up and comes to sit beside me, bringing her coffee.

'How are you holding up?' she asks, blowing on her steaming drink.

'Oh, you know – I've only just arrived, so it's not hit me as hard as everyone else.'

'But you found him?'

I try to block out the image that jolts into my mind. 'Actually, Michael found him. But Vicky and I were next on the scene. It's hard to get him . . . the image out of my head. I can't imagine what it must be like for Vicky.'

She nods. 'Such an awful business. Did you notice anything suspicious? I've heard the cops are pretty sure it's suicide . . .'

I shake my head. 'Not that I could see – but I was busy with Vicky.'

'Of course. Poor Vicky.'

'What about you?' I ask. 'How are you doing?'

'Not too bad. I mean, it's awful, of course, but, working in the office, I didn't see as much of Jamie as some of the others.' She shakes her head, then says, in a jauntier tone, 'So, that's another ghost for Ashford.'

'There are ghosts, then?'

'Oh, yes – haven't you heard? There's meant to be the spirit of a former gardener, who prowls the grounds at night, whistling.'

'You're sure that's not just Mr Blythe?'

She laughs. 'That's a definite possibility. But Lady Clara's great-grandmother is also alleged to haunt the premises. Apparently, she favours the ballroom, where she used to host magnificent parties.'

'So, there really is a ballroom?'

'Of course. And a billiard room.'

'I thought Ashford was meant to be a "small" stately home.'

'Well, compared to some of its neighbours, such as Chatsworth . . .'

'I've been meaning to visit Chatsworth, actually. I've read a lot about the grounds.'

'They're beautiful. We can go together, if you'd like, when all this calms down?'

'That sounds great.' We exchange a sad smile and she gets to her feet and heads to the office.

I go straight from the dining room to the van for my tools. Although I've been hired mainly to plan, rather than to garden, I feel the need to get stuck into a physical task. I'm planning on subcontracting the removal of most of the hundreds of box hedging plants that mark out the parterre. But today, I'm going to attack some of them myself.

As I set to work, I find that the box removal doesn't involve just hard digging – it's also a delicate operation. Many of the perennial plants have expanded, spreading right up to the parterre's box boundary, and I have to be careful not to damage the roots of any plants I might want to retain, while digging up the box roots.

There's a chilly wind, but I soon warm up, digging away under the November sun. I also become so absorbed in my task, that I lose all track of time. This is not uncommon for me. Gardening is my meditation, and I often enter a trance-like state while working on long or repetitive tasks.

It's only when Saliha appears, that I stop.

'Hiya. You're the last one to get lunch,' she says. 'Thought I'd better check you're OK.' Her voice is flat.

'Is it that time already?' I say.

'A bit past.'

I take in her appearance; her face is still blotchy.

'Are you working today?' I ask.

'Yeah . . . Everyone else is, and I don't want to sit around on my arse all day on my own.'

'Makes sense. Thanks for coming to find me.'

She loops her arm through mine and walks with me back to the house, where I give her a quick hug before we part company, and I retrieve my plate of food and a mug of fresh coffee, taking them to the tower.

Mouse is on the window seat when I reach the living room. He jumps down when I enter and runs over, his feet skidding a little on the floor, though he has got more adept on the slippery surface.

'Hey, boy. Let me have my lunch and then we'll go outside, OK?'

He makes his rumbling sound, and settles on the rug while I eat. I am finding that being still for too long brings back the previous day's images, and I'm grateful for Mouse's soothing presence. I wonder for a moment if I should be lending him out as an emotional support dog to Jamie's friends – but then I realise I don't want to be apart from him for long myself.

I remember that I've promised him to Samuel this afternoon, though. That should be fine, as I can distract myself with work. At the end of my meal, I mention Samuel's name, and Mouse goes off like a rocket. He only calms down when I say, 'Easy, mister, or we're not going anywhere.' I suspect he's reacting more to my tone of voice than my words, but it has the desired effect: he goes to sit patiently at the top of the stairs.

As we walk over to the courtyard, I remember what Samuel told me earlier, about coming upon Jamie, crying in the maze. While he's crouching to pet Mouse, I ask him, 'You know that day you were telling me about, when you saw Jamie crying . . .'

He looks up from rubbing Mouse's belly. 'What about it?'

'Whereabouts was he?'

'He was just sitting on the ground, near the centre. Why?'

'No reason.'

I take my leave of the pair of them. I want to look around the maze, just in case there's any clue as to what Jamie could have been doing there. The police conviction that it was suicide simply doesn't sit right with me. Even if it hadn't been for my promise to Oli, I would be investigating. I always need to know the answer to puzzles; it's the way I'm built. And this particular conundrum is far more troubling than the majority that come my way.

I pass Blythe on my way to the maze. He's carrying a long-handle pruner.

'No attack dog with you this time?' he says.

'I've left him to attack Samuel with licks.'

'Lucky Samuel,' he says sarcastically.

'Were you heading to the maze?'

'No. There's an oak with a low-hanging branch I need to lop off before it takes someone's eye out.'

'Oh, yes – I noticed that. Do you need a hand with anything?'

He snorts. 'Do *I* need a hand? This from the person who's trying to dig up the entire parterre, single handed?'

'Oh, you saw that? To be honest, I just needed something manual, to keep me occupied.'

His belligerent expression relaxes and his shoulders slump. 'I think we're all feeling like that. I couldn't sit at my desk any longer, checking invoices.'

'Did you know Jamie well?'

'Well enough. He used to help out when I needed an extra pair of hands. Him and Michael both.'

'I'm sorry.'

He nods and rubs his face. I notice for the first time that he's pale and his eyes are bloodshot. He's also unshaven, which is unusual. 'Such a bloody waste,' he says.

'Do you have any idea what pushed him to do it?' I don't share my conviction that Jamie didn't kill himself.

'Are you a detective or something?'

'Yeah,' I say, deadpan. 'I'm Detective Steph Marple.'

He smiles wanly. 'I keep trying to work it out. Wish I'd noticed he was struggling. Anyway, I need to get on.' He brandishes his pruning tool.

'Me, too. See you later.'

Despite the poignancy of my mission, I feel a sense of relief the moment I step inside the green enclosure of the maze. I stand still for a moment, breathing in the scent of yew. Even the brisk wind is still, here. I can see why Jamie might have choosen this place as a refuge.

I wend my way slowly, deliberately walking down every dead end. I inspect the base of the yew plants, and also search inside any patches of missing foliage that could have supplied secret storage space.

When I reach the centre, I walk around this, too. But there's nothing.

Just before leaving, I crouch down one last time, to inspect this central area. And that's when I spot it, deep beneath a corner shrub: an A5 notebook.

I lie down and stretch beneath the yew plant until I can reach the book. Drawing it out, I sit with my back to the prickly hedge, and examine my find.

It's a black, hardback book, with a red spiral spine. In case I was in any doubt as to its provenance, it has the letters 'JL' embossed on the cover: Jamie Lennox. My hands start to shake. It feels almost like a message from beyond the grave.

I wonder if the book tumbled from Jamie's lap when he stood up quickly, on Samuel's arrival.

I know I should keep my gloves on to examine possible evidence, but I can't turn the pages while wearing woollen gloves, so I compromise by balancing the book on my lap and handling it only by the edges.

My hands are still shaking as I flip open the cover. The first page contains two lines of writing, in blue ink. In extravagant loops and curls, it reads:

I know you think you're clever but you're fucking not. Put the book back where you found it, a-hole.

I can't help smiling at Jamie's colourful voice, lifting from the paper.

The following pages are full of his beautiful script, written in orderly lines. From a quick scan, I can see it's his journal. One early entry jumps out:

Called Dad. Still saying he won't fund stage school cos there's 'no work in that field'. We had another barney. Wish Mum was still around.

It's strange how wrong it feels, to be reading Jamie's private thoughts. I have to remind myself that I'm doing it for him – albeit too late to keep him alive.

I flick towards the end, and stop at a short entry that reads:

Talked to WB. Says he'll sort things out. Not holding my breath.

WB: William Blythe. What was Jamie asking Blythe to sort out? I'll have to find out.

I turn one last page. The final entry is short. It reads:

Fucking sick of this. Can't wait for Ricky's party this weekend. Get me the fuck out of here.

I turn the following pages, to check there's nothing more. But they are all blank.

I need to talk to Blythe.

16

I track down the head gardener in the woodland. He's found some more trees to prune, and is wielding his loppers like a man on a mission.

'Mr Blythe?' I say. No response. I try again. Then, I notice he's wearing earbuds. I move closer and tap him on the shoulder, leaping back as he whirls around, still holding the long blades.

He leans the loppers against the tree, peels off his gloves, takes his phone from his pocket, stops the soundtrack, then removes one earbud so he can hear me. Each of these small acts is performed slowly, to make me wait. He does not look pleased to see me.

'You really shouldn't creep up on someone when they're using anything with a blade. I would expect you to know better.'

I had been prepared to confront him, but he's wrong-footed me, and I can think of nothing to say in response.

'What did you want, anyway?' he asks sharply.

Pulling myself together, I say, 'I was just remembering a conversation I had with Jamie last week...'

I have his full attention. 'Go on.'

Watching him carefully, I continue: 'He told me you'd promised to fix something for him. Do you remember?'

His expression turns from impatient to... what? Shocked, maybe? Whatever it is, he quickly erases it and asks, in what is clearly intended to be a careless tone: 'What did he claim I'd promised to fix?'

'I was hoping you could tell me.'

His eyes narrow. 'Why are you asking me about this, exactly?'

'I'm just trying to understand why Jamie took his own life.'

He bridles at this. 'I can't see what any of this has to do with you. You've only been here a few days.'

'Anything that might help Vicky and Michael to get some closure . . .'

There's a long pause, while he reflects. Then he says: 'It was only about his pay. He was hoping for a pay rise, and he wanted me to put in a good word for him with Lady Clara.'

His eyes are avoiding mine, and he's fidgeting with the finger of one of his gardening gloves. The man is clearly lying.

'Is that all?' I ask him.

'Quite all. Now, if you'll excuse me . . .' He doesn't wait for my response before replacing his earbud and returning to his labours.

I head to the tower, where I run up to the living room and root out DS McLeod's card. As I dial his number, I perch on the arm of the sofa.

'McLeod,' he answers. I'd expected to reach his voicemail, not him *in real life*, as it were.

'Oh, hi. It's Steph Williams, from Ashford Manor. I've found something that might be important.'

'What have you got? Although my hypothesis remains that Jamie took his own life, and I believe the coroner will agree.'

I take a deep breath. 'I still don't believe he killed himself, and his older brother doesn't, either.'

'You've talked to his brother?'

'Yes, Oli, who lives in Wales. He's convinced Jamie was in trouble, but not suicidal. Also, I've found Jamie's journal. I thought you should see it.'

'When and where did you find the journal?' His voice has turned sharp, as if he suspects me of withholding evidence.

'In the garden, just now. He seems to have dropped it in the maze.'

'Right. I take it you've looked at it? Is there anything that suggests foul play?'

'Not really,' I admit. 'But he clearly wasn't happy.' Even as I say this, I realise that – from a police viewpoint – this just serves to strengthen the suicide theory.

He sighs. 'I'll send someone over to collect it at some point today. We're snowed under, so it may not be till this evening – is that all right?'

'I can run it over, if you like?'

'Oh really? That would be great, thanks. You can drop it off at the local station in Fairburn. They close at six.'

'Will do.'

After the call, I don a pair of clean, dry washing-up gloves before handling the journal again. I draw it from my pocket and set it on my desk, then take a photo of each spread, using my phone camera. When I've finished, I grab the van keys and head out to my beloved, ancient vehicle.

It takes three turns of the ignition key to spark the engine into life, but it's soon rolling easily along the driveway. I keep to a low speed until I'm past the deer and have made it out of Larkham.

It turns out that the road to Fairburn runs steeply uphill. I'm grateful that there's no one behind us on the road, objecting to my slow progress. I know I should invest in a new van – but it seems disloyal to this one, to cast it out when it's struggled on, against the odds.

I am expecting – or hoping – that the ground will level off when we get to Fairburn. It does not. When I reach the police station – a small, one-storey, cottage-style building in grey stone – I turn the van, so that it's facing downhill, pull up the handbrake, and put it into reverse gear before turning off the engine. There are no streetlights here, so I leave my headlights on.

There's a push-button doorbell, which I press. After a buzzing sound, the door clicks open and I step into a gloomy interior.

A uniformed man comes out from a door at the back and takes his position at the desk, saying, 'Afternoon. How can I help?'

'My name's Steph Williams. DS McLeod asked me to drop this off.' I walk over, holding out the notebook.

'Oh, yes, the DS just called to say you'd be coming by. Hold on.' He dons a pair of gloves and takes the book from me. But, instead of placing it inside an evidence bag, he starts to flick through it.

'Does this say who murdered him?' he asks, in an eager tone.

I draw back. 'I thought the police were certain it was suicide?'

'Oh, they are. Only, my sister did amdram with Jamie over at Farley, and she can't handle the idea of him killing himself, so I was hoping you might have something that proves *nefarious activity.*' He raises his eyebrows and puts air quotes around this last phrase.

'There's nothing definitive in there, I'm afraid.'

'Right. Lisa'll be disappointed.' With a sigh, he draws out a clear evidence bag and places the journal inside. 'I don't suppose there was anything else?' He looks hopeful.

'No.'

'OK. I'll make sure the DS gets it.'

'Thanks.'

I drive home, collect Mouse from Samuel, and feed him. When I check the time, I see there's still half an hour until my dinner. Normally, I love the peace of being alone with Mouse. But, right now, all the memories and feelings I've been keeping at bay through mental distraction and physical labour come rushing in.

It occurs to me that Danny knows nothing about what's happened. I send him a text: Please can we talk tonight, say 9?

He messages straight back: Sure.

And then I take my seat at the desk, intending to distract myself with the restoration project. But my mind is too full of Jamie's death. I find myself making notes in my notebook that have nothing to do with the gardens. Instead, I write down the time at which Jamie was discovered by Michael; the fact that Jamie had already created his flower arrangements; and the presence of his journal in the maze.

I pull out my phone and look at the photographs of Jamie's diary. I keep going back over that entry about Blythe:

Talked to WB. Says he'll sort things out. Not holding my breath.

I'm convinced it has nothing to do with Jamie's pay. Was Blythe involved in Jamie's death? He's a pretty unpleasant excuse for a human – but, however I play it, I can't picture him as a killer.

Dinner is a sombre affair. Vicky has again insisted on working in the kitchen, but the meal is uncharacteristically unappetising. The mashed potatoes are lumpy and the minced beef is dry. Michael comes in to join us after serving the food. He sits at the foot of the table, drinking beer and not touching his dinner.

The collective pain is palpable.

At the end of the meal, just as I'm getting to my feet, Olivia comes over.

'We must stop meeting like this,' I say, and she flushes, making me wonder if there might in fact be an ulterior motive to her apparent eagerness to befriend me. Does she know something about how or why Jamie died?

I decide to be cautious from now on, about how much I confide in her, just in case.

'How are you doing?' she asks.

'Not great. You?'

'Been better.' We exchange a wan smile. 'I saw you coming out of the maze earlier,' she says.

I'm taken aback. 'Right . . .'

'Did you go inside for something special?' she asks.

'Just to check the condition of the yew hedging. Why?'

'I was only wondering . . . I remember Samuel saying he'd seen Jamie in there, and . . .' She tails off.

'It's not as if that's where Jamie was found, if that's why you're asking.'

'No.' She hesitates. 'But I heard Michael say Jamie's diary's missing. I just thought . . .'

I shrug. 'Haven't seen it.'

'No. Of course not. Anyway, I'll leave you to get back to Mouse.'

'Thanks.'

She nods and squeezes my shoulder. 'Here if you need me,' she says.

I frown after her retreating back. What was that about? Did she see me with Jamie's journal? If so, why didn't she just come out with it? I rub my forehead, wishing she and Blythe didn't both seem to enjoy obfuscation. I remember how Sir Angus also talks in riddles half the time. Is it something in the Ashford air?

I video call my brother Danny from the sofa at 9 p.m.

'Hiya,' he says. 'Things must be bad, if you need to talk again.'

'Hi.' I start to cry.

'Shit! I was joking! What's wrong?'

'There was a death here yesterday. A boy – well, young man – of twenty.'

'That's awful. What happened?'

I tell him everything, from Michael's running downstairs, to Vicky and I stumbling upon the awful scene, and then the police arriving.

'Oh my god. Are you OK?'

I nod, even though I'm still crying. 'Yeah. I think I'm more in shock than anything. Some of the others were really close to Jamie. You can imagine what a state they're in.'

'I'm so sorry, sis. Do you want me to take tomorrow off work, and come up there?'

I shake my head. 'That's so sweet, but no. I'll be fine. I just needed to talk to someone.'

'Well, Karen and I are both here, if you need us,' he says. This phrase sounds so much better coming from him than Olivia.

'Thank you. Don't say anything to Mum and Dad.'

We ring off shortly after that, and I get ready for bed. It's early, but I'm wiped out. Sleep comes surprisingly easily. The dreams, though, are troubling, filled with images of Olivia, towering over me and saying, 'It's all in the journal. Haven't you done your homework?'

17

When Mouse and I return from our run the next morning, I check my phone and find a text from Dad:

Hope all good at new place. Slugs still partying on allotment. They don't like my beer. Any ideas?

I've been encouraging Dad to garden without chemicals, and the beer traps were one suggestion, which I've seen work many times before. I message back: What beer are you using?

My phone rings at once, and I pick up. 'Hi, Dad.'

'Hello! I've created my own brew by boiling up some hops and adding barley, sugar and yeast.' He sounds very proud of himself.

'I'm pretty sure there's more to the process of brewing beer. Don't you need special kit? And doesn't it have to ferment?'

'Ferment, schmerment,' he says, sounding uncharacteristically Jewish. Dad's parents were both the grandchildren of Eastern European Jews, but he rarely refers to that ancestry. I think assimilation was a big thing in his family: the need to blend in and avoid being singled out. They'd experienced first-hand what happened if you stood out.

'Anyway,' I say, 'I'm sorry to tell you that, in my experience, molluscs prefer the non-alcoholic beer varieties.'

'You're kidding. I've made loads!' Then he says, in a cheerier tone, 'Oh, well – your mum and I can drink it.'

My heart goes out to Mum. Between the glut of sprouts – her least favourite vegetable – and now the dreadful-sounding beer experiment, she's in for a tough time.

There's a pause, during which I consider telling Dad about Jamie. But I have neither the time nor the energy for his and Mum's potentially overbearing concern right now.

'I'd better go, Dad. Good luck with the slugs.'

'I'll keep you posted, send you pictures.'

'Great,' I say. 'Pictures of dead slugs. Can't wait.'

We end the call and I walk over to the dining room, where I find everyone else has already arrived.

We eat breakfast in semi-silence, then they head to their respective jobs. I've noticed none of the staff seems willing to take the proffered time off. I down my coffee and go back to the tower, to grab the plans. I hear Mouse barking, even as I'm unlocking the front door. He's waiting in the hall.

'Wow, someone's eager.' I would simply let him out, but he seems keen for me to accompany him, so I decide to return later for the plans. He runs outside, stopping impatiently a few metres away, while I lock the door. And then he's off, racing through the parterre, with me jogging behind, in an attempt to keep up. His tail is wagging hard. I wonder if Belle's back on site, though I don't think he'd be so desperate to have me along if he were going to greet her.

And then I see her: the beautiful cat, Lilibeth, walking along the rose garden wall. This time, far from running away, she leaps down and comes trotting towards us. 'Sashaying' might be more accurate: this is a feline who knows her beauty.

She looks up at us with her big, green eyes and mews once. Mouse lies down, as if to demonstrate that he's no threat, and she sniffs him briefly, before walking over to me and demanding to be stroked. I oblige. Her fur is sleek and soft. She rubs against my legs and purrs loudly.

'Aren't you a beauty?' I say.

Mouse gets to his feet and licks her face. She doesn't object. She mews once more, before deciding she's had enough and leaving at a run.

But Mouse isn't going to give up his new friend so easily. He runs after her, and I end up following again. For some reason, I think of the old woman who swallowed a fly and then a spider, a bird, a cat and a dog. In this reworked version, I am the woman who chased the cat and the dog. Hopefully, there will be no more animals joining the chase.

Lilibeth leads us to a door that I haven't noticed before, set into a tall fence between the courtyard and the deer pastures that line the long driveway. She slips through a small gap in the fence, and I open the door for Mouse and me. The area contains three sheds, all tucked away behind the courtyard wall. She slips through a cat flap, in the door of one of the sheds. This is the largest of the structures, a long, grey, windowless prefab with a corrugated roof. Mouse stands beside the door and whines.

'We can't go inside, boy. It's private.' He stares up at me with eyes that perceive great cruelty. 'Don't look at me like that,' I protest. 'It's not my fault.'

And then, Mouse starts barking and snarling. At least this prepares me for the appearance of William Blythe, emerging from one of the smaller sheds.

'You can't be back here,' he says. 'And please do something about that dog. He should be on a lead and preferably muzzled.'

It's as if our bonding conversation of yesterday never happened. We're back to being at loggerheads.

'I'm sorry,' I say, keeping a tight hold on Mouse's collar. 'He's not normally like this.'

'Well, he's been like this every bloody time I've seen him.'

'We were following Lilibeth,' I say.

'You've seen her?' He looks excited.

'Yes – she just went in through that cat flap.' I point with my spare hand.

'Fantastic,' he says. 'Lady Clara will be relieved.'

'Can I ask, why do you have a cat flap in your shed?'

'Lili's a good mouser.'

'Ah, fair enough.'

Mouse has calmed down while we've been talking, as if starting to realise that Blythe does not, on this occasion, constitute a threat to any creature that he loves, and is not about to kick him. He sniffs around near my feet, but I don't let go of his collar, just in case.

'We'll leave you to it,' I say. 'Although I'm sure Mouse would rather wait around to play with Lili.'

Blythe shoots me a look. 'Her royal feline-ness considers playing to be beneath her.'

I laugh. 'Now, that I can believe.' I look down at Mouse. 'Come, boy.' He whines and strains towards the cat flap. 'Nope, Lilibeth has work to do. Maybe she'll come by later.'

He makes one last, sad sound before accompanying me back towards the garden. It's only when we reach the parterre that I notice he has something in his mouth.

'What have you got there, boy?'

He drops it at my feet, and I see it's a flower. I bend to pick it up. It's small, white and rather lovely, clearly some kind of orchid, but not one I've seen before. I tuck it behind my ear. 'Thank you,' I tell Mouse. 'It's beautiful.' He makes a rumble of assent.

I spend the morning digging up more of the box plants and transporting them over to the bonfire heap. Just before lunch, I light the new pile. Mouse comes to find me, and he watches the fire with me for a minute or two, enjoying the movement and sound of the flames.

I take him up to the tower, where he drinks a bowl of water before curling up in his bed with Mr Rabbit. Then I head over to the staff dining room for lunch, expecting to find it empty, as usual.

Instead, Michael is pacing the room, with Vicky sitting at the table, watching him.

'I can come back?' I offer.

Michael shakes his head. 'It just makes no sense,' he says to Vicky, and she nods.

'You mean Jamie?' I say, sadly. 'It's so hard to take in.'

'No,' says Michael. 'Well, yeah, obviously Jamie. But now his room's been turned over by some arsehole. I'm fucking livid.'

'Shit!' I say, processing this information. He and Vicky nod grimly. 'And you're sure it wasn't the police, when they were doing their investigation on Monday?' I ask.

Michael shakes his head. 'This is way worse than what they

did – they called me in afterwards, in case I knew of any secret hiding places, and it wasn't too bad.'

'Who discovered the break-in?'

'Me, just now. Oli called, saying Benji had lost one of his Wednesday socks – 'cos he has different socks for every day of the week – and could I look for it? So, I let myself into Jamie's room – I've still got the key – and there was this . . . fucking, fucked-up mess.'

I have a flashback to Monday night, when I thought I heard someone in Jamie's room. 'Sorry to ask, but did you have to break the police tape to get in?'

He shakes his head. 'Turns out it had been kind of *unstuck*, you know? So it came away dead easily when I tried to get in. I should've realised that was a sign someone had got in.'

I wonder if I missed the signs of its having been tampered with on Monday night.

Something else strikes me: 'But the door . . . If you have the key, how did they get in?'

He shrugs. 'There's skeleton keys to all the rooms. Anyone here could get in.'

'Oh, Michael. I am sorry.'

'Anyway, I'm going home,' he says. 'My mum and dad are coming for me later.'

'That sounds like a good idea. How long for?'

He looks at me with hurt, angry eyes. 'I've had enough. I'm not coming back.'

Michael's parents arrive mid-afternoon. Once the car is loaded with his belongings, all the staff and the Fanshawe family gather at the front of the house to see him off. Vicky gives him a big hug, and Mr Fanshawe pats him on the back. Lady Clara shakes his hand and thanks him for his service.

After the car has vanished down the long drive, the Fanshawes go back inside. The rest of us hover, unwilling to accept that Michael has really left.

'And then there were eight,' Olivia whispers in my ear. I pull a face, but she doesn't seem to notice.

144

* * *

At dinner that evening, during a short lull between our main course and dessert, Olivia leans towards me and says, 'You look very fetching, by the way. I meant to say earlier.' I glance down at my jeans and sweater. 'No,' she laughs. 'Your hair.'

I put a hand to my hair and discover the orchid that I tucked there earlier. 'Oh!' I laugh and remove it, laying it on the table. 'I forgot all about that. It was a gift from Mouse.'

'Who needs a man when you have a dog?' says Olivia.

'Well . . .' I say doubtfully. I raise an eyebrow questioningly, and we both laugh.

Olivia picks up the flower. 'It's lovely. What is it?'

'I don't know. I mean, it's obviously an orchid of some kind . . .'

She looks surprised. 'An orchid?'

'Sorry! Obvious to a horticulturist, I mean. But it's not a species I recognise.'

She twirls the bloom between her fingers before gently pushing it back into my hair. 'The contrast with your dark curls is really lovely,' she says, smiling.

I feel myself blushing at the unexpected compliment. 'Thank you.' After dinner, I pay a quick visit to Vicky in the kitchen, to see how she is. She's busy preparing the dough for tomorrow's bread, and doesn't seem to want to talk, so I don't stay. As I'm coming out, I nearly bump into Blythe, striding towards the staff entrance.

'Watch it,' he says. 'Oh, it's you.' I can't really argue with that, so I say nothing. He stares at me for so long without speaking, I turn to leave, but he grabs my arm to stop me, and hisses, 'Where did you get that flower?'

I twist my arm free. 'The orchid? I think Mouse found it near those sheds where we saw you earlier.'

'Give it back.'

'Give it back? Are you serious?'

'It's mine and I want it back.'

Saliha and Olivia come out of the dining room at that moment, and they shoot us a curious glance. Blythe responds with a big smile, and makes a show of putting his hand on my shoulder, as if we're best buddies. I don't know if they're convinced, but they leave us to it, heading down the corridor, towards their quarters.

I shake off his hand and, with a sigh, remove the flower from my hair and hand it over. He stuffs it straight into his waistcoat pocket.

'What are you going to do with it, anyway?' I ask, 'Glue it back on the plant?'

He makes a noise that's so close to a snarl, I have to suppress a laugh. 'Well,' I say cheerily, 'I'll be on my way. I hope you and your flower will be very happy together.' And I give him a chipper wave before striding away.

A couple of minutes later, as I mount the tower stairs to the first floor, I wonder if I could train Mouse to growl at the mention of Blythe's name. It would be churlish, but also fun.

Mouse is asleep in his basket when I reach the living room, so I switch on a floor lamp rather than the main light, which might disturb him. And then I scan my stack of reference books, drawing out a rather lovely old book called *The Orchid Grower's Manual*, by Benjamin Samuel Williams. It's the seventh edition, but is still a collector's item. This beautiful 1894 hardback was a gift from my ex-husband, Ben, in the early days of our marriage, before I'd cottoned on to the fact that an expensive gift, although intended as a romantic gesture, was merely proof that he lived constantly beyond his – or rather, *our* – means.

As well as text, the book is packed with illustrations of orchids. I turn the fragile pages, examining all the detailed colour plates. But not a single flower matches the one Mouse found today. The bottom petal of an orchid is called the lip. This curves upwards, to provide a landing platform for pollinators. In Blythe's flower, the lip is more highly curved than in any of the illustrations. The book is old, of course, and more orchids are discovered all the time, but I'm surprised I can't find a flower that's even a close match.

I place it back on the stack beside the desk, turn off the lamp and head upstairs, leaving Mouse snoring in his bed, Mr Rabbit tucked like a pillow beneath his head.

Danny video calls shortly after I've got into bed.

'Hi, Lou. I just wanted to check in,' he says.

'Thanks, I appreciate it. Things are a bit weird here.'

'I can imagine. Are you doing OK?'

I pull a face. 'Someone's been into Jamie's room and ransacked the place. And now Michael's left.'

'Is that Jamie's friend?' I nod. 'So, what's going on, do you think?'

'I don't know. But I really don't believe Jamie killed himself.'

'Let me guess: you're back to your detectiving?'

I pull a face. 'Something like that.'

'I knew that blackmail investigation wasn't a one-off . . .' he muses, referring once again to the debacle I got caught up in when I was working at Beaulieu Heights.

I smile and shrug. 'So, how are all of you?'

'Pretty good, although Karen and I could do with more sleep.'

'Baby still waking all night?'

'Yup.'

'Has he got a name yet?'

'Actually, he has. We're calling him Stephen. With a "ph".'

He lets this sink in: a tribute to my name change, from Lou to Steph. 'That's lovely,' I say softly.

'We'll be calling him "Stevie" for short – you can't call a baby "Stephen". It's just wrong.'

'Like calling a dog "Kevin",' I agree.

'Or "Mouse".'

'Oy, cheeky!'

We both laugh.

'Alice adores Stevie,' says Danny.

The mention of my niece makes me yearn to see her. *When this is all over*, I promise myself.

I feel a little better by the time we finish the call – a bit lighter. Tomorrow, I will continue my investigations with a new vigour. Whatever the police may believe, there are too many suspicious happenings here at Ashford for Jamie's death to have been a suicide. I know I'm right – and I'm going to prove it. After all, I promised Jamie's brother Oli that I'd find out the truth.

For now, though, it's time to sleep.

18

Keeping my promise to myself and Oli, I embark on fresh enquiries at breakfast the next morning.

While I'm waiting for my full English to be brought through, I turn to Saliha and say, 'I've been wondering: who did Jamie work with the most?'

I'm grateful she doesn't ask why I want to know. Instead, she considers for a moment, before saying, 'I dunno. I mean, he worked a lot with Mr Blythe ... But then, he also did running around for the family, you know? He was always doing errands for Master Julian or her ladyship.'

'I've met Julian a couple of times, and he seems quite nice,' I say.

'Yeah, he's OK, for a posh git. His cousin Miles isn't too bad, either, though he's a right tart.'

I laugh. 'Has he tried it on with you?'

She rolls her eyes. 'I mean, if it, like, has a pulse, he's tried it on. Steer well clear.'

'Oh, I'm pretty sure I'm way too old.'

'Nobody's safe,' she insists.

'I'll bear that in mind. Thank you.'

Somehow, late morning, it starts to snow from an azure-blue sky. I'm in the process of unwinding some ivy from a bay tree that's been planted in the parterre for no reason I can fathom. Despite the ivy's attempt at strangulation, the bay has predictably far outgrown its spot.

Mouse appears in front of me, grumbling about the cold, wet stuff falling on him. I glance at my watch and see it's nearly lunchtime, so I take him back to the tower, and set out a bowl of water for him, before heading over to the dining room.

I'm pouring my coffee, when Olivia arrives. I'm starting to feel like she's tracking my movements. It's hard to know where the line is between legitimate suspicion and paranoia.

'Hi,' she says.

'Hi,' I reply, watching the coffee stream into my mug.

There's a silence while we both put food on to our plates. Olivia stops collecting tidbits much sooner than me, her plate only half filled.

'Is that all you're having?' I ask. 'You'll waste away.'

She pulls a face. 'I'm not very hungry. All the stress . . .'

I hold up my own, heaped, plate. 'My appetite's returned with a vengeance.'

I move to leave the room, but she says, 'What did William want with you yesterday? It looked pretty intense.'

I meet her eye. 'Am I under investigation?'

She pulls a face. 'Sorry! My mother always tells me off for being nosy.'

'With me, it's my dad,' I admit. I decide there's no harm in telling her the truth. 'You'll like this one: Mr Blythe wanted me to give back his flower.'

She raises an eyebrow. 'The orchid you had in your hair?' I nod. 'And did you?'

I shrug. 'Hey, if Mr Blythe wants to claim ownership of a random flower picked up by my dog, who am I to argue?'

She laughs. 'The man is a law unto himself.'

'He certainly is.'

We head to the staff entrance. It's stopped snowing, though the wind is again as sharp as a blade.

Olivia seems to have no more questions for me, so we part ways, she to the courtyard, for her cigarette – despite the chilliness – and I to the tower, where Mouse snoozes while I set to work on clearing my plate. There are pickles, tangy cheeses and fresh walnut bread.

After lunch, I decide to dig up some more of the infested box plants. Sir Angus comes wandering out of the house a few hours later, while I'm trying to remove an especially stubborn specimen. I've dug all around it, but it's holding fast, its roots like bunches of tiny fists. Mouse is snoozing close by, in a pile of leaves dropped by an oak. The leaves are so beautiful in their colours, they look hand painted.

I only become aware of Sir Angus's presence when he asks, in a stage whisper, 'Have you time for a wee nifter?' He glances furtively around before taking his flask from inside his coat, like a hawker of stolen goods. I'm pleased to see he's wearing woollen trousers today, in place of his usual kilt. I'm sure they breed them tough in Scotland, but Angus is a nonagenarian, and I don't want to be responsible for keeping him out of doors in November in a kilt and knee socks.

I hadn't realised but it's starting to get dark. I check my watch. It's four o'clock. 'Oh, go on.' He passes me the flask and I take a sip. The whisky flames in my throat, like a furnace. 'Thanks,' I say, handing it back.

He nods and takes a swig himself before returning the flask to his inside pocket. 'I've been meaning to talk to you, hen.' I'm beginning to suspect he doesn't know my name.

'Go on.'

'Can we sit? Louisa's bench is right here, look.'

We walk over to a nearby bench, which bears a plaque addressed to 'Louisa, beloved by all who knew her.'

'Is Louisa your wife?'

He nods. 'Aye, and a true saint for bearing with me for more than sixty years.'

I laugh. 'Were you that bad?'

'I'm not too proud to admit that I wasn't always easy to live with.'

'Oh, dear. Poor Louisa. So, what did you want to talk about?'

''Tis not an easy matter to bring up, especially when it regards kin, but I believe there's some as might be drugging me.'

I remember Lady Clara's warning to take Sir Angus's pronouncements with 'a pinch of salt'. But he seems clear headed.

'Who?'

'Who what, hen?'

'Who's drugging you?'

''Tis either the tea drinker herself or one of her henchmen. I wouldn't put it past that Blythe chappie to be growing a bit of arsenic on the side.'

I decide not to point out that arsenic isn't a vegetative crop. 'Do you think someone's trying to kill you?'

He pats my hand reassuringly. 'Oh, nay, lassie, 'tis just a wee amount, ter keep me subdued.'

'And why would they want to keep you subdued?'

'So as I can't spill the beans.'

This conversation is like pulling teeth. 'Sir Angus, if there's something you think I should know, can you just say it?'

'I saw the wee lad.'

'Jamie?' I check.

He nods. 'Aye. He was out in the courtyard the week before he died, when I was taking a midnight stroll. 'Twas a lovely full moon that night.'

'And what was Jamie doing?'

'He was carrying a container.'

'What sort of container?'

'That I cannae say. However, I did happen to see where he stowed it.' He puffs out his chest with pride.

'Why are you telling me all this?'

He reflects on this. 'The way I see it, you only came to Ashford after all this had been going on a wee while, so I don't see as how you could be involved.'

I manage not to scream with frustration, keeping my voice level as I ask, 'What's been going on?'

'That I don't rightly know. But 'tis unsettling. And happen as it's the reason for keeping me quiet.'

I rub my forehead, trying to make sense of the conversation. 'So, you think someone knows you saw Jamie that night?'

'I don't rightly ken, lass.'

I sigh and change tack. 'So, where did Jamie put the container?'

'I shall have to take you there. Meet me here at eight in the morning, and we'll take a little walk over, while the rest of the staff are at their breakfast.'

In bed that night, I wonder what – if anything – Sir Angus and I will find in the morning, when we unearth the container. Drugs, perhaps? It has to be something serious enough to be concealed by a young man who felt his life was either in danger or untenable. I should probably be notifying the police, but I don't want to waste their time if Sir Angus turns out to be as unreliable a witness as Lady Clara seems to believe. I wonder if Vicky or Michael reported Jamie's ransacked room.

I expect to be awake for hours, trying to process everything, but my room is dark and blissfully quiet, and I slide quickly into sleep.

19

Angus doesn't turn up to our rendezvous the next day. I wait for half an hour, my stomach rumbling, and then I check the Scottish Room, but there's no sign of him.

I need my breakfast, so I hurry to the dining room, where Simon greets me, saying, 'You're late.' With his slow delivery, it comes out more as a statement than an accusation.

'Sorry! I got waylaid.'

'I'll have to see if Becky's started cleaning the frying pans yet.'

'OK. Please apologise to her and Vicky from me.'

He nods. 'Help yourself to coffee.'

He leaves the room, and I walk around the table and take a seat between Olivia and Saliha.

The latter finishes her cup of tea and stands. 'Sorry to abandon you, but there's loads to do today. You know, with all the people arriving later.'

'What people?'

She stares at me. 'It's the annual family party thing. Hasn't anyone told you?' I shake my head. 'You're dead lucky – I bet you're the only who hasn't had a million jobs dumped on them.'

I grimace. 'Good luck.'

As soon as she's gone, the exodus begins, until there are only Olivia and I left.

I brace myself for the invasive questioning. But she just says, 'What are you up to today?'

'I need to get on with my surveys.' I study her for a moment. She appears relaxed and amicable, so I dive in: 'What can you tell me about Sir Angus?'

She looks surprised. Reaching for the nearest coffee pot, she tops up my coffee, then pours one for herself, adding milk and sugar to hers. While she's stirring her coffee, she says, 'I'm not sure I'm the person to ask. What do you want to know?'

I take a deep breath, 'He told me yesterday that he's being drugged.'

She pulls a face. 'Was this before or after his eighth medicinal Scotch of the day?'

'You think he was drunk?'

She leans closer. 'Last month, he was convinced he was an ageing pop star. We had nearly a week of him name-dropping Cilla Black and Lionel Richie. Apparently, he'd been to parties with them. Oh, and Cliff Richard sometimes dropped by.'

'So, I shouldn't worry about him?'

'Oh no, you should definitely worry about him. I mean, how much alcohol must a person consume to be that delusional? Or perhaps it's not even the drink any more – no one seems too sure about the state of his mind.'

'Oh . . . right.'

'But no, I don't think he's being drugged.'

'That's a relief. Have you seen him today?'

'Not yet, no. But it's early for him. He tends to get up with the . . . whatever gets up several hours after the lark.'

I laugh. 'Fair enough.'

Simon returns, and I'm relieved to see he's carrying a plate of food.

'Thank you,' I tell him, as he passes it to me. He exits without responding.

Olivia pushes back her chair and stands up. 'I'm also going to have to leave you to it, I'm afraid. I have a rather large gathering to prepare for.'

After she's gone, I eat and drink quickly, before going back to look for Sir Angus. But there's still no sign of him, either in the Scottish Room or outside, at Louisa's bench. As I'm re-entering the hall, Lady Clara's study door opens and she says,

'Ms Williams, just the person. Can you spare a minute or two?' I nod and follow her in, taking my seat in front of her desk. 'You will no doubt be aware that we have the annual family get-together here at the house this weekend,' she says. 'As you know, my family and I only moved in in February, after my mother died last year, so this is my first time as hostess. I really want it to be extra special. It's going to be quite the challenge, as most of the staff only started this year.'

'How can I help?'

She leans forward eagerly. 'A garden tour. What do you think? You could take people around, and show them the current state of the garden, while describing George London's original plans, and how you intend to restore those designs.'

'How long would you need me for?'

'Just Saturday afternoon, say from two till three thirty. How does that sound? Guests will start arriving this evening, and the boys will be taking out a rowing party on the lake in the morning, but the afternoon is still looking a bit sparse as far as activities go. Of course, we have the croquet lawn, and the tennis courts . . .'

'All right, I'll do it,' I say. 'If you think anyone will be interested.'

She clasps her hands. 'Oh, that's wonderful. I'm sure we'll get a few takers, especially among the older generation.'

'Will I need to keep my dog indoors?'

'Oh, there's no need for that. Belle will be coming, so the pair of them can entertain one another.'

'Mouse will be delighted to see Belle again. He adores her.'

'Did I hear that it was your dog who spotted Lilibeth?' she asks.

'That's right.'

'I'd been so worried about her. Thank you so much for tracking her down.'

'She was just in the grounds when he saw her. She'd obviously come back of her own accord.' Unexpectedly, I remember my ex-husband Ben, and wonder if he will also return of his own accord.

'Oh, and thank you for taking care of Uncle Angus,' she says. 'You and your dog are becoming quite the favourites around here.'

'He's an interesting man,' I say.

'That's very kind.'

'I enjoy his company,' I say firmly.

She doesn't acknowledge this, instead fixing me with a sympathetic gaze. 'Now, how are you doing, since Jamie's passing?'

'Oh, not too bad, thanks.'

'That's a relief. It must have been such a nasty thing to witness.'

'It was far worse for Michael and Vicky, of course. I don't blame Michael for leaving.'

She looks aghast. 'You're not thinking of leaving . . .?'

I hold up a hand. 'No, nothing like that. I just mean that it was a hundred times harder for Michael.'

'Still, don't hesitate to come and find me, if you need a listening ear.'

'Thank you.'

She folds her hands on the desk. 'I did consider calling off the family engagement, in view of Jamie.' She sighs. 'But it's a tradition, and one does so hate to let the family down. I should warn you that this place is going to become rather noisy over the next few days. I will try to have them keep it down, but you know what young people can be like.'

'Thanks for the warning.'

Outside, I fetch Mouse from the tower, before heading to the courtyard. I figure I have nothing to lose by taking a look around. Samuel is there, taking a ladder from one of the outbuildings.

'Do you need a hand with that?' I ask.

'No, I've got it, thanks.' He props the ladder against the building and bends down to fuss over Mouse. 'Were you looking for someone?' he asks.

'No. It's just . . .' I move closer and lower my voice, 'Sir Angus said he saw Jamie hiding something here, in the week before he died.'

'What sort of thing?'

'I have no idea. Sir Angus only saw a box of some sort.'

'So, whereabouts did he hide it?'

'I don't know that either! And Sir Angus isn't around to ask. I thought I'd just take a look about.'

'I'm out here so often, I reckon I'd have noticed anything out of place.' It's his turn to lower his voice, 'I'm afraid old Sir Angus isn't that . . .' he hesitates, presumably searching for the least offensive word, 'reliable.'

'You're not the first person to tell me that,' I say, with a sigh. 'I was just hoping there might be something to shed light on why Jamie . . . did what he did.'

Samuel nods. 'I've been asking myself that same question over and over.'

'Well, if you find anything, please can you let me know? I mean, I know you'll have to hand it over to the police . . .'

'I'll tell you if I come across anything,' he assures me.

'Thanks. Shall I leave Mouse with you?'

'Probably best not. I'll be up and down the roofs all day today, cleaning out the gutters – and we know the scene that kicked off the last time I was out of reach, with William and those kittens.'

'Fair point.' I call to Mouse, who gives Samuel a lick before trotting back to me. 'Good boy. Shall we go out to the garden?' He rumbles in agreement, and we head out through the gate.

An ice-cold drizzle starts up as we make our way between the courtyard and the parterre, and Mouse, who hates raindrops possibly even more than snowflakes, quickly finds a sheltered spot beneath a lovely *Arbutus unedo*, commonly known as the 'strawberry tree', because of its strawberry-shape fruits. While he snoozes, I put up the hood on my jacket and go back to my measuring of the parterre. The areas where I've dug out the box look almost brutal in their bareness. I must get those landscapers' quotes soon for the limestone chippings.

At lunchtime, I take Mouse back to the tower before going for my food. But there's nothing set out in the staff dining room. I try the kitchen, and find a note propped on the worktop: *In main kitchen, preparing for guests. Please help yourselves to anything you fancy from cupboards and fridge. Vicky.*

Right on cue, Olivia comes in, while I'm rooting through the fridge.

'Here,' she says, striding over to the walk-in pantry, which I'd forgotten existed. She steps inside and calls, 'Oh my god, I've just found a fruitcake. Vicky makes the best fruitcake.'

She brings it out, and we cut pieces for ourselves. It looks and smells delicious. There are several homemade loaves on the side, so we cut into one and take a few slices of bread each. Then we raid the fridge for cheese.

'I don't know how Vicky managed to get all this made when she had a party to prepare for, and she's in the middle of grieving,' I say.

'She likes to be busy. I think it keeps her demons at bay.' She gives me a sympathetic look. 'How are yours behaving?'

I shrug. 'Not great, but not awful either. I keep wishing it had been me who found Jamie, instead of Michael. Then I could have spared him and Vicky that sight.'

She shudders. 'I'm just glad it wasn't me. You're much braver than I am.'

'I doubt it.'

'No, really. I still haven't recovered from seeing *The Sixth Sense* at a friend's house when I was fifteen.' She laughs in embarrassment.

I smile. 'There's nothing wrong with a healthy imagination.'

'I'd definitely prefer an unhealthy one, if it meant not being haunted by the bad stuff.' She pauses, then says, 'Talking of the bad stuff, at least the police are sure it's suicide. You do feel the same way, don't you?' she asks, her face impassive.

'Of course!' I say, with what I hope sounds like conviction. I'm still not sure if she somehow knows I found Jamie's journal, and I have no desire to share my beliefs or findings with her. Keen to shut down the conversation, I raise my loaded plate and ask, 'You OK if I take this back to the tower?'

'Of course. Your lovely dog needs you.' She smiles and I take my leave, feeling unsettled once again by her questions.

The rain has picked up outside, along with a strong, northerly wind. I shiver and pull up my hood as I turn quickly towards the tower. But a hiss from close by has me looking around. Sir Angus is there, standing beneath a huge, black umbrella. He's wearing a long, black overcoat and a trilby, and looks for all the world like a spy from an old film noir.

'Are you free?' he asks.

'I waited for you this morning. I was a bit worried about you.'

'I told you they're drugging me, hen. I didn't make it out of bed till a few moments ago.'

Remembering what Olivia said on this topic, I'm not sure how to respond, so I just say, 'OK, well, let me take my lunch to the tower.'

He nods. 'I'll wait for you behind that tree.' He points to an oak that stands close to the courtyard door.

I hurry to the tower and return quickly, meeting up with Sir Angus behind the tree, and holding the courtyard door open, so that he can pass through.

'Now, act casual,' he instructs me. I don't point out that, in his current get-up, he couldn't look less casual if he were wielding a gun and kicking down doors.

'So, where did Jamie hide the container?' I ask him.

'Well . . .' he says. ''Twas quite dark at the time . . .'

'But you said the moon was out and you saw where he stashed it?'

'I saw the . . . environs, shall we say?'

I close my eyes for a moment. When I open them, Sir Angus is making his way slowly across the cobbles, towards the back of the big barn. I follow, hoping he saw more than he's letting on.

'That's where the lad went.' He gestures to a passageway that runs between the back of the barn and a neighbouring outbuilding. 'I'll wait here and keep an eye out.'

The gap between the buildings is quite narrow. There's just room to squeeze into it and pass along, looking to left and right, up and down, as I go. It ends at a brick wall. I run a hand up and down, checking for loose bricks, but there's nothing. I head back towards Angus, again running my hand along the bricks. Angus is whistling a tune that sounds vaguely familiar. About half way along, a brick wobbles beneath the toe of my boot.

I bend down and remove the brick, along with its three neighbours, which are also loose. Inside the cavity, I find a poster tube. I draw it out, replace the bricks and head back to Sir Angus. My hands are shaking slightly, and I realise I hadn't really expected to find anything. Sir Angus's whistling has got louder, and I wonder if he knows he's doing it. It's hardly a way of staying under the radar.

When I reach the end of the passage, I find he's blocking my egress. 'Sir Angus, I'm back,' I say.

'Well, hello there, Mr Blythe,' he says loudly. ''Tis fine weather for the ducks we're having.'

I crouch and wait for Sir Angus and Blythe to finish exchanging pleasantries. At last, Sir Angus turns to me with a wink. 'That was a close one, hen. I see you found the parcel.'

The tube is made of cardboard, so I zip it inside my jacket to keep it dry. 'Where shall we go?' I ask.

'Let's head to the Scottish Room.'

We walk back to the house and in through the front door. I notice that Sir Angus tenses as we pass the door to Lady Clara's study, perhaps expecting his niece to be behind it, ready to burst out and ply him with refreshments, like some tea-bearing version of a cuckoo clock.

When we get inside the room, Sir Angus takes a key from his pocket and locks the door. Leaving the key in the lock, he taps his nose and says, 'Now, they won't be able to spy through the keyhole.'

He leads me over to a beautiful, carved walnut table – one of the few items in the room that hasn't been plastered with tartan. 'You do the honours, hen,' he says.

I remove the white plastic lid from one end of the tube, and look inside. There's a rolled piece of paper, which I draw out. As I move to unroll it, Sir Angus says, 'Wait!' He takes his flask from the inside pocket of his coat and unscrews the lid. 'Here's to discoveries,' he says, taking a swig and passing the flask to me. It's early in the day for me to be drinking, so I take a tiny sip, to keep him happy.

And then I unroll the paper.

20

'What is that?' asks Sir Angus. He fishes a pair of spectacles from inside his coat and examines the A3 document laid out in front of us. 'Is it a map?'

'Yeah. I think it's Colombia and maybe Venezuela,' I say slowly. 'And there are Xs, like on a treasure map.'

'X marks the spot,' says Angus thoughtfully. 'But what spot would that be exactly? Or, more precisely, what is to be found at X?'

'I have absolutely no idea.' I take a picture of the map on my phone, then I check the back of the paper – which is blank – before rolling up the sheet and slipping it back inside the tube.

'Another wee dram?' Sir Angus holds out his flask.

'No, I'm good, thanks. I'm just thinking that we need to hand this over to the police. It might be important, if Jamie chose to hide it.'

He nods and swigs from his flask. 'Will you take charge of that, hen?'

'Sure. I'll call them as soon as I get home.'

'Don't get caught carrying it. Do you want to store it in my secret hidey-hole?' He makes his way over to his armchair, where he uses the bottom of his stick to lift the ruffle, exposing a gap between the base of the chair and the carpet.

'Sounds great – thanks.' I slide the poster tube into the space, and Sir Angus drops the ruffle back over it before sinking into his chair with a satisfied sigh. I perch on the chair opposite him for a moment.

'Why do you think that map was so important?' I ask.

'I haven't the foggiest hen. But let's keep this from the others hereabouts till we know more.'

'Agreed.' I stand up. 'I'd better get on. Are you OK?'

'Aye, the Grouse and I are just grand, lassie, just grand.' He waves his flask happily and I take my leave.

Back in our living room, I find a dismal Mouse watching the rain from the window seat, Mr Rabbit hanging from his jaws. He turns to regard me as I arrive.

'Do you want to watch *Boohbah*?' I ask him. This defunct psychedelic kids' TV series is his favourite viewing material after Attenborough. He barks once, jumps off the sofa and runs to sit expectantly on the rug while I set up the programme for him to watch on a loop for the afternoon. I feel like a bad parent, but I've learnt the hard way that Mouse is very difficult to persuade outside once he's decided against it. And he did have his run this morning.

My stomach's growling, but I delay eating my lunch until I've put in a call to DS McLeod. I reach his voicemail and leave a message for him to call me when he has a moment, as I have something that might have some bearing on Jamie's case.

Mouse entertains me as I eat, running right up to the television set, and making questioning sounds with his head on one side. No matter how many times he watches *Boohbah*, he always interrogates the subject matter. I am quite proud of him in this regard. I reckon another few years, and he'll be starting preschool.

Mid-afternoon, having left Mouse with the electronic nanny, I'm wading through a patch of brambles, attempting to find a water feature that's supposed to be in this spot – the mate to the limestone fountain near the rose garden – when I hear someone calling my name. Turning, I see Blythe, waving to me. I'm tempted to ignore him. But, with a sigh, I push my way back through the tangle of thorns.

'Hello,' he says.

'Hi,' I say warily.

'Look, I'm sorry about the other night. I should have let you keep the flower. After all, as you pointed out, I couldn't exactly glue it back on the plant.' He laughs, but I don't join in.

'I am quite busy,' I say.

'Yes, I can see that. Very important bramble inspection.' I roll my eyes but don't give him the satisfaction of a verbal response. 'I was just wondering...' he begins. I wait. 'I'm actually missing something, and I wondered if you might have seen it. I've asked around, but no one seems to know where it is.'

'What are you missing?'

'Oh, it's nothing very important. It's just . . . one of my plans for the gardens, so it would be useful to recover it.'

'Do you not have a copy on the computer?'

He laughs again. 'I do all my plans by hand. Silly, really, because it means this kind of thing can happen – paper notes get mislaid, you know?'

'Now you mention it, I did see something in the courtyard, but I can't remember exactly where.' I can't resist the cheap thrill of knowing I'm sending Blythe on a wild-goose chase. I wonder how long he'll spend combing the courtyard for what I'm almost certain is the item already in my possession.

His face lights up. 'The courtyard? Really?'

I'm worried he might give me a hug – or, worse, a kiss – in his enthusiasm, so I quickly say, 'Good luck finding your garden plans,' and start making my way back through the brambles.

'Thanks so much,' he calls after me. 'I won't forget this.'

I feel only a tiny twinge of guilt.

A few minutes later, my phone rings, and I see DS McLeod's name come up. Standing surrounded by thorns, I accept the call.

'Hi,' I say. 'Thanks for calling back.'

'You suggested it might be important?' He sounds stressed and distracted.

'I don't know, to be honest. It turns out Jamie hid something in the courtyard one night last week.'

I hear someone speak to him in the background, and I wait while his voice goes faint as he presumably covers the phone to respond. His voice comes back to me, 'I'm listening.'

'It's a map, showing Colombia and Venezuela, with Xs marked on it. I'm wondering if it's something to do with drugs,' I say.

'Hold on – rewind. How did you know about this?'

'Sir Angus, Lady Clara's uncle, told me about it. He saw Jamie hiding a container of some sort, and asked me to help him retrieve it.'

'So, you helped the old man. Why did he choose you? Are you two close?'

'Sort of. I mean, he seems to like confiding in me. He says it's because I'm too new here to be embroiled in anything bad.'

'What sort of bad?'

'He didn't say. I'm not sure he knows. It's more of an instinct, I think, or maybe observation.'

McLeod sighs, as if I'm talking in riddles – which, thanks to Sir Angus's general vagueness of disposition, I probably am. 'So . . . the deceased hid a map?' he says.

'That's right.'

'And we're sure it was the deceased who hid it?'

'Sir Angus saw him.'

'What time of day was this?'

'I think he said midnight.'

'So, an old man of what – eighty-something—'

'He's in his nineties.'

'Right. So, a man in his nineties claims to have seen, clearly, in the dark, not just who was hiding something, but also where they hid it?'

'He said there was a full moon, so he could tell it was Jamie.'

'We're going to have to talk to the old man again.'

'Perhaps you could refer to him as "Sir Angus", rather than "the old man"? Nobody is just their age. It's very reductionist.'

He groans. 'Please don't tell the diversity and inclusion team. They'll send me on more courses.' I wonder what courses they've sent him on so far. There's a pause before he says, 'A map . . . It seems a strange thing for a twenty-year-old to go to the trouble of hiding.'

'I know. Unless, as I said, it's to do with the drug trade?'

'Where is this map now?'

'Sir Angus has it.'

'OK. Well, we're busy – and short staffed – as ever, but this sounds like it could be important. I'll send someone over to collect it and talk to the old . . . Sir Angus.'

'There was something else.'

'What's that?'

'William Blythe, the head gardener, came to find me a few minutes ago, wanting to know if I'd come across some garden plans he was missing.'

'Garden plans?'

'Yep.' I wait for him to make the same connection I have.

'I wonder if our Mr Blythe is looking for this map.'

'That's what I thought.'

We end the call, then I spend a couple of hours happily employed in ripping away sections of the brambles that have started dying back for winter. They come away easily – though I'm all too aware that the plants' deep roots will be trickier to remove. But my focus is on finding George London's water feature.

It's only after I've cleared a small area that I notice a bamboo cane planted in one spot. I can see that the ground has been disturbed here recently. The cane marks the centre of a bald patch of earth, measuring around twenty centimetres by ten. I take out my trowel and dig. Having been dug so recently, the soil shifts easily and, in less than a minute, I've cleared a hole and unearthed a plastic sandwich box with a lid. I draw it out and open it. Inside the box, I find an envelope. This bears my name, written in blue ink.

I recognise the extravagant script immediately as Jamie's. I stare at it for a moment.

How on earth . . .? But then my mind flashes back to that breakfast, when he'd asked me – apparently casually – where I was going to be focusing my efforts over the next couple of weeks. And I'd told him about the overgrown fountain.

My heart is beating hard as I carefully tear open the envelope and peer inside. There's a glint of gold. Tipping the contents into my palm, I see that it's a thick chain, with a medallion hanging from it. I examine the pendant, which depicts St Christopher, carrying a child on his shoulder. There's a small chip missing from one of the saint's feet. I turn it over and see a pair of initials engraved into the back: GC. It didn't belong to Jamie, then. Whose was it? And why was he so keen for me to have it?

I should probably hand the medal over to the police, but – unlike the map – this item has been deliberately planted for me to find. Jamie wanted *me* to work it out.

I put the necklace back inside the envelope and place it in my jacket pocket, checking twice that the Velcro on the flap is secure. I wonder if Jamie has left me any other clues – something that would explain this one.

I return to my digging, mulling as I work. At last, just as it's starting to get dark, I reveal a corner of the fountain, gleaming white among the thorns. Focusing my attentions on that spot, I manage to clear enough brambles to uncover a good quarter of the stone base. The rest will have to wait until another day.

I collect up the piles of spiny branches and load them into the wheelbarrow, before wheeling them over to the composting area. And then I head back to the tower, where I clean myself up before updating my notes. Then Mouse and I watch some very exciting shark antics on the telly. A little before six thirty, I walk over to the house for dinner. I divert towards the Scottish Room, and quickly regret it: the hallway is filled with the Fanshawes' weekend guests, milling about and generally obstructing the way as they converse in strident tones. There must be at least twenty of them, and I wonder how they will all fit into Ashford's twelve bedrooms.

I give up any hope of reaching Sir Angus, and turn back. I'll have to wait until tomorrow to tell him about Blythe's interest in the missing map – and to see if he can shed any light on the St Christopher medal.

21

The next morning, keen though I am to discuss things with Sir Angus, I need to focus on my preparation for the garden tour. So, straight after breakfast, I let Mouse out to play with Belle, and spend the rest of the morning immersed in my notes. I'm quite looking forward to sharing my new knowledge and research on George London and his influences with members of the party.

At one point, while I'm sitting at my desk, I hear shrieking and laughter. I go to the window, where Miles appears to be entertaining a girl whose spaghetti-strap dress strikes me as far too skimpy for Derbyshire in November.

Miles glances up at the window and raises a hand, and I wave back before moving away, once again embarrassed to have been caught apparently spying.

My preparation for the tour takes longer than anticipated. By the time I've finished going through my notes, it's nearly one thirty, and I just have time to grab lunch from the kitchen and wolf it down with a mug of coffee before I'm due outside.

I'm intercepted en route by someone calling, 'Excuse me!' Turning, I see the young woman I spotted with Miles earlier. She gives me a big smile. She's white, tall and slim, with light-brown eyes and long, golden hair. I'd reckon she's around seventeen or eighteen. Rather like Miles's clothes, everything about this girl's appearance whispers *understated* and *expensive*.

'Oh, hi. You look freezing. Do you not have a coat with you?'

She laughs. 'I do, but it spoils the line of this dress.' She performs a twirl. 'Isn't it pretty?' The dress is a pale rose, with thin silver straps and a layered gauze skirt that ripples out when she twirls.

'It's lovely, but isn't it more of a summer dress?'

She pulls a face. 'I don't really do winter clothing. It's all so . . .' She wrinkles her nose while she searches for the word, 'winter-y?'

'Yes, I suppose it is. Look, I'm on my way to conduct garden tours, so I need to get on. Walk with me, if you like.'

She clutches my arm, stopping me from moving on. 'I wanted to ask you about Miles.'

'What about him?'

'Do you know if he's seeing anyone else?' She feigns nonchalance, but I can tell how alert she is to my response.

'Isn't he your cousin?' I ask.

She wrinkles her nose while she does her sums. 'Only two times removed or something.'

'Right . . . But why are you asking me about him?'

'It's just that nobody else will tell me the truth,' she says indignantly. 'I mean, Miles and Jules spend half their time whispering together. And the other girls act so . . . mean.'

'I see. Well, I'm afraid I wouldn't have the faintest idea. Have you asked him?'

'I really like him,' she says sadly. 'But I'm afraid I might scare him off if I tell him.'

'How long have you been seeing him?'

'Oh . . . we're not really *together*, you know? We meet up from time to time, during the holidays.'

'Look, I'm new here,' I say. 'But, from what little I've observed, I'm really not sure Miles is worth the anguish.'

'You're trying to tell me he is seeing someone else, aren't you?' she says, with a sob.

'No, I'm trying to tell you that you could do much better.'

She surprises me by smiling through her tears, pulling back her shoulders and saying, 'Thank you for being honest with me.'

I smile back. 'Do you fancy coming on a garden tour?'

She nods. 'I think I'd like that.'

'Go and get your coat, then,' I tell her. Even more surprisingly, she runs off to fetch it.

I follow her to the front door, where Julian and Miles seem to be in charge of shepherding the guests. There are a lot of people milling about, all talking at once. Like the previous evening, the noise is tremendous.

A woman floats by, wearing high stiletto heels with a Burberry trench coat buttoned up. Her long, light-brown hair streams behind her in the November wind. She has a young man by the hand and is leading him purposefully towards a copse of trees. I have the impression she might not be wearing anything beneath the trench coat. I make a mental note to steer well clear of that area when conducting my tour. We don't want to give any guests a heart attack.

'Here she is! Steph!' shouts Julian above the hubbub. I walk over. 'I've got some takers for your tour,' he says. He introduces me to his aunt and uncle: an uptight-looking man and woman, who are the Marquess and Marchioness of somewhere I haven't heard of, which sounds like 'Churridge'. They are clearly very pleased with themselves. From the way they look me up and down, I take it they're less pleased with me.

My phone buzzes in my pocket, so I draw it out. It's a message from Dad: Dead slugs galore!

He's attached images, which I delete without opening. As I put my phone away, the girl reappears, pushing her way through the throng with lots of, 'Sorry! Excuse me!' She arrives by my side, takes in the other two members of the party, and says, 'Oh!'

The marchioness and marquess exchange a look. I have no idea what the problem is, and no intention of asking. 'Right, shall we start?'

'Just a sec!' calls Julian. 'I have another one for you.'

A short, smiling woman bounds over to us. She's wearing an emerald-green polo neck jumper and matching corduroy trousers beneath a vibrant red coat. 'Here I am!' She turns to the others in the party. 'Binty! Jonathan! I missed you at dinner last night and again at breakfast! Where have you been hiding?' She beams at them. I wonder if she notices the look that passes between the couple. She kisses each of them on both cheeks, while they purse their lips. 'So lovely to see you,' she enthuses.

'Phyllida,' says the marchioness, with a cool nod.

'And Georgie!' says the new arrival, giving the girl a big hug.

'It's Georgina now, actually,' says the girl, but she's smiling. 'Hello, Auntie Phyll.'

'Don't you look pretty?' says her aunt, holding the girl's shoulders as she admires her.

Georgina blushes. 'Thank you.'

Binty coughs pointedly.

'Shall we get on?' I suggest.

'About time,' the marquess murmurs to his wife.

Oh, joy.

I start them off in the large parterre , where I talk them through a little of George London's philosophy. I'm just showing them an illustration depicting the garden in its prime, when I realise the marchioness is busy looking around at the current state of the planting.

'Why does the hedge look like that?' she asks in disdain, gesturing to the box edging.

'I'm afraid it's been infested by box tree caterpillar. I'm planning to have it all removed and replaced with a limestone gravel, sourced locally.'

'What a shame!' exclaims Phyll. I'm starting to realise that she can only do things emphatically. She's like a walking exclamation mark. She's also undeniably good natured, and worth several of her haughty relatives. Phyll takes Georgina's arm, and chats to her as we walk around.

After the parterre, I lead them to visit some of my favourite specimens in the arboretum.

'What about the maze?' asks the marquess, interrupting my speech about the fine collection of trees, mainly imported in the early eighteenth century, by the second earl.

'There's a maze?' asks Georgina.

The marchioness and her husband exchange another look. 'Of course there's a maze, Georgina: the famous Ashford yew maze. Honestly, has your mother taught you nothing about your heritage?'

Georgina looks doubtful. 'It's not really my heritage, is it? I mean, I'm not going to inherit Ashford Manor.'

'It's still part of your family's estate,' says the marquess briskly.

Poor Georgina looks close to tears again. I notice that Phyll, who still has her arm looped through the girl's, is holding her close to comfort her.

'It's obviously not the best time of year to view the grounds,' I say, keeping to my subject. 'Although the autumn leaf colour is pretty special. Perhaps you can come back in the early summer, when the wildflower meadow should be at its peak. I've been told there are several types of orchid which have naturalised, and there's even the occasional bee orchid in a good year.'

'I love orchids!' says Phyll. 'My husband gives me one for every birthday. I have about a hundred now.'

The marquess leans over to his wife and says, in a stage whisper, 'I hadn't realised Phyllida was so old.'

Poor Phyll blushes and then bridles and retorts: 'He doesn't only give them to me for my birthday, Jonno. He gives me one to mark every special occasion. At the last count, I had forty-three.'

'That's impressive,' I say. 'I should introduce you to our head gardener, William Blythe. He has a special interest in orchids.' The instant the words are out, I regret them. Phyll is too sweet to expose to the acid effects of Blythe.

'Oh, really?' says Phyll, her face lighting up. 'I would love to meet him!'

It starts to rain, an icy, seemingly relentless seepage from stone-grey clouds, and we wordlessly agree to terminate the tour and head indoors. I escort them to the front door, where Phyll thanks me with great enthusiasm, Georgina gives me a big hug, and the marquess and marchioness march inside with just a faint nod of acknowledgement. I spot Saliha standing in the porch, marking something on a clipboard, and I walk over to speak to her. 'Hiya! Phyllida would like to talk to William at some point, if possible. Please can you let him know when you see him?'

'Really? You're unleashing him on her? She's, like, dead nice.'

'I know. But she wants to talk about orchids.'

She shrugs. 'Fair enough. So, how was the tour?' She glances around, to check there's no one close by. 'I mean, did the marquess and marchioness make it any further up their own arses?'

I laugh. 'I don't think that would be possible. Anyway, I'll be in the tower, if anyone wants me.'

'Lucky cow, getting to escape, while the rest of us slog on.'

'Don't I know it?' I say smugly.

I turn to walk back to the tower, and see that Georgina is loitering outside, in the rain, apparently reluctant to follow the others into the house. I'm just considering what I can do for her when Mouse and Belle come racing up.

Georgina greets Belle enthusiastically, and Mouse pushes in to secure his share of the attention.

'What a lovely dog,' she says. 'Is he yours?'

'Yes, this is Mouse.'

'Oh, he's adorable.'

'We're about to go back to the tower, where I'm staying,' I say. 'Would you like to come for coffee?'

Georgina's face lights up. 'Oh, yes, please. I've always wanted to see inside the Round Wing, but Auntie Clara would never let us play in there when we were kids. She said the stone stairs were too dangerous.'

'They are pretty deadly. But I think you'll live to tell the tale.'

She smiles. There's still a sadness to her expression. Her long hair is soaked and, although she's wearing a coat, it's a wool one, which won't keep the rain off for long.

'Come on!' I say, and we run.

Once inside the tower, she brightens up, admiring the view (despite the low cloud that obscures most of it), and commenting on the way the furniture has been cleverly fitted into the circular rooms. I fish out a clean towel for her, and she walks around, drying her hair as she examines everything.

'I've always wanted to live somewhere interesting,' she says, following me into the kitchen and taking a seat at the table. I'm heating the water before pouring it over the ground coffee in the cafetiere. It's a fair trade Colombian coffee, and it fills the kitchen with its rich scent.

'Where do you live?' I ask her, setting the cafetiere on the table before getting out milk, sugar and two mugs.

'A townhouse in Bath. The house is over three storeys and it's quite big, but it's not like this. I mean, you could imagine Rapunzel living here, couldn't you?'

'I like to think she'd live here out of choice,' I say. 'None of that being held captive by a witch.'

She nods eagerly. 'And she'd paint, or take photos, of the view that she saw through the window. It must change all the time.'

'I've only been here a couple of weeks but, even in this short space of time, the leaves have been changing, and the skies are amazing. I'm really looking forward to seeing it in spring.'

Mouse and Belle come into the room, and Mouse goes to stand by the biscuit cupboard.

'Have you been good?' I ask him. He gives his affirmative rumble. 'OK, then. One each.' I take two biscuits from the cupboard and hold one out in each hand. Mouse stands back, letting Belle take hers before he accepts his own. 'What a good host,' I say, giving him a pat.

He and Belle take their biscuits through to the living room, and I sit down at the table, opposite Georgina.

After a suitable wait, I depress the coffee plunger and pour the dark liquid into the mugs. Georgina is looking thoughtful as she helps herself to milk and three sugars.

I'm about to ask what's on her mind, when she blurts out, 'I saw something earlier.'

'Go on.'

'It was . . . Do you know that woman – the really pretty one, who works in the office?'

'Olivia,' I say.

'Right. Well, she was standing in the corridor of the house, with Uncle Rupert. They were next to the door to the office.' She pauses, then adds, 'Of course, he's not really my uncle – he's a distant cousin.'

I'm waiting for her to get to the point. 'What were they doing?'

'Oh! They were arguing.'

'Really? What about?'

'She said something about sleeping tablets, and that she wanted to tell Lady Clara. And he said, "Keep your voice down, for Christ's sake." And she said, "It wasn't even my idea." Then he said something that sounded like, "Who cares whose idea it was?"'

Georgina pauses, so I break in eagerly, 'And then what?'

'I couldn't hear the rest. But she looked really angry. She walked off a moment later, obviously in a big huff. And then, as soon as she saw me, she gave me this big, beaming smile, as if I'd imagined the whole thing.'

My brain clicks into gear with this new information. *Sleeping tablets*, I think. If Jamie had been subdued with sedatives, that might have been enough to stop him fighting for his life. But surely Olivia and Mr Fanshawe wouldn't have killed Jamie?

I realise that Georgina is looking at me expectantly, and I ask, 'Are you sure you didn't hear anything else?'

But she shakes her head. 'That was it. Why? Is it important?'

I don't want to involve this troubled young woman in my theories about Jamie's death, so I just say, 'Not really. I just wonder why they would get so heated.'

'That's what I can't understand! Do you think I should talk to Uncle Rupert?'

'I'd leave it. They're both adults. I'm sure they'll work it out between them.'

She sighs. 'I hope they do it soon. I hate arguments. Mummy and her last boyfriend argued all the time.'

'Who is your mum?'

'Francesca, aka Lady Tartface. You'll have seen her swanning around, with her latest toyboy in tow.'

I remember the woman I saw leading a young man into the trees. 'She sounds quite a character.'

'She's a crap mum. She never remembers anything. One year, she forgot to collect me from school for the summer, and I had to go home with a friend's parents until we could track her down. Turned out she was in Marbella with some twenty-year-old.'

'Oh no! That's awful. You're at boarding school?'

'Of course. Francesca Fitzsimmons couldn't be seen to have a teenage daughter, could she? It might spoil the illusion that she's only twenty-eight.'

'That sounds tough.' I reach across the table and squeeze her hand. She manages a small smile.

'You're so kind. At least Elmwood's fantastic. I have mega loads of friends there.' She takes a deep breath and sits up straight. 'Anyway, I've made a decision. I'm done with crappy men. Miles can go to hell!' She sets her mug down firmly, and I feel pride rise up in me.

'It takes some women all their lives to get there,' I tell her. I check my watch. 'It's taken you about three hours.'

'I don't suppose you'd like to adopt me?' she says hopefully.

'How old are you?'

'Seventeen.'

'I'm sure you're going to do just fine.' Thinking of Miles, I ask, 'I don't suppose you know anything about a fight between Miles and Julian, do you?'

She sits forward. 'I do, actually. Miles made some joke about Uncle Rupert being boring, and Jules didn't take it too well. He kind of worships his dad.'

'What did Julian say to that?'

'Oh . . .' she blushes. 'Apparently something about Uncle Dickie not being able to keep it in his trousers!' She smiles unexpectedly: 'Like father, like son, I suppose.'

I laugh and stand up. 'I have biscuits somewhere. We need to celebrate your liberation.' I go to the cupboard and bring out a packet of Jaffa Cakes, which I set down on the table.

'Those aren't biscuits,' she says, deadpan. 'The clue is in the name.'

'Oh, dear. Well, I can always eat them all myself . . .' A knock on the front door surprises us both. 'Back in a minute,' I say. 'Help yourself to the anti-biscuits.' I run downstairs and find Phyllida on the doorstep. She starts talking as soon as I open the door.

'Steph, I just wanted to thank you for this afternoon. It was simply wonderful. I can't remember the last time I had such a lovely time out of doors. The leaves were so beautiful and I did so love hearing about Mr London's designs, and how you plan to reinstate them.'

She pauses for breath and I say, 'I'm so glad you enjoyed it. You were certainly an enthusiastic member of the party.'

She leans closer. 'Yes, sorry about the other two. My brother and his wife are always like that.'

'The marquess is your brother?'

She sighs. 'Yes. You wouldn't think it, would you? He got the brains, the looks and the inheritance.'

She looks so sad that I quickly add, 'Well, I'd far rather spend time with you.' Seeing her expression lift, I say, 'Listen, Georgina's here, and we're having coffee. Would you like to come up?'

'Oh! Only if you're sure I wouldn't be intruding?'

'I'm sure.'

She claps her hands. 'I've always wanted to see inside the Round Wing!'

I lead her up the stone staircase to the top, where she exclaims at the curved living room, before following me into the kitchen. She meets Georgina's eye. 'Isn't this glorious?' she says.

'I love it,' says the girl. 'I could live here.'

'I think you'd start to miss your grand lifestyle after a while,' I say.

Georgina shakes her head determinedly. 'No. I'm sure I'd be happy.'

I gesture for Phyllida to take a seat at the table while I make more coffee. 'Ooh, Jaffa Cakes!' she says. 'May I?'

'Of course – they're there to be eaten. Though you might want to avoid getting into a debate with Georgina on the difference between a cake and a biscuit, and whether it's purely etymological or there's an actual chemical basis to the construct.'

Georgina laughs. 'I only said you can't call them biscuits.'

Phyllida smiles before asking her niece, 'How are you, love? I noticed your mother has a new beau.'

'I'd be more worried if she didn't,' says Georgina bitterly.

'Well, I'm here if you ever want to talk. And I'd love it if you came to stay for a while over Christmas, if you don't have other plans.'

'That's kind, Auntie! I'll give it some thought.'

After I've set down a freshly filled cafetiere and taken my own seat, Phyllida addresses me.

'Thank you so much for telling me about Mr Blythe. Do you know, he's going to acquire some new orchid specimens for my collection? I'm so excited. He can get varieties I've never even heard of! Of course, Rufus might not be too impressed when he sees the price tags!' She laughs.

I don't like the sound of this. 'Has Mr Blythe told you where he's sourcing the plants?'

'Oh, he says he has contacts who supply him,' she says vaguely. She chats on about the unusual colours he's promised her, and how he's given her some great cultivation tips to achieve longer flowering times.

I recall Blythe's reaction to seeing the white flower, tucked behind my ear. And I remember the map, highlighting areas in Venezuela and Colombia.

And then, with a shiver that runs down my spine, I realise exactly what Blythe is up to. He isn't dealing in drugs, he's smuggling rare orchids – one of the most valuable imports in the world. It's also one of the deadliest trades.

Is this why Jamie was murdered? Did he find out too much?

22

After Georgina and Phyllida have left, while the dogs are curled up together on the rug, I grab my coat and head out into the rain, in the hope of catching Sir Angus.

When I reach the main entrance hall, I again find it teeming with guests, all of whom have now returned from their various jaunts. Young people are gathered, laughing, around someone's phone; children are running up and down the wide staircase; and older family members are standing in a group, talking seriously, still wearing their wet coats, as if they've become too engrossed in their conversation to remember to take them off and sit down. There's no sign of Sir Angus, so I try the Scottish Room. I find him in his chair, snoring loudly. As I move to creep away, the telltale floorboard wakes him. He snorts and starts awake, reaching for his glasses.

'Oh, it's you, hen. I thought it was the abominable tea monster.'

'Just me. I have something to tell you.'

I sit opposite him, and fill him in on Blythe's enquiries after the item Jamie hid, and the conversation I had with DS McLeod.

'I like that bobby,' he says.

'Me, too.'

''Twasn't him as came to see me this time, mind. It was her nibs. You know the one: all bark as well as bite.'

'I know the one,' I agree.

'She wanted to know how I knew this and that and the other. By the end, I didn't know what I knew and what I didn't. I was glad when she finally took the map and left me to kip. My brain felt like mashed spud.'

'She is a bit aggressive. I'm surprised she's the one McLeod sent to talk to you.'

'I reckon as he just likes to get her out from under his feet.'

I laugh. 'I bet you're right. There are a couple of other things, by the way.'

'What's that, hen?'

I tell him about the St Christopher medal.

'And you're sure he intended it for you, hen?'

'He addressed the envelope to me.'

'Can I see the medal?'

I fish it from my pocket and hand it to him, and he draws a magnifying glass from down the back of his cushion and proceeds to examine it. 'It's an old one,' he says, as he hands it back. 'And I don't know if you noticed, but the text is in Spanish.'

'Is it?' I squint at the minute text around the edge of the circular gold pendant. It reads, 'San Cristóbal' at the top and 'patrón de los viajeros' at the bottom. 'I hadn't seen it was in Spanish. Do you think that means it's linked to the map of Colombia and Venezuela?'

He nods thoughtfully. 'Aye, could be, could be.'

'I keep wondering if Jamie knew you were watching him that night,' I say. 'Maybe he wanted you to find the map.'

His eyes grow wide. 'That didn't even occur to me, hen. But aye, it would fit with his burying something for you. He was leaving us a trail of breadcrumbs, just in case the worst should happen. I only wish we knew why the laddie was killed.' He hands back the St Christopher and I stow it away.

'You'll like this next part,' I say. 'I told Blythe that I'd seen something in the courtyard, and it might be the "plans" he's looking for. I didn't tell him we'd already removed it.'

He wheezes with laughter. 'He'll be out there for hours!'

'I know. I might feel bad about it, if I hadn't worked out what he's up to.'

Sir Angus peers around his chair to check the door is closed. Then he leans forward, his hands on his knees. 'What is it, hen? Is it the opium trade?'

I shake my head. 'It's orchids.'

He sinks back. 'Well, that's a new one on me. Are they dear to buy, then?'

'The rare ones can sell for thousands of pounds.'

He whistles. 'I've been on this earth for ninety-odd years, yet I never cease to be gobsmacked at what folks will throw their money at. But why so cloak and dagger?'

'It's an illegal trade. I mean, there are legal trade routes, but I'm pretty sure William Blythe is engaged in illegal trading – smuggling. Orchids have become highly collectable in certain wealthy circles, with no regard for the environmental impact of digging them up in their native habitat. The rare ones are protected species. That's why it's banned – it's highly destructive, on a par with trading in threatened species of wildlife. I think Blythe might be propagating them in the large outbuilding between the courtyard and the deer paddocks.'

Angus considers this. 'What makes you so sure it's these orchid flowers that are the loot?'

'I found one of the flowers – well, my dog did – and Blythe got very worked up, demanding it back. And the countries on the map definitely have a problem with people digging them up in the wild, and smuggling them out.'

He lets out another low whistle. 'So, the bobbies will be wanting to hear about all this, then?'

I shake my head. 'I don't think so. From what I understand, the regional cops won't have the resources to deal with this. I'm not sure even Scotland Yard would.'

'You mean we can't turn him in, hen?'

'Well, not until we find out why Jamie was murdered, at any rate, and how Blythe was involved.'

'And so we keep investigating,' he says, with some relish.

'And so we do. There's one other thing.' I tell him about the conversation Georgina overheard, between Mr Fanshawe and Olivia.

'Sleeping pills?' he says thoughtfully.

'I was wondering if someone might have used them to drug Jamie, so he couldn't fight.'

He nods seriously. 'Aye, that might explain things. But surely not that lovely Olivia?'

'I don't think so. Although she does seem very interested in my findings.'

He raises an eyebrow. 'Does she, now?'

'But I just can't see her as a killer.'

He shakes his head. 'She's a sweet lassie, that one – always bringing me hot toddies and warm blankets, now the temperatures have dropped.'

'So, we're still looking for our murderer.'

'Aye, that we are, lassie, that we are.'

When I come to take my leave, Sir Angus says anxiously, 'Make sure that door closes firmly behind you, hen. The place is crawling with those people, and they won't leave me alone.' He assumes a high-pitched voice: 'Do I want tea? Am I warm enough? Can I tell them stories about the old days?'

Sure enough, as I step out into the hall, a woman I don't recognise says, 'Oh! Is Uncle Angus awake?'

I shake my head, sadly. 'No. I'm afraid he drifted off before I left him. He'll be out for the rest of the day, I should think.'

She regards me suspiciously, but turns away nonetheless, and is swallowed back into the fray.

In bed that night, while I'm mulling over everything, it occurs to me that I still don't know the identity of Olivia's boyfriend – is he really someone from outside the Ashford crowd? And what are she and Mr Fanshawe up to, that involves sleeping tablets?

Also, why does she seem so interested in my investigations? I keep trying to give her the benefit of the doubt, but I find it hard to trust her overtures of friendship.

While I'm lying there, Mouse begins to bark downstairs and, a minute later, loud music starts up outside. I climb out of bed and walk to the window. Parting the curtains, I see a group of young people gathered around a fire in an incinerator bin. They're laughing and drinking, their faces lit partly by the flicker of the flames and partly by light spilling out from the house.

Mouse is still barking, so I call to him. He comes running upstairs and leaps on to my bed, where I stroke him for a few minutes, and he falls asleep. I, meanwhile, lie awake for hours, hearing the rise and fall of voices and laughter, the bass of the music, and the occasional shout from a first-floor window of the main house, as a parent or other guest becomes infuriated by the disruption to their sleep.

By the time six o'clock comes around, I have had three hours' sleep, and am very glad it's Sunday.

23

As I do my stretches in the bedroom, my mind wanders to Blythe's map. Why did Jamie hide it? Was Blythe threatening him? If I'm right about the orchid trading, Blythe won't be alone in the business.

It occurs to me that I've been assuming it was Blythe who ransacked Jamie's room, looking for the map. But what if it was someone else? Perhaps Jamie hid the map as a kind of insurance. Someone dangerous wanted it, but he believed he was safe as long as they didn't know where to look.

Once I've finished stretching, Mouse and I go out for our run. I'm just locking the door behind us, when Mouse starts barking. At least this prepares me for the arrival of Blythe.

He speaks while I still have my back to him, 'Why did you tell Sir Angus I was involved in orchid smuggling?'

I pocket the key and turn to face him. Mouse is snarling, preventing the man from coming close. I keep the lead short, so Mouse can't go for him. Blythe says, 'Will you call off that sodding dog?'

'Not until you tell me why you're here.'

'I just want to talk to you.'

'In that case, you might want to come up with a less controversial introductory line. Now, if you'll excuse me, Mouse and I are going for our run.' I move to pass him, Mouse still snarling and pulling on the short lead.

Blythe blocks my path, though he keeps a wary eye on Mouse. 'Why didn't you tell me you'd found the map?' He has to raise his voice to be heard.

'I thought you were looking for garden plans?' I say.

'You knew perfectly well I was looking for that map. You deliberately kept it from me. I only found out you'd got it when I spoke to Sir Angus, after I'd spent hours searching the courtyard.'

I really will have to ask Sir Angus to be less keen to share.

I try to get past Blythe, but he grabs my arm. Mouse pulls harder on the lead and looks ready to go for Blythe's jugular. I hold his lead tightly. 'It's OK, boy,' I murmur.

'Why did you tell Sir Angus you thought I was an orchid smuggler, of all things?' asks Blythe again.

'Aren't you?'

'Of course not,' he says. 'I'm a skilled breeder. To be more precise, I use *micro*propagation, whereby small pieces of plant tissue are grown on, in a nutrient-rich jelly, to create more plants.' His tone is pompous and self-righteous.

I rub my spare hand over my face and sigh. 'I know what "micropropagation" means.'

Mouse has calmed down a little. He isn't taking his eyes off Blythe, but he is no longer snarling, or straining at the leash.

'Show me inside your shed,' I say.

'I beg your pardon?'

'If you want me to believe you aren't dealing in smuggled orchids, you need to show me the contents of your shed – the big one, on the far side of the courtyard.'

He eyes me. 'How much do you know about orchids?'

'Very little,' I admit. 'I wouldn't know a rare one from a common one. Unless it has a monkey face – those are quite rare, aren't they?'

He smiles, which is almost more unnerving than his usual glower. 'Leave the dog here.'

'I'd rather bring him with me.'

Blythe's gaze moves from Mouse to me. 'It's your choice. Either leave the dog here and come with me, or go for your run. I am not going anywhere with that mutt in tow, and he's certainly not gaining entry to my propagating lab, which is filled with delicate equipment.'

Reluctantly, I tie Mouse to a nearby tree. 'It's just for a few minutes,' I tell him, as he whines anxiously.

Blythe doesn't speak as we walk towards the fenced-off area where the sheds are situated. He takes fast strides and, despite my long legs, I have to run to keep up. When we reach the largest shed, he takes a bunch of keys from his pocket and, selecting a square-headed, silver one, turns it in the lock and opens the door. He enters ahead of me, and holds the door. As I step over the threshold, I notice a video camera above the door. This seems superfluous for a normal shed – one in which rare orchids are not being propagated and sold on the black market.

I'm about to ask about the camera when Blythe shuts and locks the door.

'Why did you lock it?' I ask.

'Security,' he says. 'I always lock the door, whether I'm inside or out.'

I glance around, for an alternative exit. But the roof is made from corrugated metal and there are no windows.

I should probably be panicking, but curiosity is keeping anxiety at bay.

A huge, black tent has been erected within the shed. Blythe parts the cloth door flaps and steps inside. I weigh up my options, which are limited. I follow him into the tent.

The first thing that strikes me is the heat. It's warm and humid, like the tropical house at Kew Gardens. Long rows of tables are set out with modular plant pots, each with seedlings growing inside. Specialist lighting provides warmth and light. It's an impressive set-up.

As I pass through the tent, I take the opportunity to study the nursery. On some tables, plants are already in bud, or even flower. I haven't experienced scented orchids before, but some have a strong perfume. The scents mingle in a heady mix, making me feel slightly nauseous. The heat is also intense, and I'm glad I have my running gear on, rather than thick gardening trousers and a sweater.

Blythe stops to alter the position of small stakes which are supporting several of the plants. I take advantage of his distraction to snap photographs of some of the flowers.

I quickly slip my phone into my pocket as he turns back to me.

'Let me show you my masterpiece,' he says, beckoning for me to follow him towards the end of the tent. Here, an orchid with a single bloom is set apart. Its flower is white and has delicately frilled petals. 'Meet Rita,' he says, gazing at the flower in something close to worship.

'Rita?'

'After Hayworth, the beautiful actress.'

'Ah. It is a lovely flower.'

He shoots me a scornful look. 'Rita is a one-off. It's taken me ten years to persuade her to bloom from the original seed. She is the only hybrid of her kind.'

'Gosh, quite a rarity then.'

'Indeed.'

I wave a hand to take in the whole tent. 'This is a big operation,' I say.

He nods. 'I'm very proud of what I've achieved here.'

'But you can't be doing all this on your own?'

'Well, I've had some help, if that's what you're getting at. Jamie, Michael, Simon . . . They've all shifted compost and jelly, fetched containers – that kind of thing. But the bulk of the work is down to me – it's far too delicate an operation to entrust to anyone else.'

'What will you do with all these plants?'

'Oh, I have plenty of buyers, through the internet. There are no worries, there. So, you see it really is just a normal propagating suite.'

I make a noncommittal grunt, which he appears to take for agreement.

He escorts me back to the door. 'Now you can stop telling people I'm running an illegal operation.'

'Of course,' I say. I don't point out that I'd agree to anything while he's got me locked in.

He unlocks the door and I step outside into the cold air, and hear Blythe locking the door behind me. After all his bluster and protestation, I am utterly convinced of one thing: Mr Blythe is a liar – and not even a plausible one.

24

Mouse is overjoyed to see me still in one piece when I return. I untie him, and we enjoy a reassuring cuddle. Then he and I jog through the fields, while I think through all that Blythe just told me. Like many people, I do some of my best thinking while running. Occupying the body with a repetitive, rhythmic movement frees the brain to mull and process.

Blythe's tour of his propagating shed has done nothing to lessen my conviction that he's part of a smuggling ring. If Jamie was threatening to expose them, this might be motive enough to kill him.

Jamie was tall – over six foot – but Blythe, at around five eleven, is broad and muscular. He could easily have overpowered the younger man. But, even with motive and means – and his unprepossessing personality – I'm still struggling to reconcile Blythe as a killer.

Mouse can tell I'm distracted. He keeps running back to me, until I pack away my concerns and get properly into our run, picking up my pace and drowning out everything but the regular beat of my feet on the ground. He's grinning, tongue lolling, as we run side by side, our pace perfectly matched, the sky the perfect pale blue of a chicory flower. When we're nearly back at the gate to the grounds, Mouse lets out an excited bark, and breaks into a sprint.

By the time I catch up, it's no surprise to see Belle waiting for us on the other side of the gate. The two dogs escort me to the tower, where they race upstairs ahead of me. I set out a bowl of food for Mouse, plus two water bowls, before pouring a bowl of cereal for myself. After they have had their fill, they run to the stairs, where Mouse barks once and I, his biddable human, go downstairs to let the pair of them out to play.

After they've gone, I return to the living room, where I make a few more notes, going through what I know as fact, versus what I merely suspect.

There's the map of Venezuela and Colombia. I am now pretty sure that the Xs mark the spot of a number of rare – and therefore endangered – orchids. But I have no way to prove this. There is also the entry in Jamie's journal – *Talked to WB. Says he'll sort things out* – but again, it's too vague to be taken as proof of anything. Regretfully, I have to accept that I don't yet have enough tangible evidence on Blythe to report him.

Then I remember the photos I took in his shed. A quick search online reveals an orchid specialist at Oxford University. I email over the pictures, asking if she can identify them, as I'm concerned they may be from illegal imports.

Pleased to have done something productive, I spend the rest of the morning immersed in the book on Victorian plant hunters. It's filled with sketches from various explorers' notebooks, and makes for a fascinating read.

I'm brought back to the subject of orchid hunting when I reach a section on the British naturalist, William John Swainson. In 1818, Swainson sent back an orchid from Brazil. This was the first of these exotic blooms ever seen in the UK, and it gave rise to an obsession for orchid collecting, lasting right through Victorian times and into the early 1930s. This period of orchid-collecting frenzy has more recently become known as 'orchidelirium'. During this time, many collectors hired orchid hunters. The whole enterprise was not only risky (as well as traversing dangerous terrain, people sometimes fought and were even killed for their spoils), but there was not even any guarantee the thousands of plants gathered and packaged would survive the journey to their destination. Those rare specimens that did make it were sent into auctions, where plants often sold for eye-wateringly high prices.

The story seems strikingly similar to what I've heard about today's secret trades. I wonder, yet again, if Jamie died because he posed a threat to the orchid smugglers. Had he been threatening to go to the police? Blythe said Jamie had helped him with some of the lifting and carrying work for the propagating shed. Did he somehow find out that Blythe's orchid breeding was not legitimate? Perhaps Jamie even had a role within the smuggling operation. Whatever happened, it's clear from his notebook – and the gold chain he hid for me to find – that Jamie was troubled.

I need a sounding board. It's nearly lunchtime, so I decide to seek out Sir Angus. I walk around to the staff door, and from there through to the family section of the house. There are no guests milling about in the hall today. I'm not sure if they've already left, or if they're simply out and about. I find Sir Angus in the Scottish Room, asleep in his chair. He looks uncomfortable, with his head too far back, and I grab a cushion to slip behind his head. As I'm gently holding his head with one hand and sliding the cushion into place with the other, I notice he's shivering, despite the warm tartan throw over his lap. I say his name, 'Sir Angus?' but get no response. I shake his shoulder, and he snorts but doesn't wake. At least the snort means he's breathing. I feel his hand and find it's icy cold. His nail beds are a strange bluey-yellow. On closer inspection of his face, I can see that his complexion has a grey tinge.

My hands are shaking as I draw out my phone, and it takes me two attempts to input 999 and press the green call button. I ask for the ambulance service and report his symptoms to the operator.

'Is he breathing?' he asks.

'Yes.' I lean my head closer to Sir Angus. 'But it sounds laboured.'

'I'm sending an ambulance now. It should be with you in twenty minutes, hopefully less. Are there any access problems?'

'No. I'll leave the front door open.'

After I end the call, I run out of the room, fling open the front door, then bang on the door of Lady Clara's study.

'Just a minute,' she calls, but I'm already stepping inside. 'I'll call you back,' she says to the person on the other end of her phone. She hangs up and looks at me with concern. 'What is it?'

'It's Sir Angus—'

I don't even finish the sentence: she's already racing from the room, her neat court shoes clipping on the tiled floor of the hall.

I run after her to the Scottish Room, and see her crouch beside Sir

Angus. 'Uncle Angus!' she says. 'Wake up, please.' Her voice sounds breathless and scared.

If there has been a plot to poison Sir Angus, Lady Clara is either a very good actor – or has had nothing whatsoever to do with it.

25

Lady Clara travels in the ambulance with her uncle. I follow in the van, which feels like a reassuring friend as I drive slowly the length of the deer pastures, in case an animal should bolt across the road.

The ambulance is long gone from view, but I know the paramedics are taking Sir Angus to A&E at Highfield Royal, so, from Larkham, I head out to the main road, where I follow signs to Highfield. When I get close to town, there are signs to the hospital. On arrival, I find a parking space and pay for three hours. Parking is dear. I hope I won't need to stay longer. The cynical voice in my brain reflects that there's always money to be made when people are sick and vulnerable.

Inside A&E, I find Sir Angus still on a stretcher, while Lady Clara is standing beside him, holding his hand. I walk over.

'Has he not been seen yet?'

'He's been triaged, apparently,' she says crossly, 'which appears to mean they've taken one look at him, deemed him too old, and decided there are younger lives more worth saving.' She looks close to tears.

'Do you want me to have a word with them?'

She shakes her head. 'I'm just being emotional.'

'Has he ever had an episode like this before?'

'No, never. He tripped over his cane once, but that's the only other time we've had to call an ambulance for him. He's remarkably fit for his age. Or he was.' She draws out a handkerchief and blows her nose.

'I'm sure he'll be fine,' I say. 'I'm just going to see how long the wait is.' I walk over to the reception desk, where, in a hushed voice, I tell the woman behind the screen that I have reason to believe the elderly man on the stretcher may have been poisoned.

She raises a sceptical eyebrow. 'Really? Or is this just a way of skipping the queue?'

'He told me himself, a few days ago, that he thought someone was drugging him.'

She picks up a phone receiver and nods for me to leave it with her.

Within two minutes, Sir Angus is being wheeled into an examining room, with Lady Clara close behind. I sit in the waiting room, picking up newspapers and magazines, and putting them back down without reading them. In the end, I get up and walk around the room. I regret this as soon as I see how ill some of the people are. I find myself wondering what diseases Sir Angus might be exposed to in this environment. Hospital is really the worst place to take a sick person. You never know what they might catch.

Lady Clara reappears while I'm pacing in the corridor that leads from A&E to other departments.

'How is he?' I ask.

'They started asking me about toxins he might have been exposed to. I had no idea what they were talking about. I told them he drinks a lot of whisky, but I'm not sure they were listening. In the end, they dismissed me and said they'd run some tests. They were all wearing white, full-length protective gear, with those masks that are like space helmets. I can't help thinking how frightened Uncle will be when he wakes up and finds himself surrounded by people who look like spacemen.'

I touch her arm gently. 'I'm sure they'll reassure him. Would you like a drink?'

'Oh, I'd love a cup of tea.'

'I can't promise it will be drinkable.'

She doesn't seem to hear me. I walk over to the vending machine a couple of metres away. When I glance back, she's hugging herself, as if she's cold. Without checking with her, I select white tea with sugar, and wait while the hot water drips into the paper cup. After giving it a short time to brew, I remove the bag and take the tea to her.

'Would you like to sit down?' I gesture to some metal seats fixed along the wall, and she sinks into one without speaking. 'Are you cold?' I ask. She shakes her head, but I take off my jacket and drape it around her shoulders. 'I think you're in shock,' I say. 'Take this. I've added sugar.'

She takes the cup and starts to sip, without waiting for it to cool. 'Thank you.'

I sit beside her. 'Did they give you any idea what tests they're going to run?'

She shakes her head. 'They said his heart was behaving erratically, but that's about all.' She starts to cry.

'I have to tell you,' I say. 'The reason they were asking you about toxins is because Sir Angus believes he's being drugged.'

She jerks her head and nearly spills her tea. 'Drugged? What on earth . . .? But . . . why?'

'He said that he frequently has trouble staying awake. I think he often feels sluggish.'

'He's ninety-two! What does he expect to feel like?'

'It's just . . .' I tail off and she waits. 'I was wondering about digitalis – foxglove.'

Her expression grows fierce. 'If you know that he's been given something, you have to tell the doctors—'

'No, I don't know anything. It's just that some of his symptoms match. Or, at least, the erratic heartbeat. As you probably know, the medical profession uses digitalis as a heart medication. When I was doing my gardening training, we did a short course on poisonous plants. If I remember rightly, the effects would be worse if Sir Angus were dehydrated.'

'Which he almost certainly is. His doctor keeps telling him he isn't drinking enough water. I'm always trying to persuade him to drink tea in place of that awful whisky.'

'I'm pretty sure there's an antidote for digitalis poisoning.'

'I think we need to talk to the doctor.'

I shake my head. 'They're already checking him for toxins, and we're not sure. I don't want to send them down the wrong path.'

She stares at the surface of her tea. 'Who did he think was poisoning him?' I hesitate, but she lifts her eyes to mine and says, 'It was me, wasn't it?'

'I'm not sure. He wasn't very forthcoming on that point.'

She shakes her head. 'You don't have to protect me. I've tried so hard to look after Uncle Angus since Auntie Louisa died, but he always acts as if I'm trying to kill him with tannin or something. I've heard him refer to me as the "abominable tea monster" when he thinks I can't hear.' There are tears in her eyes.

'I'm sure he knows really that you're just looking after him.'

She sighs and sips her drink. 'We should go back to the waiting room, in case they need us.' I nod and we get to our feet and walk the short distance back.

It's another two hours before a nurse comes to find us. 'We've given your uncle a lot of fluids, and he's doing much better,' she tells Lady Clara. 'Would you like to see him?'

'That really depends on whether he believes me to be the cause of his incapacity,' says her ladyship.

'I'm sorry?' says the nurse.

'Does he believe I hurt him in some way?'

'Not that I'm aware of . . .' I can see her starting to wonder if she should be calling social services, so I step in. 'Sir Angus can get a bit confused,' I say. 'Her ladyship is just checking he's not having one of his delusions, where he believes people in the family are out to harm him.'

'Oh no, nothing like that,' says the nurse, with a reassuring smile. 'He's looking forward to seeing you. I'll take you to him.'

The nurse turns to leave, and Lady Clara moves to follow her. She glances at me over her shoulder. 'Do please come with me. I don't think I'm quite up to going in on my own.'

I accompany her to the small curtained 'room', where Sir Angus is still on his stretcher, but someone has raised the head end so that he is almost in a sitting position. His skin has regained its pink hue, and he's looking far healthier. He smiles as we enter.

'Hello, dear ones.'

Lady Clara hurries over to take his hand. 'Oh, Uncle, I've been so worried about you.' Her voice breaks.

'Now, now, dinnae get yourself in a state, Clara.'

'What caused it? Did the doctor say?' she asks.

He thinks for a moment. 'Hyper-whatever.'

'Hypertension?' she suggests.

'Aye, that'll be it. Or maybe dehy . . .' He catches my eye. 'Hello, hen.'

'Hi, Sir Angus. It's good to see you doing better. You gave us a scare.'

He beams, clearly loving all the fuss. 'They're keeping me in overnight, for more testing. I reckon they're nae used to a fossil like me. Doctor said as I was an "interesting case".' He puffs out his chest with pride.

I smile. 'You didn't have to make all that fuss just to get some attention, you know?' He chuckles.

Another nurse comes by, to check Sir Angus's monitor, and tells him, 'We should have a bed for you soon.' He turns to Lady Clara, 'Dr Bridlington would like a quick word before you go. She's in the sister's office.'

Lady Clara places a kiss on Sir Angus's forehead, and walks away. I'm about to take my leave when Sir Angus says, 'Come here.' He beckons urgently to me and I walk closer. He grabs my arm with a surprisingly strong grip. 'Watch your back,' he instructs me. 'They didnae reckon with how tough I am. They'll nae make that mistake when they come for you.'

I feel a sudden chill. I'm about to ask who he's talking about, when two orderlies come in, ready to wheel him to a ward. Sir Angus waves me away, saying, 'Goodbye, lass. And dinnae forget what I said.' This seems to be his favourite instruction. It's a shame he doesn't favour filling in the blanks in his directions. As I walk back to the waiting room to wait for Lady Clara, I remind myself that Sir Angus's improvement with fluids suggests he was not poisoned, but merely dehydrated. His active imagination can be surprisingly persuasive.

I drive Lady Clara back to Ashford in the van. She sits very upright, knees together, incongruous in her tailored shift dress and navy wool coat among the wear and grime of my old workhorse. My stomach rumbles, and I realise I never had lunch.

'How long have you had this vehicle?' she asks me.

'Only a couple of years. It was all I could afford after Ben lost everything.'

'I keep meaning to ask: has there been any news as to your ex-husband's whereabouts?'

'Not yet. I thought he'd called me a few days ago, but if he had, he wasn't able to talk. There was just static, or perhaps his phone was in his pocket.'

'How disconcerting.'

'Yeah. To be honest, I don't know why he'd ring me instead of his girlfriend, so it's probably just someone who has his phone. He may have sold it on, to get money. He probably forgot to delete the contacts.'

'Oh, I should mention, I did email one of my contacts at Scotland Yard about Ben, but I'm afraid they said that they couldn't get involved.'

I don't bother pointing out that I'd told her that. 'Thank you for trying.'

'Hopefully, someone will find something. You must be beside yourself.'

'To be honest, I keep forgetting about him.' I don't add that I feel guilty every time I remember he's missing. Sometimes, I go a whole day without thinking about him.

I'm focusing on the driving – it's dark, there are no street lights, and the road winds steeply downhill – but I sense a shift in the atmosphere at my confession. I change the subject: 'Did the doctor say any more about what happened to Sir Angus?'

'She suggested it was a combination of dehydration and old age. I'm never very happy when clinicians use old age as if it were an ailment in its own right. It suggests limited . . .' she searches for the word, 'understanding. Or downright ignorance.'

I bite the bullet. 'Was any more said about possible poisoning?'

'Yes, Dr Bridlington did bring that up. She asked if he might have been exposed to any poisonous substances or plants. I said, not so far as I was aware, but that my uncle has a healthy imagination, and had informed a member of our staff that he believed he was being drugged.'

'And what did she say?'

'Nothing. She just looked at me as if I might be the one drugging him. It was a rather unpleasant experience.' She sighs. 'I do love Uncle Angus, but he is not always the easiest person to care for.'

'He's certainly strong willed.'

She laughs. '"Stubborn as a hungry mule," Auntie Louisa would have said.'

We finish the drive in silence, and as we come up Ashford's long driveway, I wonder if Belle is still around, keeping Mouse company. I hope so.

I park the van beside the garages, and Lady Clara thanks me for keeping her company. 'I hate hospitals,' she confides. 'They smell of death.'

Personally, I think they smell of disinfectant, but perhaps it depends on one's associations, so I don't contradict her. I walk with her to the front door of the great house. She's just ringing the bell when she turns to me and says,

'You don't really believe someone is drugging him, do you?'

The door is opened and we stand, blinking, in the orange light that floods out. Simon is standing beside the door. 'Good evening, ma'am,' he says.

'Good evening, Simon.'

'I don't know,' I say quietly.

She takes my hand and whispers, 'Please don't say anything to anyone at Ashford, at least until I've had a chance to look into the matter.'

I wonder how she's planning on doing this. She can't exactly ask the staff if one of them is poisoning her uncle. Nor is there likely to be a jar in the kitchen, labelled 'Deadly Nightshade', next to the ones marked 'Coffee' and 'Sugar'. But perhaps she has someone on the staff she can trust, who can investigate more easily.

I walk back to the tower, where I find Mouse and Belle lying outside, beside the front door, curled around each other. As I approach, Mouse stirs and gets to his feet, greeting me enthusiastically, and Belle follows suit.

'Were you not meant to be going home today?' I ask her. She nudges my hand, and I stroke the wiry fur on her head. 'Come on,' I tell them. 'You can both come up to the tower. At least until someone comes to take you home, Belle.'

* * *

A little later, at dinner, Olivia walks over to sit beside me. We have a cold buffet – which is understandable, after all the hot meals Vicky has had to prepare this weekend for the party. But, instead of everyone taking their plates back to their own rooms like the last time we had a buffet, there's an unspoken consensus that we want to be together. Jamie's death has shaken us, and the one positive seems to be that we are drawing closer as a group.

'Hiya,' says Olivia. 'Is Belle over with Mouse in the Round Wing?'

'Yes. Is she wanted?'

She shakes her head. 'Actually, I was going to ask if you'd mind keeping her overnight? Dickie's helping Lady Clara out with arrangements for their uncle's return from hospital, so he's going to stay another night.'

'Sure. We're happy to have her, no problem. Mouse adores her.'

'That's great, thanks. I'll let Dickie know.'

'Is Sir Angus due out tomorrow, then?'

She crosses her fingers. 'Not tomorrow, but we're hoping later this week.'

I'm just chewing on a miniature pepper, stuffed with a delicate, herby cream cheese, when Saliha says, 'Did you hear the police are planning on releasing the body to Jamie's family on Friday?'

I swallow quickly. 'This coming Friday?'

Saliha nods. 'Jamie's dad's seeing if the church can fit them in next week for the funeral. It'll be in Liverpool, though.'

'So, they've ruled it a suicide?' I check.

Olivia chips in, 'I don't think that was ever in doubt. They were just dotting their i's, as it were.'

'Right . . .' I say.

She raises a perfectly tailored eyebrow. 'Did you have another idea?'

I try not to show my panicked calculations. It's now Sunday night. That gives me only four full days to prove Jamie was murdered, and find his killer.

I shake my head and smile. 'No. I'm glad it's all resolved. Sorry if the funeral's a bit far for you to go, Saliha.'

'Maybe we can have our own ceremony that day,' suggests Olivia.

'Maybe,' says Saliha.

The rest of the meal passes in general chat about the party, which has dominated the weekend for most of the staff. The marquess and marchioness did not make a good impression.

'Maybe they'll drop dead before next year,' suggests Simon hopefully. Then his face changes, as he realises how tactless he's been. 'I mean . . . I didn't . . .'

'It's OK,' says Vicky, who's sitting at the table with us for once, instead of working in the kitchen. 'We know what you meant.'

He looks relieved.

I glance at Vicky. She's pale and drawn, but her inner resilience is showing through.

This is grieving, I realise: believing you aren't going to make it through the loss, and then discovering you're stronger than you ever imagined.

26

I check my emails on my phone after breakfast the next day, and am surprised to see there's already a response from the orchid expert. Mouse is out, roaming the grounds with Belle.

I take my seat at the desk and open my laptop emails.

The message reads:

Dear Ms Williams,

Thank you so much for sharing your findings with me.

You are absolutely right in your concerns. Several of these specimens appear to be endangered orchid types, which exist only in South America, where they are protected species. I can also see a rare *alba* form of one of these species – as you may know, the white forms are considered especially desirable among collectors.

The presence of these orchids in this country can unfortunately mean only one thing: that they have been plundered from their natural habitat and illegally imported, in direct contravention of CITES (the Convention on International Trade in Endangered Species of Wild Fauna and Flora). As you may be aware, this activity is a treacherous one for the hunters. Many participants are focused only on the prize, and have no respect for human life.

I would recommend that you report this situation at once to the National Wildlife Crime Unit. Although they are somewhat overstretched, I believe – or at least hope – that they will intervene in this important matter. Back in 2021, Border Force seized an enormous cargo of imports of protected

species, including some orchids, thus setting a precedent
for action regarding this important issue.

The professor signs off. I scan her email a second time, my heart beating hard. At last I have proof that Blythe is involved in the illegal trafficking of rare orchids.

My heart slows as I realise that I still have no proof to tie him and the illegal trade to Jamie's death.

I pull up the website for the National Wildlife Crime Unit. At first glance, it appears to be more concerned with the protection of UK wildlife than with preventing the importing of protected species from elsewhere in the world. Nonetheless, I forward the professor's email to the unit, together with an introductory note from me. I attach the photographs of Blythe's orchids. I'm about to press send, when it occurs to me that I have nothing to lose by copying in DS McLeod. I find his email address on his business card, type it in, and press send.

Having done all I can for the time being, I decide to get to work. I'm determined to finish unearthing the limestone fountain today, so I set off for the wild blackberry patch, where I spend a rewarding morning digging out bramble roots, until the entire structure is revealed. It is identical to its mate, with an octagonal base designed as a pool, and small fountain heads surrounding a large central head. The feature will need to be reconnected to both the water and power supplies, but the joy of being a consultant is that I don't need to do this part of the job myself. I make a note to call in a specialist.

I spend the afternoon finishing my survey of the trees. The grounds are beautiful today, lit by that Midas light that turns the amber autumn leaves to gold.

As it starts to get dark, the dogs and I head indoors to rest. Just before dinner, when we're installed in the cosy living room, Mouse and Belle start barking, and there's a knock at the door. From the eager way in which Belle runs to the landing, it's clear that Dickie has arrived to fetch her.

The three of us head down the stone stairs and I open the front door to Dickie, whereupon Mouse makes sure he receives almost as many cuddles as Belle.

Dickie laughs. 'He's a friendly chap, isn't he?'

'Sorry if he's a bit full on.'

He shakes his head and pats Mouse, who's twisting himself around Dickie's legs in excitement, like an oversized cat. 'He's a lovely boy.' Dickie stands up. 'I can't thank you enough for having Belle,' he says. 'My sister was in quite a state about Uncle Angus, and Rupert asked if I'd mind staying over.' He runs a hand through his hair. 'It's just easier if I know Belle's being looked after, you know?'

'Of course. Any time.' I glance at the dogs, who are nuzzling one another outside. 'To be honest, Mouse pines the whole time Belle's away.'

'Oh no, really?' He looks at Mouse. 'I'm sorry, chap. I'll try to make sure she comes again soon, all right?'

As soon as our guests have left, Mouse races upstairs to sit by the window and whine quietly. It's heartbreaking. I set out his dinner in the kitchen, and it takes a lot of cuddles from me to persuade him to eat it. When he's finished, he curls up in his basket with Mr Rabbit.

'Right, it's time for my dinner. I'll be back in a bit, boy,' I tell him, giving him one last stroke.

In the dining room, I find myself seated between Olivia and Saliha. Despite my misgivings about Olivia, I'm grateful for the normality of her and Saliha's chat this evening, while my head is full of puzzles and unanswered questions.

I sit mulling, joining in the conversation occasionally on the subject of art schools (Saliha) and the horrors of doing taxes (Olivia), and savouring the homity pie made by Vicky. This is followed by banoffee pie, which is one of my favourite desserts.

I tune back into the chat when Saliha solemnly says, 'So, it's all set for Friday.'

'Is that for the release of Jamie's body?' I ask, and she nods.

'Jamie's dad's in a right state, according to Oli.'

'It must be hard, if they were arguing so much before Jamie died.'

She nods again, her big eyes serious. 'Oli says their dad rang him yesterday. He's had this letter arrive, offering Jamie a place at some stage school. Apparently their dad cried all the way through the call. Oli says he's never heard him cry before.'

We sit in silence. It's almost too much to process. For a moment, I wonder if Jamie's dad would have allowed him to accept the place on the course. But there's nothing to achieve by such speculation.

I'm keen to get back to Mouse, so I slip away soon after.

Outside, the November wind slaps me like a cold hand. I take my orange woolly hat from my jacket pocket and pull it down low over my ears, despite the brevity of my walk to the tower.

As I turn my key in the door, step inside and lock it behind me, I remember my email to the National Wildlife Crime Unit. Now, I just need to establish the link between the illegal orchid trade and Jamie's death. I still have three days. That will have to be enough.

Mouse is sound asleep in his basket, with Mr Rabbit tucked between his paws. I am careful not to disturb him. Soon tucked up, too, I pick up my book, *Bluebird, Bluebird*, from the bedside table. The story features two bodies for the detective to investigate. But my mind keeps wandering to my own, very real, murder case. I find myself lying awake for hours, going over everything I know, in case I've missed something.

Who could have killed Jamie? Blythe is an obvious suspect – but I still doubt he'd be capable of an intentional murder. I try to pin down what it is about him – it's certainly not because he's compassionate. I decide it's his natural cowardice. His strong need for self preservation would make him too scared of getting caught.

So, either he had an accomplice, or someone else entirely is responsible for Jamie's death. Olivia has been following my investigation a little too closely for my comfort. Might she have carried out the murder, as Blythe's accomplice? They make an unlikely duo, but they do spend some of each day side by side in the office.

I remember the conversation that Georgina overheard, between Olivia and Mr Fanshawe – something about sleeping pills. I try to imagine the pair of them having drugged Jamie and strung him up . . . But what on earth would be their motive? And Mr Fanshawe seems even less likely to be a killer than Olivia or Blythe.

I keep coming back to the chain that Jamie buried for me to find. This has to be the clue that makes sense of the whole puzzle, but I'm at a loss to solve it. Who could 'GC' be, and why did Jamie have their St Christopher medal? Perhaps more importantly, why did he want *me* to have it? My mind goes round in frustrating circles as tiredness sets in. Has Jamie left me another clue, to explain this one? Maybe the map bears a code? I take out my phone and examine the photo I took, but there's nothing.

When I finally drift off in the early hours, my dreams are disquieting. In the worst one, Blythe has me tied to a chair in the propagating shed, and he's advancing upon me with a pruning saw, saying, 'You'll grow much better once I've given you a hard prune.'

27

After my bad night, I oversleep – it's eight thirty by the time I roll over to squint at the clock on my mobile. With a groan, I roll out of bed, taking the duvet with me and upending poor Mouse, who was stretched across my feet. He must have migrated to the bed at some point in the night. He lies back down and regards me with reproving eyes.

'Sorry, boy!' He goes straight back to sleep, so I guess I'm not the only one who doesn't fancy a run this morning. Besides anything else, I want my breakfast. I pull on jogging bottoms and a T-shirt and jumper, and head downstairs to get my coat before walking over to the house.

The dining room, when I reach it, is warm and cosy. Someone has lit a fire – the first in this room since I've been at Ashford – and the staff are looking more relaxed than I've seen them since Jamie's death.

I take a seat beside Saliha and pour myself a coffee. After Vicky has come in to take my order, I turn to Saliha.

'I've been meaning to ask you about something,' I say quietly.

'Uh huh?' she says, biting into a jam-smeared slice of white toast.

'Sir Angus told me he thinks he's being drugged.'

Her eyes grow huge and she's so excited, she speaks with her mouth full: 'I saw Lady Clara crumbling something into a cup of tea one day! I just thought it was paracetamol or something – you know how some people can't swallow tablets?'

She puts down the slice of toast and we sit in silence for a moment, both considering the new possibility. But then she shakes her head, 'No, Lady C wouldn't do that . . .'

I remember how distraught her ladyship was, upon discovering her uncle in an unresponsive state. But the momentary suspicion has raised a sense of disquiet. Neither of us wants to believe Lady Clara could be drugging her uncle, but we can't entirely dismiss it either.

Saliha stuffs down the rest of her toast and stands up. 'Right – see you.'

'See you.'

My breakfast arrives, and I eat it quickly and down my coffee before leaving. Olivia calls to me in the corridor when I've just reached the staff exit. 'Steph! Hold on a sec and I'll walk out with you.'

I nod and hold the door for her, then we start walking the short distance to the tower. I realise I'm holding my breath, on the alert in her presence.

'Have you heard any more about how Sir Angus is doing in the hospital?' I ask, to break the silence.

'Oh, he's great. Having a whale of a time, by all accounts. Honestly, he'll outlive all of us.'

'It sounds like he was dehydrated. Do you think he'll start drinking more water?'

She shakes her head. 'Sir Angus lives according to his own laws.'

'I suppose, once you get to a certain age, you might as well enjoy life,' I say.

'I certainly don't intend to give up my red wine and chocolate.'

I unlock the door. 'Do you want to come up for a moment?' I'm hoping I might be able to get her to relax enough while chatting, to let something slip that would help in my investigation.

'I'd better not,' she says. 'There's a pile of invoices waiting for me in the office. Lady Clara also asked me to look over the joint bank accounts. Dickie has loaned her a large sum of money for work on the house and gardens, and we need to keep tabs on it all.'

'What does Dickie do?' I ask.

'Oh, he's the director of an import/export firm, and also sits on the board of a couple of property companies. He should be quite wealthy, but the poor thing got taken to the cleaners by his ex-wife, in the divorce courts.'

I wonder if Dickie has lent all that money to his sister in order to avoid paying it to his ex-wife. But I just say, 'It's great that Lady Clara can afford to go ahead with the garden renovations.'

She nods. 'Yes, it's perfect timing, with her and Rupert having moved in so recently. They'd been wondering if they'd even be able to keep the house. Thanks to Dickie's generosity, that's all been resolved.' She looks at me. 'Don't mention any of this to anyone, will you? I shouldn't really be discussing private family business.'

'My lips are sealed.' She bids me good day, and heads off to tackle her various administrative tasks, while I go upstairs to fetch Mouse.

He's in a happier mood this morning. Out in the grounds, he races off towards the woods. It's a fine day: cold and windy, but with a bright-blue sky and scudding white clouds.

My job for today is to remove all the diseased and damaged branches of the specimen trees. I've noticed that Blythe only removed low-hanging ones, and then only if they posed a safety concern.

I fetch my extendable ratchet loppers from the van, and begin with all the easy-to-reach branches. I love using this cutting tool: the ratchet mechanism turns cutting slim branches into a simple, satisfying process. The blades close in increments, slicing effortlessly through the wood.

Just before lunchtime, I call to Mouse and take him inside, where he empties his bowl of water and settles for a nap in his bed, Mr Rabbit tucked between his front paws. I check for emails on my laptop, hoping for an acknowledgement from one or both police departments. But there's nothing.

I've just reached the dining room when Simon intercepts me: 'Lady Clara wants to see you.'

'Can it wait till after lunch? I'm starving.'

He shakes his head. 'She said it was urgent.'

'OK . . .' With a last, wistful glance into the dining room, where the table is laid out with the customary picnic-style treats, I walk to her ladyship's study, where I'm about to knock on the door, when I hear her voice coming from inside, raised in anger: 'You had no right!'

A response comes – calmer and quieter, pacifying. I'm sure the voice is her husband's. I don't catch everything, but I hear him say, '. . . for his own good.'

I know I should move away, but I'm frozen to the spot.

'It was not your decision to make!' she shouts.

He says something else, that I can't make out, to which she makes a frustrated sound before shouting, 'Ohhh, just get out! I can't bear to look at you right now, Rupert!'

I jump back, as the door opens, and Mr Fanshawe comes striding out. He starts when he sees me. 'Ms Williams! Have you been there long?'

'I just arrived. I didn't mean to . . .'

He nods and says quietly, 'I'm sorry you had to witness that. My wife and I don't row very often, thank heavens. I'm sure it will all blow over by dinnertime.' He knocks on the door and pokes his head into the study, in the manner of a soldier warily putting his head above the parapet.

'What do you want *now*?' she snaps.

'Ms Williams is here to see you, my love.'

'Oh! Send her in.'

As he leaves, I enter the room, cautiously.

But Lady Clara is all smiles: 'Oh, Ms Williams, thank you for coming. I was wondering, might you be able to have Belle again, while my brother Dickie goes away overnight on business? I know you've only just had her, but this trip is unexpected. Normally, he'd board her in the kennels, but your sweet dog seems to love having her around.'

'We both love her,' I say. 'We'd be happy to have her.'

'Thank you so much. I'll have Dickie drop off her bed and food later today.'

'How is Sir Angus?'

She pulls a face. 'Stubborn.' She laughs. 'But I suppose that means he's on the mend! I'd worry if he suddenly became biddable. Of course, he's charming to the hospital staff.'

'I hope you can persuade him to take more soft drinks in future.'

'I find that very unlikely,' she says sadly.

My stomach growls loudly and she says, 'Do get back to your lunch.'

I laugh. 'I think I'd better!'

I'm the only person in the dining room when I get there, so I put together a plate of food, which I take back to eat in the living room while Mouse dozes. While I savour one of Vicky's delicious Cornish pasties, I can't help wondering what Lady Clara and her husband could have been arguing about. I've never heard her sound that angry.

At around two thirty, I'm removing some dead branches from a *Sequoiadendron giganteum* when Belle comes racing over. The tree is one of my favourites: one of those giant redwoods that I read about as a child and longed to see. Again, this specimen was not part of London's original late-seventeenth-century planting. It would almost certainly have been imported in the eighteenth century.

I'm crouching, making a fuss of the wolfhound, when Dickie arrives.

'Ms Williams – thank you so much for agreeing to mind Belle again.'

I stand up. 'It's my pleasure.'

'I have her things in the car. I'll bring them now, if you're OK to let me into the Round Wing?'

'Sure. Mouse will be thrilled to see Belle,' I say.

While Dickie goes to his car, I lay down my gloves and loppers, then walk over to the house. He meets me at the corner, laden with Belle's possessions, and I take one of the bags from him as we walk the remaining short distance to my front door, where Belle is already waiting for us.

I can hear Mouse barking behind the door, so I open it and stand back, so that he and Belle can enjoy an enthusiastic reunion in the hall before Dickie and I enter. We laugh as the two of them race outside to play, barking excitedly.

'I don't think I've ever seen Belle so happy,' he tells me, as we step inside and start the climb to the first floor. 'It makes me realise it's quite cruel, leaving her alone on the days when I go to the office.'

'Well, we're always delighted to have her.'

We deposit Belle's belongings in the living room. She has several soft toys, and Dickie places these carefully in her large bed. He hands me a bag of food for her, which I take through to the kitchen and put away in a cupboard.

At last, I say, 'Right. Well . . .' and gesture towards the landing.

'There's just one thing,' he says, eyeing me thoughtfully.

'What's that?'

'A little bird told me that you've been conducting your own investigation into Jimmy's death.'

'Jamie,' I say automatically.

'That's right.'

We stare at each other for a moment, and I feel my skin begin to prickle under his gaze. Keeping my voice steady, I say, 'What about it?'

'Oh . . .' he says casually. 'I just wondered if you'd turned anything up? Such an awful business.'

I shake my head. My palms are sweating now, and all I can think is that I'm trapped in this tower, with a man who is considerably bigger and stronger than I am. I edge backwards, towards the kitchen, where I can grab a knife if necessary.

But at that moment, he puts up his palms. 'I'm so sorry – I shouldn't have brought it up. I can see I've upset you. Please, forget I said anything.'

I hold his seemingly sincere gaze, my mind turning over. What just happened? I definitely felt threatened, but is my imagination working overtime? It wouldn't be the first time, after a night of poor sleep and worse dreams. After a beat, I decide to test him, 'You seem very interested?'

'Oh, no, not really.' He hesitates, then adds, 'It's only if you've found something that suggests foul play. The poor boy's death was so shocking. I know my sister and Rupert have been distraught over it. I just . . . well, I'd appreciate it if you could be discreet with anything you find out. They don't need any more upset.'

I want to believe him.

'Of course,' I say. I gesture towards the stairs. 'Now, if you'll excuse me . . .'

'Sure, sure. I'll let you get on.' He glances at his watch. 'I need to be off, in any case.'

We go downstairs, and he heads back to his car. I lock the front door and check it's secure. The encounter has left me feeling vulnerable. And I don't like it.

I walk on autopilot back to the giant redwood. I keep reflecting on how trapped I felt, with Dickie in the tower. I'd been so aware of his looming presence, and of how isolated we were from the rest of the house. Was he really just asking me not to stir up more upset for his sister, or was there a threat hidden in his enquiries? As for the 'little bird', I can think only of Olivia. She is the one person to have noticed my 'investigation' – and to have repeatedly questioned me about it. I zip up my jacket, for comfort as well as warmth. I'd already suspected Olivia of having more than a passing interest in my findings. What are she and Dickie up to?

I remember how sympathetic she sounded towards him, when telling me earlier about his ex-wife 'taking him to the cleaners'. Are the two of them romantically involved? My mind flicks back to my first week here, when I spotted her in an intimate encounter with a man outside my window. I'd assumed it was someone who had no connection to Ashford, but could it have been Dickie?

I find myself wondering how well Jamie knew both Dickie Spencer and Olivia.

I take up the loppers and set to work, removing dead segments from a number of other trees. Blythe seems to have missed quite a few, and it takes me a couple of hours before I'm satisfied I've cleared the worst of the damaged and low-hanging branches. During the whole of this time, I'm sorting through the bits of information I've gleaned, and processing the fact that Dickie and Olivia have both moved up to prime suspect slots. I need to talk to Olivia again.

It's around three thirty by the time I collect up the cut branches and wheel them over to a log pile I've started building near the wildflower meadow, to provide a home for insects and hedgehogs. Then I stow away my loppers in the back of the van, before making my way around the back of the house to the staff entrance, from where I head to the office.

Olivia is sitting at her desk when I walk in. There's no sign of Blythe. She looks up from her screen and smiles. 'Steph, hi.'

'How are the invoices?'

'All dealt with.' She folds her arms with pride.

'Excellent.' I point to the chair in front of her desk. 'Can I?'

'Of course,' she says with a smile. 'Though I'm afraid my aunt would point out that it should really be "May I?".'

I laugh. 'May I?'

She bows her head in mock courtliness. 'You may.'

I sit down and say, 'Dickie came to visit me a couple of hours ago. It was ostensibly just to drop off Belle's belongings, but he seemed to have another agenda. And he appeared to know a lot more about my activities than I might have expected.' I look her straight in the eye.

One thing about her peaches-and-cream complexion is that she blushes easily. The flush rises to her cheekbones, a beacon of guilt.

'I've been wondering,' I say pleasantly, 'did Dickie know Jamie?'

She regains her composure impressively quickly. 'Well, only so much as he knows all of the Ashford staff,' she says. 'He visits his sister several times a week, after all.'

'So, you don't think he knew Jamie well?'

'I doubt it. Anyway, why on earth are you asking?'

'All I want to know is why Dickie is so concerned about my investigation,' I say. 'He seems to have some . . . vested interest in the case.' Seeing she's about to contradict this, I add, softly, 'As do you.'

She laughs. 'What *do* you mean?'

'Only that you wanted to know what I'd found in the maze . . .'

'So, you did find something!' she says, smugly. 'I thought as much.'

I raise my eyebrows. 'I rest my case. Meanwhile, tell me something: how long have you been involved with Dickie Spencer?'

She looks about to protest, but then she changes her mind and sinks back in her chair. 'Since before he and his wife separated,' she admits quietly.

'So, he was having an affair with you?' At least Miles's warning about Olivia now makes sense – he must see her as responsible for his parents' break-up.

'Dickie's wife was a total bitch,' she says defensively. 'She was only ever interested in his money.'

'I see. And what reason did he give you for keeping an eye on me?'

She shakes her head. 'He's very protective of Clara. He doesn't want some big scandal that might upset her and the family. I should probably have told you why I was asking questions. But he asked me not to say anything that might create any kind of fuss. He's very kind and thoughtful in that way. Clara's so lucky to have him as her brother.'

It's clear I'm not going to get an objective view of Dickie from Olivia, so I take my leave.

I don't believe, for one minute, that Dickie's interest in my findings has anything to do with protecting his sister. So, was Dickie involved in Jamie's death? If he was, I'm certain that Olivia, deeply in love, suspects nothing.

It's close to four and getting dark as I leave the house, so it's not worth starting any more gardening tasks today. I walk over to the tower, calling to the dogs as I go. Belle and Mouse come running over for a quick cuddle, but immediately race off again.

Back in the living room, I write two sentences into my notebook:
Is there a link between Dickie and Jamie?
Is there a link between Dickie and Blythe?

I'm pretty sure that the answers to these questions, and unravelling the mystery of the medallion, will solve the puzzle of Jamie's murder.

The dogs only return to the tower when it's pitch dark outside, summoning me with a chorus of barks. When I open the door, they're panting with exhaustion, and their slow, weary climb to the first floor is almost comical to observe. I set out their dinner, along with bowls of water, in the kitchen. As soon as they've finished, they squeeze together into Belle's bed, which is huge and highly padded, and a far more luxurious item than Mouse and I ever knew existed.

Olivia and I are seated quite far apart at dinner. She waves to me, and I wave back, with a smile. But underneath, I am troubled. She is bound to have told Dickie that I confronted her, and that I now know he asked her to keep an eye on me.

By bedtime, I'm feeling nervy. If Dickie was responsible for Jamie's death, what might he resort to, if he suspects me of knowing too much? I curse myself for my carelessness in seeking out Olivia.

I go down to the entrance hall twice, to check the front door is locked. As well as the lock, there are two bolts and a chain, and I use each piece of this hardware.

At least I have two large dogs to keep me company, and to warn me if anyone approaches. Not that Belle would view Dickie as any kind of threat.

Once again, I lie awake for hours. Finally, I take my duvet down to the living room and settle on the sofa, my feet hanging over the end. Mouse is snoring loudly in Belle's bed, but tonight it's a comforting sound. Nonetheless, it still takes me a while to get to sleep. The wind has picked up and is driving rain against the window panes. The sound is like Morse code, or the tapping of a hundred urgent fingers.

28

By 6 a.m., even though it's still dark out, everything seems less menacing. I berate myself for my night-time paranoia, and take both dogs with me for a restorative run. We have a lovely time, jogging through the fields.

Back in the tower, I set out their food and water and go for my shower.

As I squeeze out a dollop of shampoo and start lathering my hair, I think about Jamie's death, and the way he buried that medallion for me to find . . . I know it's right at the heart of what happened, I just can't work out how.

I wish I had something to tell DS McLeod, a reason to ring him. A hunch that I've pinpointed Jamie's murderer is not going to get me far in the eyes of the police – especially while they're convinced it was suicide.

I leave the dogs to nap on the window seat, and head over to the house for breakfast.

Saliha greets me with a smile as I sit down. 'Hiya.'

'Hi,' I say, smiling back and pouring myself a mug of coffee.

'I've got some news,' she says.

I set down the coffee pot and turn to look at her. 'Go on.'

'I've got a place for next September, on a fine art degree course.'

I grin and squeeze her shoulder. 'Oh, that's brilliant!'

She leans closer and whispers, 'I'm going to hand in my notice here and take some art classes near home, till the course starts.'

'That sounds like a great idea.'

'I haven't told anyone yet. I'm going to talk to Lady Clara today, after I'm dressed.'

'My lips are sealed.'

Her face turns grave and she lowers her voice: 'Do you think it's possible that Jamie didn't . . . kill himself?'

The question comes out of the blue, and I'm not sure how to answer it. I say carefully, 'What makes you ask that?'

'I found something.'

She's in her big, fluffy dressing gown today. She fishes in the large patch pocket, and draws out a rolled-up A5 notebook.

'What's this?' I ask. But my hands are trembling as I take it from her and unroll it. It has the initials JL on the front. 'Is this one of Jamie's journals?' I whisper. I glance around to check no one is watching, and slip the book into one of my coat pockets.

She shakes her head. 'It's his sketchbook. I realised no one had done his washing since he . . . died, and we need to send his clothes on to his family. And I was, like, checking the pockets, you know, like we always do, and I found it in the back pocket of his jeans when I went to wash them.'

'Did you go through it?'

She nods. 'It's just portraits of people from Ashford. There's also this man who came over from South America – Colombia, I think. He was called Gabriel.' She pronounces it the Spanish way: *Gab-ree-ell*. 'He wasn't here long, but he and Jamie got on really well.'

I freeze.

'I just think Jamie would want his friends to know the truth,' she says. Her eyes are wet. 'I mean, I don't know if there's anything in there . . .'

'Can I ask do you know Gabriel's surname?' She shakes her head. 'OK. Well, thank you for sharing this with me. After I've had a look myself, I'll make sure the police see it.'

'Thanks. I think Jamie would've wanted that.'

I nod. 'I just want justice for Jamie, like you do.'

She gives me a hug. 'I have to get going.'

'Good luck with Lady Clara,' I say quietly, and she pulls an anxious face.

Soon after she's left, Simon brings in my breakfast, and I eat it quickly. I have an urgent appointment with Jamie's sketchbook.

* * *

When I get back to the tower, I find Mouse and Belle have once again squeezed on to the window seat, where they're snoozing, both bottoms hanging off the edge. They have a luxury bed to sleep in, but they've chosen to cram themselves into this spot. It looks desperately uncomfortable.

I take a seat at the desk and open the book. It turns out that Jamie was a proficient artist, and there are lots of intricate sketches of plants, beautifully detailed and coloured.

I keep turning the pages, until I come to a section filled with sketched portraits of Ashford familiars. They are all easily identifiable, and I marvel at the range of Jamie's talent. There are sketches of his brother Benji, as well as Julian Fanshawe, Michael, Vicky and Samuel. Lady Clara and Rupert appear to have posed for him together, and their portrait is more formal than the others. And then I come to two sketches of Gabriel. Jamie has written 'Gabriel Cortes' beneath the pictures. GC: just like the St Christopher medal.

Gabriel is wearing a T-shirt and shorts, and is sitting, facing out, in the first sketch, whilst the second shows him in profile. The man's gaze in the first portrait is thoughtful, looking past Jamie, past me, to another place entirely. From his lined face and sun-darkened skin, I would guess that he's used to working out of doors, in a country where the sun beats down. I wonder how he came to be at Ashford. Around his neck, there hangs a St Christopher. I grab the medal from my desk, and squint at the one around Gabriel's neck. They are identical, down to the small chip at the bottom.

After studying Gabriel's intense expression for a while, I turn the page and find a portrait I was not expecting.

Dickie Spencer is looking out at me.

29

A shiver runs down my back as I meet Dickie's gaze. There is something both gratifying and awful in this confirmation that he knew Jamie as more than just a passing member of staff. The drawing is lifelike, perfectly capturing his air of self-confidence and entitlement.

Dickie has been depicted sitting in a chair, one arm slung over the back, his legs stretched out, and a smile playing on his lips. The portrait markedly lacks the formal posing of Lady Clara and Mr Fanshawe. Dickie looks completely at home in Jamie's company.

If my growing suspicions about Dickie's guilt are correct, it strikes me that Jamie may have spilled secrets to this man, not realising that he was entirely the wrong person to confide in. Drawing out my mobile, I take pictures of every page, before texting DS McLeod:

Now have a sketchbook belonging to Jamie, if you're interested?

I walk through to the kitchen, where I make coffee and give space to my brain to whirr. I still don't know why Jamie had Gabriel's medallion – nor why he left it for me.

I'm walking back into the living room with my mug when the dogs jolt awake and start barking. Mouse nearly falls, bottom first, off the window seat, but Belle leaps gracefully to the floor, and runs to the top of the stairs. Mouse sorts out his balance and follows her.

I immediately start to sweat, at the anticipation of Dickie Spencer on my doorstep. Why didn't I keep the dogs outside today? I could have put Belle's stuff in one of the garages, and then I wouldn't have set myself up, like a fly waiting in a web for the spider's return. For a moment, I consider hiding Jamie's notebooks.

But another glance at Belle calms my breathing. Although her tail is wagging, she is not in the exalted state that means her human has arrived. I go downstairs, and find Simon outside.

'Master Dickie's sent me for the dog and its things.'

I smile, relieved to learn that Dickie isn't planning on coming over to the tower. 'OK. Come up.'

On the first floor, I load Simon up with Belle's bed, bedding, toys and food, then show him out with Belle. As soon as I've shut the front door behind him, I run up to check on Mouse. He's at the window, gazing out, making his sad little whining sound. I crouch beside him and stroke him.

'Do you want to come outside?' He turns a lugubrious expression towards me, before climbing down and getting into his basket with Mr Rabbit.

I spend a few minutes sitting on the floor by his side, stroking him, until he falls asleep. Then I fetch my notebook from the desk and head downstairs. I can't help checking all around me as I step outside and lock the front door. After my encounter with Dickie, I'm feeling on edge.

I spend the rest of the morning digging out patches of the invasive campanula, while trying to work out what hard evidence I can put together to inform the police. It's now Wednesday, and they're due to release the body on Friday. Time is running out.

Just before lunchtime, I see Lady Clara drive up to the front of the house in a gleaming white Mercedes. It's the first time I've seen this car, which she presumably keeps in a garage. It's the new S-Class 580e hybrid model, and I know that prices start at over £100,000. It's a real beauty.

She parks, and walks around to the passenger side, where she helps Sir Angus to climb out. She hands him his cane, and the two of them walk inside.

I choose this visual interruption as a good moment to break for lunch. As usual, I take my plate of food up to the tower, where I find Mouse still sleeping, curled around his toy. I hope he'll be feeling less sad by the time he awakes.

After savouring my delicious meal of olive bread, locally produced cheese, homemade houmous and a fruit salad, and downing my strong coffee, I head over to the house, hoping to find Sir Angus in the Scottish Room. But his chair is missing. As I walk back into the hall, I hear voices, emanating from Lady Clara's study. I walk over and knock on the door.

'Come!' she calls, in a cheery tone.

I push open the door and step inside, where I'm met with a wall of heat from the blazing fire. I take a step back, and her ladyship says,

'Yes, it is rather warm in here, but I'm not risking my uncle having another episode. It was far too frightening. Do come in.' She smiles first at me, and then at Sir Angus, who I now see is seated near the fire, in his tartan wing-back chair that has been carried through from the Scottish Room.

'Hello, hen!' he greets me. I greet him, taking in his appearance. If possible, he looks even more shrunken than before, but he's smiling cheerily.

Lady Clara tells him, 'You owe Ms Williams a debt of thanks, for having found you and sounded the alarm.'

'Aye, thank you, Ms Williams,' he says. I notice he uses my name for the first time, possibly because his niece has just supplied it. 'I've had a grand old time at the hospital.'

Her ladyship turns to me. 'He loved having all those nurses fuss over him. He was quite the favourite.'

'Why am I not surprised?' I say.

'Won't you join us?' Lady Clara asks me. 'We were about to have some tea.'

'She's back ter poisoning me,' says Sir Angus.

'Oh, come now, Uncle, you know I'm doing no such thing. The doctors said—'

She doesn't manage to finish sharing what the doctors said, because Sir Angus interrupts, 'I've lived to the grand old age of ninety-seven, and I've never had ter drink so much tea in my life. 'Tis my insides as will be swimming with the murky stuff.'

I laugh. 'I'm sure you've aged several years since you last told me.'

Lady Clara rolls her eyes. 'You're ninety-two, Uncle, as I'm pretty sure you know.'

He shrugs, but there's a cheeky gleam in his eyes.

Her ladyship turns to me. 'Where are my manners?' she says. 'Please, Ms Williams, do take a seat.' She gestures to the chairs in front of her desk.

I shake my head. 'I just wanted to check on Sir Angus, but I have work to do.' I don't add that I couldn't bear to spend another moment in that furnace of a room. If Sir Angus was dehydrated before, he'll be desiccated by the end of the day.

I realise I've left my gardening gloves in the tower, so I walk back to fetch them before returning to work. Mouse is awake when I reach the living room. He's still lying in his basket, and is viewing me with sad eyes. I sit back on the floor beside him, stroking his head and ears.

'Would you like to watch some Attenborough?' I ask him. 'Sharks?' I'm distressed to find that this enticing suggestion elicits no response. 'How about *Boohbah*?' Again, nothing. I hate seeing him depressed like this, and I consider staying with him but I have work to do.

'I'm going outside,' I tell him. 'Do you want to come?'

I'm amazed when he barks once and gets to his feet. 'OK, boy!' I say, laughing. 'Let's go outside together.'

As he carries on barking, it takes me a moment to realise his excitement has nothing to do with my invitation. There's someone outside. Surely Belle can't be back so soon? Perhaps it's Lilibeth, the cat.

But when we get downstairs and I open the door, it is indeed Belle on the doorstep. I step outside and glance around, but there's no sign of Dickie. I'm not as relieved as I might be. I'd rather know where he is. Did he not leave after all?

Mouse races outside, and the two dogs lope off together. I wonder idly if Dickie would allow me to adopt Belle. But, if I'm right about his involvement in Jamie's death, and I end up exposing him, it's unlikely I'd be his on his list of preferred carers for his beloved wolfhound.

I fetch my gloves and leave the tower, checking around me before locking the door. As I walk back to my digging, I remember the previous time that Belle appeared unexpectedly at the tower, early one morning.

And then, stopping abruptly with a shiver, I remember exactly which morning it was: my second Monday at Ashford.

The day that Jamie was hanged.

I'm sure Belle's presence at Ashford that day means that Dickie was also here, so I have the beginning of – admittedly slim – evidence that Dickie is implicated in Jamie's death. But I still don't know his motive.

Did Jamie witness something that led Dickie to silence him? Where does Gabriel Cortes fit in?

I summon up an image of Jamie, with all his natural charm and kindness. I remember how he made me feel so welcome when I first arrived; the way he had all the staff in stitches at his impersonations. How could anyone bring themselves to end such a generous and vibrant personality?

I'm determined that his murderer will be exposed. If my hunch is right – that the orchid smuggling is the key to it all – then I need to uncover how Jamie got involved, and why that led to his death.

I decide to start with Blythe. Slippery though he is, he might give something away.

30

I come upon Blythe as he's stepping out of his propagating shed. He jumps when he sees me, standing close by, on the concrete.

He shuts the shed door behind him – without locking it, I notice – and says, overloudly, 'Steph! You gave me a shock.'

'I was hoping to talk to you.'

'We can talk in the orchid shed,' he says, still in an artificially loud voice, as if ensuring he's heard by someone who's out of sight – presumably inside the shed he's just left. I step quickly behind him and open the shed door. Sure enough, Dickie Spencer is standing within earshot on the other side.

'You caught me!' he says, his hands up in mock surrender. He steps out and comes to stand beside Blythe, a jovial smile on his face. 'We were just talking about you, weren't we, Billy boy?' He puts an arm around Blythe's shoulders and squeezes. The head gardener is socially awkward at the best of times, but this is the most uncomfortable I've seen him.

I look from one man to the other, weighing up whether to cut my losses and run. While I'm deliberating, Dickie smiles and says, in a jocular tone, 'You're always digging aren't you, Ms Williams? If it's not in soil, it's in other people's business.'

I put my hand into my jacket pocket and rummage surreptitiously until I locate my pruning knife. It's small, but I keep the blade good and sharp.

Dickie continues, 'What did you want to talk to William about, anyway?'

Determined not to appear intimidated, I take a deep breath and say simply, 'I just had some more questions about his orchid trading.

It's quite the side gig.'

Blythe says, with obvious exasperation, 'I already told you everything. I even showed you round the lab.'

I force him to make eye contact with me. 'With all due respect, a young man is dead, in suspicious circumstances. And I believe it has something to do with your orchids.' Blythe tries to interrupt, but I cut him off: 'Just listen,' I say firmly, 'I'm going to tell you both what I know, and we'll see where that takes us, shall we?' My legs have started shaking but I'm hoping I appear confident from the waist up.

I hold up my thumb. 'Number one: Mr Blythe is running an illegal orchid trade.'

As he looks about to object, I see Dickie kick him on the ankle, and Blythe shoot Dickie an indignant look. That's all the encouragement I need to amend my wording. 'Actually, scratch that. Dickie here is running it. Our head gardener's role is to breed more plants from the specimens collected by the orchid hunters overseas.'

Dickie stands silently, arms folded, a mocking look on his face. Blythe, meanwhile, has turned a strange reddish purple.

I hold up my forefinger. 'Number two: Jamie was involved in the scheme. I have yet to work out in what role.'

This time, Blythe blurts out, 'It is a *legitimate* business, and Jamie was just helping out with some of the logistics: packaging up online orders, that kind of thing.'

'Will you shut up?' snaps Dickie, breaking his pretence at nonchalance.

I nod to Blythe. 'That makes sense. Now, number three: Jamie believed he was working for a lawful side business.' I decide to go out on a limb. 'He only started to have concerns after what happened with Gabriel Cortes,' I say.

There's a satisfying, stunned silence.

'What do you know about Gabriel?' asks Dickie, warily.

'He was an orchid hunter,' I say, with more confidence than I feel. Remembering the professor's email, I add, 'And he was murdered.' Watching the shock on their faces, I continue, with more assurance, 'And Jamie knew about it . . . Was Gabriel here when he was killed?'

Blythe splutters. 'Of course not! He only came here the once, to escort a particularly delicate specimen. It was just after his return to Colombia that he was savagely attacked, by a rival. Orchid hunting is a dangerous profession—'

'William . . .' Dickie says, in a warning tone, without taking his eyes off me. Blythe promptly shuts his mouth.

'So, that was number three,' I continue, getting into my stride. Fixing my gaze on Dickie, I say, 'Number four. Jamie and Dickie knew each other well enough for Jamie to sketch Dickie's portrait.'

Dickie scoffs. 'That's hardly proof of anything, now, is it? He sketched everybody.'

'But you were the last person he drew. That sketchbook is now in the hands of the police.' They won't know this is a lie.

The sequence of events is clicking into place in my mind's eye as I lay it out, presenting me with Dickie's motive. It's like one of those puzzles, where you slide one tile at a time, until you finally have the complete picture. 'Oh, and Jamie didn't know you were the big boss, did he, Dickie? In fact, he didn't know you had anything to do with the orchid trade.'

Before he has a chance to object, I continue, holding up my little finger. 'Now, where was I? Oh, yes, number five: Jamie was thrown into a panic by Gabriel's death . . .'

At this, I glance at Blythe, whose anxiety is palpable, and I hear him mutter, 'I should never have told him,' under his breath.

I continue: 'That's when he realised the whole enterprise was dangerous, and probably illegal, and started to fear for his own life. So he came to you, didn't he, Mr Blythe? He wanted out. When you seemed a bit . . . unmotivated, he secreted your copy of the map, showing the location of the orchids, to ensure he had something with which to barter.'

When Blythe seems about to object, I say brightly, 'It's all in Jamie's journal. You said, and I quote, you would "sort things". I bet you promised to make sure all the workers in the chain were protected from now on. You ran to your boss, but only because you were scared Jamie might report you. How am I doing?' Blythe looks pale. I turn to Dickie, 'And then *you* said . . .' Here, I deepen my voice to mimic

Dickie's, "Leave it with me, old chap: I'll talk to him. There's nothing to worry about."'

'For fuck's sake,' says Dickie, anger flaring in his eyes, 'this is completely delusional, even by your standards. You seem to have taken some innocent plant business and an unfortunate suicide, and blown the whole thing up into a mystery worthy of Nancy Drew. Do you not have enough to do here, Ms Williams?' His voice is dripping with sarcasm, but he's not done. 'Your entire "theory" is based on the premise that our orchid trade is illegitimate. But Blythe here applied and obtained licences for the entire trade. Isn't that right, William?'

Blythe is looking scared, but he nods. 'I've told you that over and over again. The operation is completely above board . . .'

I put up a hand to stop him, saying, 'No. You are not going to fob me off with stories of licences or permits to trade. I have it on good authority – from an orchid expert, no less – that the species you are cultivating have been obtained illegally. The devastation of valuable habitats, and the destruction of threatened species are just two of the reasons why this practice is outlawed.'

Believing himself on safe ground, Blythe recovers enough to scoff, 'I know for a fact that you have not shown any so-called "orchid expert" around my propagation shed.'

'You're right,' I say. He looks smug for a split second before I add, 'I sent photos.'

He stares at me. 'You have photographs? When would you . . .? How did you . . .?'

'I took some while you were otherwise occupied in re-staking your plants,' I say.

'For fuck's sake, William!' says Dickie, through gritted teeth. Blythe turns redder.

I meet Dickie's gaze and plough on: 'You couldn't risk exposure, so you needed to know how much Jamie had found out. You approached him, pretending to be his friend. You even agreed to pose for a portrait.

'Jamie was horrified by what had happened to Gabriel and desperate about his situation, what he'd got himself into. He confided in you, didn't he? He didn't realise that he was spilling his secrets to the mastermind behind the whole operation. And, when you realised he had worked out that the business was not only dangerous but also illegal – and, crucially, that he was planning on going to the police – you killed him.'

'Of course he didn't kill him!' interjects Blythe with spirit. 'That's absurd! Tell her . . .' He turns towards his boss, and I see the colour drain from Blythe's face.

And then I look at Dickie, and see he is staring at me, a cold half-smile playing on his lips.

'Leave now, William,' he says, without looking at Blythe.

A shiver runs down my back and I grasp the knife in my pocket more tightly and attempt to open the blade.

'Dickie,' says Blythe, in a worried tone.

'I said, go.'

With a concerned glance at me, Blythe hurries away, across the concrete, to the door in the tall fence that will take him back into the gardens. Dickie waits until the door has opened and Blythe has passed from sight. At last, he says, 'How much do you want?'

My grip on the knife loosens in surprise. 'What?'

He rolls his eyes. 'Come on – I did a bit of digging. You lost all your money in some bad deals. How much do you need?'

I stare at him. 'You think this is about money?'

'It's always about money. Look at my sister: she's so delighted to have funds for her precious restoration projects, she hasn't once asked where I acquired it all.'

At least that confirms my belief that Lady Clara is not involved in any of this mess.

I hear familiar barking from the other side of the door in the fence. My beloved dog knows I'm in trouble. I wonder if I could get over there, and make a run for it, with Mouse covering me. But Dickie sees my eyes move in that direction and says, 'Don't even think about it.'

My hand tightens again on the knife. 'I don't want your money,' I tell Dickie. 'I just want justice for Jamie. And to close down your smuggling operation before there are no orchids left in the wild.'

He laughs scornfully. 'Oh, come on: you can't really be naïve enough to believe closing us down will make any sort of difference? We're small fry. The trade is global, and the demand is huge.'

'The police are closing in,' I say, somewhat desperately.

He raises an eyebrow and looks around. 'I don't see them, do you? In fact, I don't see anyone but you and me.' He lets this sink in – as if I hadn't already noticed we were alone.

I tell him, 'The detective has Jamie's journal and his sketchbook. And I've emailed them the orchid specialist's information, about how your company is dealing in illegal imports.' I take a deep breath, 'I've also told them you are my primary suspect in Jamie's murder.'

He shakes his head in patronising fashion. 'Oh, Ms Williams . . . As you would know – if you'd actually looked into the facts before accusing me – I was not at Ashford when Jimmy died.'

I eye him coolly. 'So, who *did* kill Jamie?'

'He killed himself, Ms Williams,' he says, as if explaining something to a child. 'Such a shock. One minute, he was arranging flowers in little jars, and the next I was hearing that he'd been found hanging in his bedroom. An awful waste.'

A fist clenches in my belly, my usual response when faced with fear or cold certainty. 'How did you know about the flower arranging?' I ask softly.

His expression registers his error, but he tries to bluff his way out: 'Oh . . . I think my sister mentioned it,' he says, waving a hand dismissively. 'Or perhaps Rupert.'

'Belle was here, when Jamie died,' I say, testing his response.

His eyes narrow briefly, though I can't tell whether it's in anger or shock. Perhaps he didn't know I'd seen Belle that morning. Then he recovers himself and, with a broad smile, says, 'As you know, my sister frequently gives Belle the roam of the place when I'm putting in a long day at the office.'

'Strangely, your sister was as surprised as I was at Belle's appearance in the early hours.'

I remind myself a little too late that cornering a murderer is only a clever move if you have set up an escape route for yourself. I take a step away from him and say, 'Well, I think we're done here, so . . .'

He grasps my wrist in a movement that's both fluid and unexpected, like the strike of a cobra. I dimly wonder if he has trained in martial arts. I can hear a regular thudding from the door in the fence, as Mouse throws himself against it, trying to gain access. And then, all of a sudden the door, bursts open, and Mouse comes racing across the concrete, a black streak of muscle and determination, travelling faster than I've ever seen him move before. I twist my arm sharply and, as it comes free, Mouse leaps at Dickie's chest, the full force of my magnificent dog taking him down to the ground, where Mouse barks and snarls in his face. I tense as Belle arrives, racing towards us. But she simply runs to Dickie's side and licks his face, making no attempt to defend him against Mouse. It looks as though – so long as Mouse only growls and snarls, but doesn't hurt Dickie – she will not intervene.

'Good boy!' I tell Mouse.

And then I pull out my phone and dial 999.

31

My mobile rings almost immediately after I've hung up and I see it's DS McLeod.

He starts speaking as soon as I answer the call. 'Ms Williams, is everything all right? I heard your name go out over the air.'

I fill him in quickly on everything that's happened with Dickie.

'And you're there with him now?'

'Yes. Mouse – my dog – has knocked him over.'

'Right. I want you to go over to the house, find a crowded room, and stay there. I'm on my way and I'll bring back-up.'

He hangs up before I can tell him that I have no intention of leaving Mouse. While we wait, Dickie manages to struggle into a sitting position, but my brave dog simply snarls and bares his teeth, forcing Dickie to wriggle backwards, until he's up against the shed.

'Can't you call him off?' asks Dickie, after Mouse has prevented him from getting up for the third or fourth time.

'I could, but I'm not going to,' I say calmly.

Belle is sitting close to Dickie, but she does nothing to help him. It's as if this sensitive dog has an innate understanding of the situation – of just how badly her human has behaved.

Much sooner than I'd dared to hope, I hear sirens in the distance. A couple of minutes later, my mobile rings again, and McLeod asks me for Dickie's location. I give him directions to the sheds, and three police officers appear, alongside the DS. Strangely, I feel both comforted and unnerved at the sight of them. The gravity of their demeanour reinforces just how dangerous Dickie Spencer really is.

I stand back as two officers escort a handcuffed Dickie towards the door in the fence, and their waiting cars. Poor Belle runs along beside them.

DS McLeod approaches me, saying, 'Well done for this. I'll need to talk to you – probably tomorrow now.'

'How did you come so quickly?'

'You weren't the first person to call in. Your friend Mr Blythe had already dialled in a few minutes earlier, reporting a murder, and saying that you were in trouble. Luckily, we were already in the area, for a burglary.'

I stare at him, no words coming. William Blythe dialled the police *on my behalf*? It's unthinkable.

He coughs. 'Sorry I hadn't found the time to respond to you, about the orchids or the sketchbook. Do you have the book on you?'

'No, it's in the tower.'

'All right. We can pick that up tomorrow as well. We're going to place a couple of police guards for now, but we need to prioritise getting our little friend here processed and locked safely away. Are you all right? Do you want us to call anyone for you?'

'No, it's all right, thanks. I'll go over to the house.'

'Right, then. I'll be in touch.'

When Mouse and I reach the house, Lady Clara is standing outside, watching the cars drive away.

She turns to me, her eyes full of dismay and bewilderment. 'Steph! What's going on? The sergeant wouldn't tell me. They've got Dickie.'

I am not ready for this conversation. My legs are still trembling, but I need to be calm for Lady Clara.

Belle is standing whining, one ear cocked, as if hoping to hear Dickie calling to her. Mouse runs over to her, licks her face, and brings her back to us.

'Well?' says Lady Clara when I stand watching the dogs instead of answering her question.

'Come inside to the Scottish Room, and I'll tell you and Sir Angus together,' I say. 'You might want to ask Mr Fanshawe and Julian to join us.' I remember Miles – whose father has just been arrested. 'And is Miles here today?'

'The boys are out somewhere on their motorcycles,' she says impatiently. 'Please, just tell me what's happened.'

Without another word, I lead her into the house and through to the Scottish Room, where I gesture for her to sit in my usual chair, opposite Sir Angus, who is back in place with his beloved armchair. I perch on another close by, while the dogs curl up together on a plush rug.

'What's going on, hen?' asks Sir Angus. 'Did the bobbies get the perpetrators?'

I look at Lady Clara. 'Do you want to call your husband before I start?' but she shakes her head.

'Please, just tell me.'

Apart from the occasional exclamation, Sir Angus and Lady Clara are quiet while I give them a potted version of the orchid trade, and Jamie's murder at the hands of Dickie. Of course, Sir Angus knows much of it already, but he didn't suspect his nephew.

'So, it's not Blythe?' he says, sounding stunned.

I shake my head. 'He was in on the trade, but he doesn't seem to have been involved in Jamie's murder. In fact, he's the one who just reported it to the police.'

Lady Clara looks at me through tear-filled eyes. 'This must be a mistake,' she says, in a pleading tone.

Sir Angus leans across to take her hand and she bursts into loud sobs. I quietly call to the dogs, and we leave the two of them to comfort one another.

32

The next morning, after a long and seemingly dreamless sleep, I walk through the garden, mulling on the events of the day before, and looking for a job to occupy me. I'm due at the police station later today, to make my report. There are two police guards on the house, and another in front of the orchid shed.

I've heard the police are pretty busy with Dickie for now. An officer I didn't recognise came over to collect the sketchbook after breakfast – but the sketch only serves to prove that Dickie knew Jamie. I'm aware of how slim the evidence is – I just hope they'll have enough to nail him. At the very least, they should be able to get him for the orchid smuggling. I wonder if Blythe might be able to earn a reduced or suspended sentence, through cooperating. I am still not sure if Olivia will admit to having spied on me, at Dickie's behest, which could go some way towards strengthening the case.

My mind takes me back to last night. I'd been nervous upon entering the dining room for dinner, unsure of the reception I might receive from Jamie's friends. I'd half expected them to resent me – for interfering, or for not allowing him rest in peace. I was taken off guard when I instead received a round of applause. Saliha drew out the chair beside her, and planted a kiss on my cheek as I sat down.

'That's for Jamie,' she said, with a smile.

The meal itself was full of questions, fired from all around the table: What had made me so sure Jamie had been murdered? How had I come to suspect Dickie? How had I persuaded the police to listen to me?

Olivia, further down the table, looked as though she'd been crying. But, when I met her eye, she offered me an apologetic smile. In the gap after the main course, while we waited for Simon to bring dessert, she came to crouch beside me.

'I'm so sorry – I had no idea,' she said, a tear rolling down her cheek.

'I know,' I said gently, placing a hand on her shoulder. 'Was it you who searched Jamie's room, the night after he died?'

She nodded. 'Dickie said there might be a sketch of him, and that it would make it look like he was involved in some way.' She pulled a face. 'It never occurred to me that he really was involved. I genuinely thought Jamie had killed himself.'

'Can I ask you: someone told me they'd overheard you talking with Mr Fanshawe about sleeping tablets?'

'Oh!' She flushed. 'Why do you ask?'

'I think Dickie must have drugged Jamie, so he could hang him.'

She looked horrified. 'Oh my god! That hadn't occurred to me ...'

'So . . . the tablets?'

She sighed. 'Lady Clara has a stash, which she rarely uses. She was getting so upset about her uncle's night wanderings . . .'

'You mean you and Mr Fanshawe really were drugging Sir Angus?'

'Only for his own good!'

It was the same phrase Mr Fanshawe had used, when he'd been arguing with his wife. I shook my head. 'You have to tell Sir Angus.'

'Lady Clara did that already. And he's decided he wants to keep taking them.'

'You're not serious?'

At that moment, the door opened and Simon came in, pushing a trolley laden with apple strudel. Olivia went back to her seat.

My overloaded mind snaps back to today, and I find I'm standing in front of another large patch of the sprawling campanula, which I've not yet got around to removing. Today's the day, I decide.

I fetch my spade from the van and dig away at the invasive plant, until there's a huge pile of it in my barrow and I'm pretty sure I've got all the roots. Stepping back to get an overview, I see that the removal of the invasive evergreen has already made a difference. There's a new openness to this section of the parterre, which highlights the intricate shapes made by the surrounding hedging. I'm eager to get the dead box removed and replaced with the planned gravel, so I draw out my phone and call a local landscaping firm that I found online. The person I speak to informs me that they've just received a cancellation for a large job. As a result, they can come out next Tuesday, to begin digging out the box. I'll have to run the quote by Lady Clara, but it's pretty reasonable.

Saliha comes out for a tea break mid-morning, bringing me a mug of coffee, and we sit together on a large tree stump.

'Oh!' I say, 'I forgot to ask earlier: how did Lady Clara react to your resignation?'

She pulls a face. 'I mean, she wasn't thrilled about it. She kept talking about how they've lost Jamie and Michael, so they're already short staffed.'

'Ah. Not great.'

She shakes her head. 'She asked me to wait till they've got at least one new hire.'

'How do you feel about that?'

She shrugs. 'I wasn't planning on leaving much before Christmas, in any case.'

'At least that means I get to have you around for longer.' She grins and gives me a one-armed hug, and I hug her back.

Just before lunch, I'm sitting on Louisa's bench, when a police van arrives. A small group of officers spills out, enters the guarded house, and brings out computers and box files. When they've finished, they visit Blythe's orchid shed and remove more evidence. Then the guards leave with the others in the van.

I spend the afternoon at the station, sitting in an interview room with DS McLeod and another officer, running through all of my observations and discoveries. When I've finished and we get up to leave, McLeod shakes my hand.

'I owe you an apology,' he says. 'My instincts are normally pretty reliable, but it turns out yours were better than mine, on this one.'

Later, back at Ashford, after the dogs have been fed, I walk over to the house as usual for dinner. Vicky, Becky and Simon join us at the dining table after dishing out. Vicky takes the seat opposite me.

Smiling sadly, she says, not for the first time, 'I hate thinking he'd have got away with it if you hadn't been here.'

I reach out to squeeze her hand on the table. 'He'd have been found out at some point.' I look around at the assembly. 'Why did the police seize all the family's files and computers?'

'Nobody knows,' says Samuel. 'You don't think they were involved, do you? In this illegal orchid stuff?' Samuel has taken the news badly – not just of Jamie's murder at Dickie's hands, but also of the illegal business that was being conducted, without his knowledge, on the estate for which he's responsible.

I shake my head. But then I remember that Dickie had given over large sums of money from the orchid trade to Lady Clara, presumably with plans to recover the bulk of it down the line, when it would be harder to trace. I wonder how the manor house's finances will be extricated from those of Dickie. At least that explains why all the files and computers have been confiscated.

I glance at Olivia, who is once more sitting in silence near the bottom of the table. Her hair is loose and unwashed. My heart goes out to her.

After dinner, I go back to the tower, where I collapse on to the sofa. Mouse and Belle are stretched out on the floor in front of the television, watching a David Attenborough programme on humpback whales, with the sound turned off. I am waiting for Lady Clara to realise Belle's missing, and demand her back. In the meantime, I'm making as much fuss of her as possible.

33

The following Tuesday, I oversee the team of landscapers who are undertaking the box removal. I'd thought I was efficient, but I am in awe of the way they work together, swiftly digging out whole swathes of the diseased box, and transporting it to a bonfire. Soon, the parterre area starts opening up.

Caz, the woman in charge, comes over to me. 'We should be able to start on the trenches tomorrow, if the weather holds.'

'That's fantastic.'

Sure enough, by the end of the week, the trenches have been dug, filled with aggregate, tamped down, and topped with the white gravel, which I've had delivered from a local quarry. Saliha has let me view the parterre from her second-floor window, and the effect is spectacular: a geometric delight of which George London himself would have been proud.

My prime remaining concern is with Sir Angus and the sleeping tablets. I bring up the subject with the man himself, during one of my frequent visits to see him in the Scottish Room. He's trying to teach me to play a card game called cribbage. I still don't understand the rules, but I suspect this suits his purpose, as he keeps winning.

'So, you're OK with taking sleeping tablets?' I ask him.

'Eh, lass, what's that? Oh, aye, the pills.' He shrugs and moves a peg along a wooden score counter, called the cribbage board. ''Tis better than being shipped off to the death house.'

I've learnt that 'death house' is Sir Angus's term for a care home.

'But . . . drugging yourself? And knowing you were being drugged for all that time . . .?'

He puts his cards face down on the table and looks at me. 'Listen, lassie, I've lived to the grand old age of ninety-eight...' I don't correct him. 'And I reckon as I'm doing pretty well on it.' He squeezes my hand, then picks up his cards. 'So, let's play on. You still owe me fifty pence from the last time, and I'm about to beat you again.'

'I'm not playing you for money,' I tell him for the umpteenth time. 'Besides anything else, I'm pretty sure you cheat.'

He feigns indignation, then shakes a card from his sleeve and starts to cackle.

'I give up,' I say, putting down my hand and standing up. 'You're incorrigible.'

I can still hear him laughing as I step out into the hall and close the door.

34

In December, Saliha moves back to her parents', ready to attend art classes in January. I spend a week over Christmas in Peterborough, with my brother and his family. On Christmas Day, our parents come round, and we eat too much and laugh at the children's antics. Baby Stevie sleeps all day, while his siblings rush around – and sometimes over – him in his baby chair. I am presented with a beautiful, bright-green tool belt, chosen by Alice. Designed to hold all my gardening tools, it means that I no longer have to rummage for them in my jacket pockets.

Back at Ashford, the rest of the winter passes in relative calm. Dickie is still in jail, awaiting trial. From what little I can glean – largely through Mr Fanshawe's general lack of discretion – Dickie's case is bulking up, with evidence from Blythe and even Olivia, who has messages on her phone which prove he was at Ashford on the morning that Jamie was killed.

In March, at my suggestion, all the staff and Lady and Mr Fanshawe gather in the grounds for a small tree-planting ceremony, in Jamie's memory. With my help, Vicky has selected an ornamental cherry, *Prunus subhirtella* 'Autumnalis Rosea', which will burst into spectacular bloom each year, in full view of the house. Michael returns for the ceremony, and Oli comes with Benji and a large Labrador puppy called Dog. Oli and Vicky say some beautiful things about Jamie. After the ceremony, Oli leaves Benji to play with the dogs for a few minutes, and walks over to me.

He takes my hand and says, 'Thank you. I couldn't have rested till the truth came out.'

'Neither could I,' I admit. 'I'm so sorry about Jamie.'

He nods. 'It's hard. Benji misses him a lot. We all do.'

We turn to watch Benji, who's running and laughing, as the three dogs bound beside him.

'You did well getting Dog for him,' I say.

He smiles. 'Yeah, Dog has been brilliant. He can sense when Benji's sad or frustrated, and he goes to him and calms him down.'

'That's great.'

We smile at one another, then he lifts a hand in farewell. I watch as he walks off to reclaim his brother, putting an arm around his shoulders and saying something to him. I hear Benji laugh in response. I'm glad they have each other.

March proves to be a wonderful time at Ashford. Each day brings fresh shoots in the flowerbeds. The parterre comes into its own, with the fresh white gravel providing the perfect foil to the green shoots that are bursting up inside the intricate patterns. I take to squeezing on to the window seat beside Mouse in my free time, admiring the view over my end of the parterre. I have an order placed with a local nursery, to source the dwarf evergreens and white-flowered perennials needed to complete George London's vision, all of which I plan to plant – with help from a local gardening firm – in April or May, after the last frosts.

Belle was eventually claimed by Lady Clara, which has proved the perfect compromise: I don't need to feed or care for the huge wolfhound, but Mouse can enjoy her company every day.

I was more than a little surprised that I was encouraged to stay on at Ashford, after my part in exposing Dickie's crimes, but Lady Clara seems ashamed of her own complicity.

'I shouldn't simply have accepted his explanations at face value,' she has said to me on several occasions over the past months. 'As if my brother ever had the nous to make so much money in a legitimate way.' She sighs each time. 'Thank goodness you came along, or he'd still be involved with those terrible crooks. I only hope prison can set him on a better path.' I have my doubts about this, but I keep them to myself. Sir Angus regularly denounces his nephew as a 'nincompoop' – which seems far too mild, given that one of his crimes was murder. In fact, I'm pretty sure both he and Lady Clara have chosen to reject all proof that this heinous crime was ever committed by their much-loved family member.

I've heard from Vicky that not all of the family have shown such equanimity. The marquess and his wife, for instance, have severed all links with this part of the family.

Vicky cheered up considerably when she told me this, adding, 'So at least that's one bonus that's come out of all this: they won't be at next year's family party.'

Saliha messages me regularly, often attaching a photograph of her latest artwork. She's very talented, and I love seeing her creations, which are usually acrylic paintings in unexpected colours. Michael has a new job, as a learning support assistant for children with additional needs, at a local primary school. By all accounts, he's loving it.

Thanks to his cooperation with the police investigation, Blythe received a suspended sentence. He has moved to Cornwall, where I hope he will be better behaved. There's a new head gardener, due to start later in the month, to replace him. I helped with the selection process. She's bright, energetic and doesn't suffer fools. I think she'll fit in brilliantly. Samuel, meanwhile, is talking about retiring and getting a pair of golden retrievers.

Lady Clara and Mr Fanshawe – who had to take out a large loan against the house to finance the garden restorations – have been discussing the idea of opening up the gardens to paying visitors, with Vicky running a cafe for them in the grounds. It's all change, and there's a sense of excitement in the air, that fits in well with the rising sap of spring.

Since his hospital admission, Sir Angus has been slightly more inclined to drink Lady Clara's much-plied tea. I know for a fact, however, that he still keeps a flask of Scotch whisky secreted down the side of his seat cushion in the Scottish Room.

I have received no more phone calls from my ex-husband's phone. Late at night, I sometimes lie awake, wondering if that call came from him, or if someone else has acquired his phone. Is he all right? There's a part of me that refuses to believe he could be dead. For all his faults, Ben is very charming. I like to imagine he could talk himself out of any tricky situation. Hopefully, one day soon, Caroline or I will hear from him.

In June, I pack up our belongings ready for my next assignment, and Mouse and I say goodbye to the tower, the staff and Belle. We've made some good friends here, and I feel especially sad about leaving Sir Angus and Samuel. I also hate separating Belle and Mouse. I did ask if I could adopt her, but Lady Clara wouldn't hear of losing her.

Apart from the new placement, there is one other, more personal, event, which I am anticipating with a mixture of excitement and nerves: I have reached out to my birth mother – and we've agreed that we will meet, in a few weeks' time, in a London park.

After breakfast, Mouse and I climb into the van. There's a small gathering to see us off. I've already said my goodbyes so I give a quick wave and turn the ignition key. It takes a couple of tries, but at last the old engine catches.

We're heading to Coleton Fishacre, a National Trust property in Devon billed as a '1920s country retreat, complete with tropical garden by the sea'. Built for the wealthy D'Oyly Carte family, the house is to host its first ever flower show, and I am one of six designers invited to create a show garden. From stories I've heard of some of the others taking part, there may be some big egos involved. Still, it should be a breeze after Dickie and Blythe.

For now, I glance at Mouse, who is sitting very upright, watching the deer on either side of Ashford's long driveway.

'We'll stop for lunch and a walk in about an hour, boy, OK?'

He rumbles his approval at two of his favourite words, and settles down on his seat, Mr Rabbit snug beneath his head.

Acknowledgements

The Gardener Mysteries would not have come into being without the support, expertise and persistence of my wonderful agent, Jenny Todd at The Literary Office, or the confidence and vision of Embla Books' Editor at Large, Jane Snelgrove. Huge thanks to you both.

Thanks also to Melanie Hayes at Embla Books, for overseeing everything with energy and enthusiasm, and to the rest of the amazing Embla team, who go to great lengths to ensure that every book is the best it can be: Emilie Marneur, Anna Perkins, Hannah Deuce, Danielle Clahar-Raymond, Katie Williams, Marina Stavropoulou. If I've missed anyone, please accept my apologies and thanks for all you do.

I am grateful, too, to my copy editor Laura Gerrard, for spotting inconsistencies and inaccuracies with her eagle eye, as well as proofreaders Kay Coleman and Dushi Horti for their brilliant catches.

I have been blown away by my beautiful covers, designed by the talented Lisa Horton: thank you.

Meet the Experts

My heartfelt thanks go out to the following people, for so generously sharing their expertise:

Dr Amy Hinsley, co-chair of the IUCN SSC Orchid Specialist Group, for taking the time to share her extensive knowledge on the illegal international trade in orchids. I look forward to hearing such dramatic words as 'plundered' used widely from now on in her profession.

DI Scott Kingsnorth, for his amazing patience with my ignorant civilian questions. ('What colour is police tape for sealing off a crime scene?' and 'Is it sticky?' are just two examples that spring to mind.)

Jamie Abinger, for his kind help in navigating the complex world of hereditary peerages.

Garden writer, historian and generous mentor, Tim Richardson, for his advice on George London's (rather minimal, as it turned out) tree introductions.

Garden designer and horticulturist extraordinaire Christina Erskine of The Urban Hedgerow (urbanhedgerow.co.uk) for once again preventing Steph from making some potentially embarrassing horticultural mistakes!

Dawn Vincent and Vicky Matthews for early reading and advice.

As ever, any mistakes in the above fields are entirely my own.

Read on for an extract of *Seeds of Murder*...

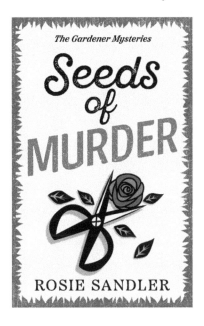

Prologue

It is cold in the paddock. The two Shetland ponies have taken shelter in their shed. The small and expensively dressed group of mourners huddles together against the wind as the coffin is lowered into the grave. One of the group, a woman, is sobbing hard. Now and then, she looks towards a man who is standing slightly apart, his face closed and inscrutable. He has his arm around a girl of about ten, who stares at the coffin with big eyes. When the priest finishes the service, the man takes the girl by her gloved hand and they walk quickly away, across the rough grass towards the far gate.

The woman collapses to the ground, sobs racking her body and a wail wrenched from her throat. The others look on, their faces a tight mix of sympathy and distaste. Then a small woman in high heels steps out from among them, approaches the wailing woman and crouches down to pull her into her arms, her heels sinking deep into the earth. The onlookers shift, uncomfortable voyeurs, then reach a silent consensus: they pick their way back through the field, stumbling in the rabbit-pocked earth, grateful to leave the raw scene behind them.

The two women remain in the paddock until the keening finally eases and the friend supports the bereft woman for the short walk home.

1

Mouse is whining quietly on the passenger seat. He likes to go for drives, but this has been a lengthy one, with only a couple of stops for him to exercise his long legs. A large black dog, he is quite shaggy – and very opinionated.

'It's OK, boy,' I tell him. 'We're there; you can get out soon.'

I swing the van off the main road and on to the private lane, slowing my speed to obey the fifteen-miles-per-hour signs. I whistle under my breath at the smoothness of the tarmac beneath my old vehicle's wheels. There are immaculately trimmed standard bays in planters all the way along the lane, and at the end, there's a pair of those giant gates they have only on really exclusive housing developments. These bear a sign, BEAULIEU HEIGHTS. I was surprised to hear during my online interview that this is pronounced 'Bewley' rather than 'Bowlyer' – more East London than French Riviera. There's a buzzer to press for access. A man's voice issues tinnily from the speaker, asking for my name.

I lean out of the van window, 'Steph Williams.'

There's a pause, then the voice says, 'And whom are you visiting, ma'am?'

I like being addressed as *ma'am*. 'I'm the new gardener,' I say.

There's a satisfying buzz as the gates swing open – and I'm through.

I nearly swerve, staring at the houses as I drive. They're all arranged part-way up a steep slope to my left, to maximise views out to the right, where the land falls away to woodland and farmland, before London raises its metropolitan head.

The first dwelling is so out of place in Old Blighty, I laugh. It's a concrete-and-glass, California-style arrangement – all whitewash and palm trees. The sign on the gate reads: LA JOLLA.

Mouse raises himself to see what's amused me. He's in time to see the next place, which comes into view within another minute or so. It is a pink stucco affair: VILLA SPLENDIDA. 'More like a birthday cake than a house, eh, boy?' I say, and he makes the rumbling sound in his throat that I like to take for agreement.

The van, Mouse and I keep going, and the houses don't stop delivering. From a gleaming, four-storey rectangle that looks like it's built from granite (THE MOUNT) to a building that resembles a miniature castle, complete with crenelations (THE TOWERS), they scream *Money lives here!*

I have been told that there are only five of these big houses, but they take up as much land as a small village. I reckon I drive a quarter of a mile from the start to the end, where I park my van in front of a small one-storey lodge on the right, as per my issued instructions. It has a sign, GARDENER'S COTTAGE, and with its irregular stone walls, blue-painted front door and climbing roses, it's quaint and charming. And, compared to some of the places I've stayed recently, it's a palace.

'Well, we're here, Mouse. What do you think?' He turns a doleful face towards me. I jump down and go round to let him out. But when I open his door, he stays put.

'It's OK, boy. This is our new home.'

Mouse stares straight ahead, as if he's waiting for me to chauffeur him to somewhere more to his liking.

'Suit yourself, but I need to start unpacking.' I leave his door open and walk over to the house. The key's been left in the front door as promised.

I'm reaching in to take the third box from the van when Mouse starts barking and a smallish, stocky woman of around fifty appears. She's dressed in pristine blue jeans with a checked shirt tucked into them, and a thigh-length Barbour jacket; her prematurely white hair is cropped short, giving her a no-nonsense appearance. I recognise her as Mimi Purdue, the chair of the residents' committee, who interviewed me for the job. In person, she bears more than a passing resemblance to my strict English teacher from school, and I have to swallow back the urge to say, 'Good morning, Miss Turner.'

'Hello, Steph,' says Ms Purdue. 'Welcome to Beaulieu Heights.'

I perch the box on the tailgate and hold out a hand. It's only then

I realise how grimy my palms are, from the dust and dirt in the van. I snatch my hand back before she can touch it. 'Sorry! I'm filthy,' I tell her.

'Well, no one expects a gardener to have clean hands, do they?' she says, with a smile. 'As you know, I'm Mimi Purdue. I live at The Chimneys – the end house you see there.' She points to a rooftop dotted with chimneys, a little way along from the cottage and just visible above a line of trees. It's the last house in the road.

'Ms Purdue – thank you for hiring me,' I say.

'Well, as you know, I'm only the chair of the residents' committee. We sifted through the applications together.' She looks me in the eye. It's a direct appraisal, and I stand my ground: I'm not easily intimidated. 'It's nice to get a woman gardener,' she says at last. 'I think you said early thirties when we spoke?'

I nod, 'Thirty-one.'

'So . . . according to all this new-fangled liberal nonsense, I'm not allowed to ask if you're going to start a family and leave us in the lurch, am I?'

I smile politely. 'No, you're not.' There's an awkward pause, which I break: 'I remember you said I could call in support staff as and when. Looking at the scale of the grounds, I'm sure I will need some back-up.'

She nods. 'Just give us notice before you call anyone in – the committee will need to approve any expenditure. A day should be enough. Of course, as I said at your video interview, you won't have to maintain everything – there are tennis courts, a swimming pool, various paddocks, which you won't need to trouble yourself with. The ponies are in the top paddock . . .' She falters and breaks eye contact, and I wait.

'Do the other paddocks not need mowing?' I ask at last, when it's clear she isn't going to finish her sentence.

She looks back at me, and I can see the effort it takes her to refocus. Then she shakes her head. 'No – there are also a couple of horses; and the ponies get moved between the others, so that keeps the grass in check.'

Mouse chooses that moment to stop sulking. He jumps out of the van and leaps at Mimi before I can stop him. Mimi simply stands her ground and says, 'Down!' in such a firm voice that Mouse lies down and whimpers. 'Nothing was said about a dog,' she continues, turning to look at me.

I pull an apologetic face. 'Ohhh. Mouse always comes to work with me. He's very well behaved.' I cross my fingers and hope he doesn't choose that moment to leap up at her again.

She studies him. 'What is it anyway?' she asks.

'He's a cross,' I tell her.

'A cross between what? A giraffe and a sheep?' She snorts. Luckily, Mouse is too good-natured to realise she's mocking his long, skinny legs and unruly fluff. There's definitely some poodle in the mix, and I've always wondered if his legs owe their length to a sighthound of some kind. His tail – the only part of him that dares move – twitches in eager greeting.

I think I'm extra sensitive about Mouse's gene pool, as I've recently discovered I'm something of a mixture myself – Eastern European Jewish on one side and Scottish Presbyterian on the other. There was an African great-grandmother on my father's side, and I don't know if my mass of black curls is down to the Jewish or the African heritage. Either way, I'm tall; at five foot ten, I tower over Mimi, though she seems undaunted. She's still studying Mouse, who is looking up at her meekly. At last, she nods.

'We'll see about the dog,' she says, somewhat ominously. 'Now, do you need a hand?'

'No, we've got this, thanks. Haven't we, boy?'

Mouse barks once, and Mimi says, 'Right, I'll leave you to get settled in. Come to The Chimneys at eight tomorrow morning and I'll show you the ropes.' I watch her stride away – and look back just in time to see that Mouse has jumped into the back of the van, and is nudging the next box towards the tailgate.

'Good boy!' I say, grabbing it before it crashes to the ground. I read the label: CROCKERY. 'That would have made a very fine mess,' I tell Mouse, who makes his rumble of agreement.

For some reason, I'd expected the cottage to smell damp, but the only scent is of cleaning products. It's spotless, with a slate floor in the kitchen and beautiful wooden floors elsewhere. It's also freezing cold, and I have to go around shutting all the windows. Mouse has already discovered the garden and he's learning its nooks and crannies scent by scent. I can see him through the kitchen window as I unpack the utensils and crockery. He stops at every step, smelling the ground, the plants, the air, and examining the trees for new birds to bark at and squirrels to torment. The garden ends at woodland, and he soon vanishes from sight. He'll be back when he's done exploring.

Home, I think, looking around the pretty interior with its beamed ceilings, whitewashed walls, and paintings of woodland scenes and country paths. There's even a large TV set in the living room, which Mouse is going to love.

Things could be a whole lot worse. The involuntary thought brings a shiver.

At that exact moment, my phone beeps. Generally, I keep my mobile turned off or on mute, but I used it to navigate my way to Beaulieu. I take it from my pocket and check the screen. It's from Ben:

Thinking of you and hope your journey went well.

There was a time when a message from Ben would have lit up my world. Right now, I don't want to think about him at all. I turn off my phone and leave it on the worktop before going back out for another box.

It's gone seven by the time I carry in the last box. I have so few possessions, I can't understand how it's taken me over an hour to get them inside.

For dinner, I heat some beans in the microwave and pour them over toast made from a loaf of bread someone's left in the fridge for me. There's a dishwasher – luxury! – so I place my used plate, glass and cutlery inside it.

I can hear Mouse start up barking outside. He's probably found a hedgehog – or, worse, a fox or badger. He's earned himself some pretty bad injuries through run-ins with wildlife, so I open the door and call him, but he doesn't come.

With a groan, I pull on my wellies, grab a torch that's been left beside the back door, and go out to look for him. I find him standing at the end of the garden, where it borders the trees, barking into the darkness.

'What is it, boy?' He glances up at me, but continues barking. He runs toward the trees, then back to my ankles. From his tense stance and upright ears, I'd say he's scared.

I murmur to him reassuringly, but there's something unnerving about standing in that unfamiliar spot, not knowing if the threat is animal or human. I weigh the torch in my fist, glad of its heft.

And then, Mouse stops barking. He emits a last, low growl, before looking up at me.

'Is it gone?' I ask. His body eases and he lets me pet him, his tail swishing gently.

'Well done, boy. You saw them off.' I have no idea what spooked Mouse, but I feel uneasy as we walk back inside the house, and I double-check all the doors and windows before bidding him goodnight.

I leave him guzzling his meal, clean my teeth and head into the bedroom. The lovely carved oak bed has been made up with a pretty patchwork quilt in shades of blue and purple; I instantly decide my old checked duvet can remain in the boot tonight. I slide beneath the covers and lie on my back, relishing the contrast between this cottage and the grotty bedsit I've been renting. My thoughts stray to Mimi Purdue. She'd seemed so in control, and then she'd lost her train of thought entirely over . . . what was it? The paddocks?

I'm too fatigued to wonder for long, and soon I'm asleep, dreaming that I'm mowing a giant lawn while Mimi barks orders:

'*You need to mow the swimming pool after this. And don't forget to feed the giraffes in the paddocks. But watch out for the man in the woods.*'

The Gardener Mysteries

Seeds
of
MURDER

ROSIE SANDLER

Steph Williams has arrived at the wealthy, gated community of Beaulieu Heights ready to start her new position as head gardener. Surrounded by mansions and acres of land, it's worlds apart from the life she knows, but she's determined to give it her best shot.

If she happens to accidentally overhear private conversations while trimming the bushes, or is refused access to a locked shed, she knows not to question it - after all, gardeners should be seen and not heard.

Until notes start turning up, threatening to reveal the deepest secrets of the residents. Suddenly Steph finds herself the prime suspect, and now she must leave the shelter of the gardens behind to clear her name and save her job.

The seeds of suspicion have been planted, but the case is turning out to be no bed of roses. And when the investigation puts her life at risk, Steph is up against the clock to weed out the real culprit before it's too late...

The third book in The Gardener Mysteries series, *Murder in Bloom*, is coming in Autumn 2024.

Available to pre-order now!

About the Author

Rosie Sandler lives in Essex, UK, where she writes novels, poetry and short stories, and is an editor and creative writing tutor. She loves dressmaking and wearing colourful outfits, which often leads to joyful encounters with strangers. Although she enjoys visiting beautifully tended gardens, Rosie's own garden is a bit on the wild side (her excuse is that this encourages hedgehogs and other wildlife). She dreams that she and her husband will one day live beside a lake. Or at least a big puddle. Rosie is co-author of the Agatha Oddly trilogy of children's detective novels.

About Embla Books

Embla Books is a digital-first publisher of standout commercial adult fiction. Passionate about storytelling, the team at Embla publish books that will make you 'laugh, love, look over your shoulder and lose sleep'. Launched by Bonnier Books UK in 2021, the imprint is named after the first woman from the creation myth in Norse mythology, who was carved by the gods from a tree trunk found on the seashore – an image of the kind of creative work and crafting that writers do, and a symbol of how stories shape our lives.

Find out about some of our other books and stay in touch:

X, Facebook, Instagram: @emblabooks
Newsletter: https://bit.ly/emblanewsletter

Milton Keynes UK
Ingram Content Group UK Ltd.
UKHW010250150524
442697UK00046B/40

9 781471 416200